MURDER RUNS DEEP

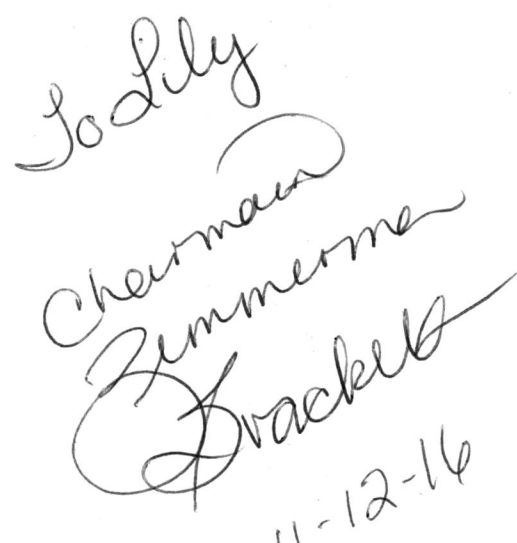

A Collection of Victoria James Murder Mystery Novellas

C. Z. Brackett

Murder Runs Deep by C.Z. Brackett

Copyright 2014 - All rights reserved.

This material may not be redistributed without written consent of Charmain Z. Brackett.

This is a work of fiction. Any likeness to any person living or dead is purely coincidental.

MURDER RUNS DEEP

MURDER RUNS DEEP

MURDER AT TWIN OAKS

A Victoria James Mystery

Diamond Key Press

1

Victoria James parked as close as she could to the white-columned Greek Revival mansion. About a dozen cars with their blue lights flashing from the local Bennettsville Sheriff's Department as well as cars from the Georgia Bureau of Investigation and three nearby counties were parked outside the ivy-covered brick walls in the middle of the hot Georgia July afternoon. She parked her vehicle and tried to push her way through the throng of law enforcement who blocked the wrought-iron gates.

"I'm sorry ma'am, but you can't - " started one of the deputies from another county.

"She's fine," interrupted Deputy Jefferson Hawes of the Bennettsville Sheriff's Department, who saw her pull up and had been awaiting her arrival. "You can't stop Victoria James when she's on a story. I'll handle Ms. James' questions."

The other deputy nodded and backed away, and Victoria smiled at Jeff.

"What took you so long, Vic?"

"Couldn't get past all of the police cars, Jeff. What is going on?"

Jeff shook his head.

"We were trying to keep this one quiet," he said.

Victoria laughed.

"Then, you've failed miserably. Besides you should know you can't keep anything quiet in this town. People know what color my underwear is, and you think you can hide a murder? I got a phone call the minute three deputy cars passed Myra Evans' house."

"Good old Miss Myra. God love her," he replied. "And how do you know it's a murder investigation?"

"You know you really should hire her. I think she solves most of your cases. She said there are two dead bodies in Twin Oaks."

"Shh. That's between you and me, but it's going to take a lot more than the town busybody to solve this one. And that is off the record so don't quote me on that."

"Mysterious, are we?"

"No, but I can't let you leak any details on this one. It's a gruesome crime scene." Victoria stared at Jeff and started to say something when a black sports car roared onto the scene. Its driver jumped out of the vehicle and headed up the perfectly manicured lawn, pushing past every deputy she could find and throwing off her heels before she reached the door. Allison Blake's shrill screams sent a shiver down Victoria's spine. The young heiress darted back out the front door screaming. She collapsed on the lawn and cried convulsively.

"Well, it's not Allison, so who?" Victoria asked.

Jeff stared at her and shook his head.

"I can't officially release the names yet. We still have family to notify."

"Jeff, what is going on?"

"I can't tell you yet, but I promise to let you know."

Victoria grimaced and looked as a couple of deputies tried to console Allison who still lay in a crumpled heap on the ground.

"Why is the GBI here?"

"Stop asking so many questions."

"I'm a reporter. That's what reporters do, Deputy Hawes. Is there anything you can tell me?"

"This is something not even Myra Evans know the answers to," he said. "I have to go back inside, but under no circumstances are you allowed in that house. Do you understand?"

"Only because you have the power to put me in jail," she answered.

Jeff winked before he turned and headed toward the house. She watched him as he stopped to talk to Allison. The other deputies had helped her up from her heap on the ground. She leaned against one of the female deputies; her body shook as she continued to sob.

Cassandra and Charles Madison Blake VI were in their late 50s and were pillars of the Bennettsville community. They were the owners of the massive Greek Revival home, which had been built prior to the Civil War. The Blakes could trace their roots in the Bennettsville community prior to its founding in the Colonial era. They owned huge parcels of land. When many lost their fortunes during the Civil War, the Blakes were among the few to survive with money. The Blake ancestors invested wisely in the Georgia railroad and the textile industry. They parlayed these earnings into countless other ventures, even managing through the stock market crash of 1929.

Over the years, the land had been parceled out, but they still owned Twin Oaks and about 100 acres. The youngest Blake was among the last of the direct descendants and had made his own small fortune in real estate. He developed a country club and an award-winning golf course which drew small numbers of extremely wealthy international guests each year. The family, which included multiple cousins, had its hand in almost every business in town. In addition, Mr. Blake had served as mayor for two terms, only recently retiring from public life to focus on his businesses and charity, and Mrs. Blake, known as "Cassie," was on the boards of all of the local charities. Not only were they well-known in the hamlet of Bennettsville, but their reach extended into nearby larger cities, where they were patrons of the arts and the university which bore the family name on its business school.

Victoria scribbled some notes on her pad, taking in the mood of the scene. People in town had heard the news by now. She turned around and looked down the long winding brick driveway and saw clusters of gawkers standing at the road. Several deputies were now blocking the entrance to the country road leading to Twin Oaks. People typically didn't end up at the Blake estate by chance. They had to go there on purpose.

Victoria wondered what was going on. Judging from Allison's reaction, Victoria was sure at least one of her parents was among the dead. Miss Myra was often right about things. No sign of Charles or Cassie. Could it be a double murder in Bennettsville? There hadn't been a serious crime involving Bennettsville's upper crust since debutante, Hillary Vincent, got drunk at the annual Bennettsville Masquerade Ball and drove her Mercedes into the town fountain five years before.

As Victoria contemplated the horror that had taken place inside Twin Oaks, she heard another shrill scream from Allison. She noticed as the coroner and his team brought two body bags from the house. She also hadn't seen their other daughter, Cynthia, better known as Sissy, who spent most of her evenings in bars and at parties in Bennettsville and bigger cities. Who knew where she was? Maybe she was the next of kin who needed to be contacted. Maybe there were three victims? Victoria would have to await the official word, and on a sweltering July day in south Georgia, she wished she could do it inside.

Allison was the opposite of her sister, Sissy. She wanted to become a fashion designer. She moved to New York right after she graduated from college. It wasn't what her parents wanted, but she was determined. Things didn't pan out as she'd planned so she moved back home, and her parents helped her set up her own boutique in one of the historic buildings downtown. Allison was trying to make a name for herself, and she proved she had business savvy. People wanted her clothing and were willing to travel to get it. Her business acumen only added to her father's choice of her as the favored child. Everyone knew she was the apple of her father's eye, much to the chagrin of her younger sister, whose attention-getting sprees landed her in jail on more than one occasion; they were mainly misdemeanor offenses, and her daddy's money always got her off the hook. As she watched, Victoria suspected Allison's display of grief was no act.

There wasn't much written in her notebook. Jeff barely said anything even "off the record." She could see the headline "Former Mayor and Wife Found Dead," but what could she write? Interviewing Allison wasn't happening - not in the state Allison was currently in.

Victoria felt her cell phone vibrating in her pocket. It was Ed Grady. He was the managing editor, but he liked to keep close tabs on stories, especially one focusing on Bennettsville's elite.

"I don't know anything yet. They just removed two body bags, and there's an heiress in shock," she said

"Do you have any IDs?"

"Not yet. It's probably Charles and Cassie Blake, but I don't have it officially yet."

She interviewed some of the bystanders at the gate in the 45 minutes before Jeff emerged from the crime scene. He gave instructions to two deputies and noticed she was still there.

"Waiting for me to let you see the crime scene?" he asked.

"No, I'm sure there will be plenty of photos at the trial."

"Let's find the killer first."

"I need some info for my article. What's the official line?"

"The official line is an apparent homicide of the former mayor and his wife. We have a few leads we are investigating, and we don't know the cause of death yet. We'll need an autopsy to confirm it," he replied.

"Double murder in Bennettsville. That's a headline."

"Yes, it is."

"Is there anything else? Possible cause of death? Give me something to go on, Deputy. I've been out here for a couple of hours now."

"Autopsy, Vic," he said.

"Fine."

The newsroom was practically empty when she returned to her cubicle so she took advantage of the silence, putting the cold words on the page. Two prominent citizens dead, and no answers.

"James!"

Ed usually bellowed her name from across the newsroom when he needed her. Victoria slowly walked to his office and knocked on his door.

"You know the Blakes were friends of our publisher?" he asked without looking up.

It was a rhetorical question that he did not allow her to answer. He kept talking.

"We have to be sensitive on this one. What do you know?" he asked.

"On the record, I know Cassie and Charles Blake are dead. Autopsy results are pending. Deputy Hawes said they'll let us know when they have more information."

"That's it?"

"Deputies from three other counties and the GBI were at the crime scene, and Allison Blake was overcome with grief. It wasn't pretty. She walked into the house and ran out screaming. She collapsed in the azaleas. I think she threw up."

"Leave out the Allison part. I still have a few more years until I can retire."

"I can do that."

"You've got 20 minutes, and call Hawes back."

Victoria rushed back to her desk and churned out the first draft. She sent a copy to Ed before she called Jeff.

"Jeff, I just submitted my first take of the story. Do you have anything else for me?"

"Just say we've gotten some tips from local residents, and we appreciate them all. We are following all the leads," he said.

"You are so official sounding," she said

"Off the record, it's going to be a long night. People are calling in with all kinds of crazy conspiracy stories, and don't be surprised when they start calling you, too."

"Thanks for the warning."

2

Bennettsville was a town of about 40,000 people - just big enough for Victoria, a 30 year-old with shoulder-length, curly, light brown hair and soft hazel eyes. She lived in a loft apartment over a book store in an historic downtown building. It was in walking distance of the news building. Actually, it was in walking distance of most of the places she needed to go. Victoria lived alone except for her 3 year-old Yorkie named Augustus, who she called Auggie. At times, she felt guilty for having a pet. She worked so many hours, even at home with her laptop. Tonight was no different. She had turned in her story on the Blakes, but she knew there would be lots of follow-up stories on this one. She curled up in bed with Auggie and perused the internet on her laptop. She wanted to find out everything she could on the Blakes. Most of the news articles were about their businesses or them smiling at charity events.

"Auggie, I think I need to take a drive," she said.

He tilted his head and stretched out his left paw.

"No, I don't think it's a good idea for me to take you this time, and yes, I promise to be careful."

He seemed forlorn as he dropped his head and rested it on her bed.

"I'll be back. I promise."

She took the drive back to the Blakes slowly. On paper, they seemed to have no enemies. A burglary gone bad, maybe? Jeff hinted that it was a brutal crime. Lots of questions and no answers.

She parked her car on the county road out of view from the house and walked toward the locked, wrought-iron gate. The full moon and the stars were the only lights. Twin Oaks was too far off the beaten path for city-owned street lights. There were a couple of lights on in the house but not the front parlor. She wondered if that's where the bodies were found. Despite being covered in sweat as she stood outside the gate, she was oblivious to the Georgia summer heat, which was present long after dark, and her thoughts were so loud they drowned out the usual calming sounds of the chirping of the crickets and the songs of the tree frogs.

She wondered about Jeff's statement to her about conspiracy theories. A family with that much money and influence surely had some skeletons in its closet. But there were never any allegations; no history of wrongdoing and seemingly no enemies. Even as mayor, Charles Blake was a likeable person who won by a landslide both terms. He'd probably still be mayor if he hadn't maxed out his terms. He'd served on the city council and school boards as well during his lifetime. The Blakes seemed to be law-abiding, taxpaying citizens, but after a couple of years in journalism, Victoria knew things weren't always as they seemed.

A door slammed, and the sound of two female voices broke through the night air.

"This is all your fault." One of the voices was shrill.

Victoria moved from the gates to hide behind the ivy-covered walls. She found a spot in the wall missing a brick and tried to peer through it. The moonlight shone down on the two women, who appeared to be Sissy and Allison Blake. Sissy was shouting, but Allison attempted to keep her voice down. Although their voices carried well, it was difficult to make out everything Allison was saying.

"They wouldn't be dead if it wasn't for you," Sissy continued to rant, and she began walking across the expansive front yard.

"Come back here," Allison began to follow her. As they moved closer to the driveway, Allison began to raise her voice, and Victoria could hear everything clearly.

"No, I can't stand to see that room. I can't look at it. I have to get away from it," Sissy said.

"I didn't kill them."

"Yes, you did, Allison. No one wants you to lead Blake Enterprises. You would destroy everything he worked so hard for."

"You're a drunken idiot. You think you should be the one in charge?"

"Why not me? I can do a lot more than people think, and it definitely should not be you. And everyone knows it. And that's why they are dead."

"I have a degree, and I run my own business. Why not Blake Enterprises? I'm capable," Allison said. "And why would Daddy's appointing me head of his company cause someone to kill both of them? Besides, where were you when all of this was going on? Do you even remember last night? Are you sure you weren't on some drunken spree and killed them because Daddy loved me best?"

Victoria heard the sound of a slap. She could only imagine it was Sissy hitting Allison in the face.

"I would never kill them, you witch," Sissy screamed.

"There was one thing you could always do better than. Daddy always wanted to take you hunting with him because you could handle a shotgun. Who's to say you didn't use it on them? And he taught you how to field dress a deer. Did you use your skills with a knife to cut off his hand too? Were you going to mount it like you did that deer you shot last fall? "

"I hate you, Allison. If I was going to kill anyone, it would be you."

Allison turned and walked back to the house while Sissy ran toward the garage. Within a few minutes, Victoria heard the sound of an engine, and she fell face to the ground as she heard the gates open and shut. She stayed there for a few minutes until the roar was gone. She didn't think anyone saw her until she heard a voice.

"That reminded me of your softball slide from high school. You could fall to the ground quicker than anyone else on the team, and you didn't mind getting that red Georgia clay on your white uniform."

It was Jeff. He leaned against the ivy-covered walls with his arms folded.

Victoria stood up and began to wipe dirt and grass off her pants.

"Working late tonight?" she asked.

"I always work late," he said. "What brings you out at this time of evening?"

"Sometimes, fresh air is good. Big story. I have to clear my mind."

"Leave the investigating to us," he responded.

"I'm not investigating. I came to stand outside a house and think."

"Vic, you have never been a good liar."

"Two victims killed by a shotgun? What about the hand? Allison said his hand was missing."

"Yes, it appears they were killed with a shotgun, and Charles Blake's right hand was cut off the body," he said.

"Is that on the record?"

"It's not supposed to be, but it sounds like you got quite an earful out here," he said.

"Their sibling rivalry has never been a secret."

"Yeah, tell me about it. Vic, I need to ask you a favor. You can have the missing hand info on the record if you promise to give me any info you get. If you uncover something, I want to know it from you and not find out by reading it in the paper. Give me a heads up?"

"I've always cooperated with the Bennettsville Sheriff's Department, Deputy Hawes. I don't understand why you are being so cryptic."

"Vic, drop the formalities. You aren't at a news conference," he said. "But I expect people will be telling you things."

"We don't print everything we hear. We have to check it out," she said. "Why are you here anyway? It's after midnight."

"There's a deputy watching the place. He knew who you were, and I told him to call me if anyone from the media started snooping around."

"I guess I should have known I wasn't alone."

"Definitely not alone."

She glanced at her cell phone to check the time. It read 12:35 a.m. "Good morning, Deputy. I'm sure we will be talking again soon."

As soon as she got in her car, she called Ed. She had just enough time to get the hideous detail in her story online and in the final edition before everyone left the newsroom for the night. Ed was pleased. He actually said, "Good job, James," before he hung up.

She smiled. She didn't hear that often.

She also sent Jonathan Marlowe, the business editor, a quick text to let him know what she'd overheard in Sissy and Allison's argument. His response was "hmm, interesting."

Victoria tried to imagine the crime scene on her ride home. Jeff never said how they were killed, but he did say it was gruesome. Why cut off his hand?

She parked in her usual spot when she arrived back at her apartment. As she walked toward the door, she was thankful for a full moon. The corner of the block wasn't well lit, and she often returned home after dark. It wasn't bad if she was running from the news building to her house, but she often attended meetings or events after dark. The building had a locked exterior door, which led to a set of stairs. There were three loft apartments on her floor, and her apartment was on the front of the building. As she approached her door, something caught her eye. She saw a large brown envelope propped against it. She looked around, but she didn't see anyone.

How did someone get in the building? she wondered. She felt a shiver down her spine in the sweltering, un-air-conditioned hallway. She felt uneasy as she opened the door. Auggie didn't come to her right away. He whimpered when she came in, and she could see him hiding under a chair.

"Some watchdog you are," she said. "Come here."

He came out of hiding and jumped into her lap when she sat down. She held him in one arm and inspected the envelope in the other. She realized he was shaking uncontrollably.

"It's okay, Auggie," she said trying to soothe him.

Despite the size of the envelope, it was practically weightless. She carefully opened it. Inside was a single sheet of paper, and on it was typed, "Don't let your eyes or ears deceive you." It wasn't signed. She picked the envelope up and peered inside. She held it upside down and a business card and photograph fell out. The card read Davenport Travel Agency, Birmingham, Ala.

She reached for her cell phone, but it was after 1 a.m. She was sure the good deputy was not interested in talking to her at this hour, and she wasn't sure she wanted to talk with him again either.

"So, I'm not supposed to believe anything I see or hear?" she asked Auggie, who was beginning to calm down.

She grabbed her laptop and sat down on her bed. She did a search for Davenport Travel Agency in Birmingham. No results. She looked up the address. It seemed to be a private residence. She looked at the photograph. It was Charles Blake, but she didn't recognize the pretty, young woman he had his arm around. They were dressed in business attire. It looked like it could have come from a conference or something. It didn't seem to be blackmail material. What did she have to do with the Blakes?

Victoria closed her laptop and tried to sleep. She couldn't. There was something about seeing Jeff twice in one day. She didn't see him often. He'd only been the department spokesman for about six months. Most of that time, they simply exchanged brief phone calls or emails. She picked up most of her information on her regular rounds to the sheriff's department and saw him in passing on occasion. She had his work cell number just in case, but she was hesitant to use it.

She and Jeff had known each other since they were children. They dated in high school and off and on when she went to college. Her senior year involved internships and a heavy course load, and she and Jeff drifted apart during that time. Victoria wanted to see the world when she graduated - or so she thought. Instead she got a job at the Bennettsville Herald, but when she moved back home after graduation to start her job, she found out he'd met someone else. A year later, they were married, and two years later, they had a daughter.

Victoria tried to forget Jeff. She moved to South Carolina for a year, but she missed her roots, her family and friends. She missed Bennettsville, and she came back. Some world traveler she was. She'd dated a couple of others but never for a long period of time. She couldn't commit to any relationship. She couldn't forget her first love with his light brown hair and his blue eyes that twinkled when he smiled. And that smile. When he smiled, he had a single dimple in his right cheek. She loved his smile. He also had a faint scar on his chin. That was Victoria's fault. She got mad at him when they were 7 years-old, and she pushed him off of his bicycle. He fell and hit his chin on a rock.

"Stop it, Victoria!" she said to herself, pulling her pillow over her head. Auggie licked her hand.

She moved the pillow and hugged her dog.

"Yes, Auggie, you are the only man in my life."

He barked in approval.

Jeff was the real reason she never found anyone else. It wasn't the long hours at the paper; it wasn't anything but Jeff – the one who got away.

She fell asleep thinking about that smile.

Her cell phone began ringing around 7 a.m. Auggie licked her face until she woke up. She glanced at the phone. It was Ed.

"I need you to come in here now," he said and abruptly hung up the phone.

She looked at Auggie.

"It's too early for this," she said. Auggie licked her nose.

She took a quick shower to try to wake up and prayed there would be coffee on when she got into the news building. She knew this would be a long day.

"It's about time," Ed said as she walked into his office.

"Good morning to you, too," she replied.

Ed stared at her over the top of his glasses and blinked slowly. He was too serious all of the time. She wondered if he might keel over dead at his desk from a heart attack especially on the days when she could see the veins bulging at his temples from the stress. She knew that he ran five miles a day. He stayed in shape. Maybe that's what kept him from complete meltdowns. He scared her too. She cringed when he called her name. That usually meant she'd made someone mad, and all he seemed concerned about was making himself look good, at her expense. He was always worried about his job and any mistakes that were made didn't reflect well on him. He had glimmers of moments when he was tolerable, but they were rare. He had retirement on his brain, and he didn't want anyone rocking that boat.

"This Blake case has hit the national news. Rich people having their hands cut off is apparently something people want to hear about in other parts of the country," he said. "Do you have anything else? Other news outlets have some details that are not in your story."

He showed her the websites of newspapers in bigger cities such as New York and Washington, D.C., which had posted stories on the Blake murders.

"I got the hand detail. I was the first to get that. Besides, I thought you weren't ready to retire yet?" she asked as she glanced at the pieces. "I have sibling rivalry and a cat fight outside Twin Oaks last night - but I wasn't supposed to see that."

"Which we can't print. Sometimes, there are things our paper needs to know because we are close to the story. Get Hawes on the phone and get me some copy now."

She knew that pat on the back at 1 a.m. was too good to be true.

"I need coffee," she said as she dialed Jeff's number.

He answered right away.

"7:30. That's much later than I thought," he said.

"Really? I didn't think you'd answer this early."

"Please. I haven't slept. The minute your story about the missing right hand hit the paper's website my phone blew up."

"That's what happens when you are the spokesman for the department and a high profile double murder takes place. Didn't they tell you that when they gave you the job? Ed said there's stuff in these stories that I didn't have. Is there any more information you can give me?"

"They didn't have much more than you, but someone else, not me, leaked info about them being shot at close range with hunting rifle, but you knew about the gun. What I can tell you is there is a vehicle missing. Allison was too distraught to question, but Sissy noticed his hunting pickup wasn't on the grounds. It wasn't in any of the places he usually parked it. She even went to their hunting lodge, and it wasn't parked there."

"Hunting pickup? With all those high-priced sports cars in his garage, our killer is a redneck?" she asked.

"How do you know what's in his garage?"

"I did a story one time. I got a grand tour. "

"The point is we think they were killed with a shotgun, and it could have been Blake's own gun that killed them."

"So is this on the record?"

"Yes."

"And do I get this before everyone else?"

"I haven't told anyone that yet. We found out about an hour ago. Sissy has been up all night. We are planning a press conference at 11 o'clock."

He paused for a minute.

"What about you? Do you have anything for me?"

Victoria was afraid he might ask that question.

"Why do you think I know something?"

"Vic, you are the hometown girl. Your parents, grandparents and great-grandparents all lived here. People around town trust you because you are one of them. You know they don't trust outsiders. If they are going to talk to anyone, I'm banking on you first."

"Yes. I do have something for you."

"That's what I thought."

"Can I meet you at the station in about an hour?"

"Sure."

"That will give me enough time to get this story filed and Ed off my back."

"See you then."

Victoria wrote her update for the newspaper's website and stopped by Ed's office before heading to the sheriff's office.

"It's in. There's a news conference at 11 a.m., and I'm meeting Deputy Hawes before it."

"Well, you have a little info. Go get more. Dan Kennedy is breathing down my neck on this. He and Blake were close friends. He wants justice."

Victoria nodded. Dan Kennedy was the newspaper's owner and publisher.

When she arrived at the sheriff's department, there were news vehicles from around the state parked outside. Her cell phone rang. It was Jeff.

"Meet me at Jake's," he said.

"I can do that. I'm outside now."

"I'll be there shortly," he said.

Jake's was a hole-in-the wall greasy spoon diner where the locals tended to flock. The blue haired ladies or blue hairs, as Victoria called them, was a group of older ladies who liked to gossip at breakfast while playing canasta. Jake started the diner in the 1950s, and his grandson kept the place going. It hadn't changed its decor since it opened. It had the best grits in town, but Victoria's favorite breakfast in the summer months was the bacon and tomato sandwich.

Jeff ordered a cup of coffee as he sat down in front of her.

"So what do you have for me?"

"I'm not sure. When I got home from Twin Oaks last night, I found this envelope in front of my apartment door – not outside the building itself but inside. It was scary because that outer door stays locked."

He pulled out the note and the business card, staring at them with a puzzled look on his face. While he was looking at the envelope's contents, their food arrived.

"Can I keep these?" he asked.

"Go right ahead," said Victoria, who'd made copies of them for safe keeping. She kept the photograph. "Is there anything you can tell me?"

"That this note is probably right. You are going to hear a lot of stories over the next few weeks, and you won't be able to believe them all."

"Can I get a sneak peek into the press conference?" she asked.

"At this point, you could give the press conference," he said.

He stood up.

"I've got to run. I'll check into this and see what I find," he said.

As Victoria ate her breakfast, she wondered about more than just the obvious questions. Everyone had secrets, and she knew the Blakes must have had more than their fair share.

The press conference wasn't spectacular. Jeff was right. Victoria knew more than everyone else at that point. It was simply a way to fill in the details for all of the outside media that had descended on their small town. He released the info about the stolen vehicle and gave a description for people to be on the lookout for. He fielded questions, but he said he couldn't answer many of them or didn't know. It sounded like there might be a lot of waiting by the phone for Victoria over the days to come.

Victoria's mind drifted to the card and the note as the press conference droned on. Birmingham was about a five-hour drive. She thought about placing a phone call when she got back to her desk.

Wanting the press conference to end, she posed her question.

"Deputy Hawes, do you have any suspects at this point?"

"No, Ms. James, not at this time," he replied. "We will keep the press informed as we uncover details. That's all the information I have. Thank you for coming."

She wanted to call that number before Jeff had a chance to. She rushed back to the office and pulled her copy from her desk drawer. It went straight to voicemail; no rings at all.

"Hi, this is Amy. Leave a message."

Victoria wavered before hanging up. Something told her not to leave a message.

With no new leads on the murders themselves, Victoria's focus was on how the community would remember the dead. It was going to be a long day.

3

Myra Evans lived in an early 20th century craftsman cottage on the edge of town not far from the road leading to Twin Oaks. At 84, the retired librarian was the town historian and had served as president of the Bennettsville Historical Society for many years. She was also the town busybody and a lifelong friend of Victoria's grandmother.

"So lovely to see you, my dear," Miss Myra greeted Victoria with a hug. "Come and have some iced tea with me in the parlor."

She led Victoria into the front room of the home. It was furnished in antiques, and the iced tea in its clear crystal pitcher sat on top of a lace tablecloth on the coffee table.

"I haven't seen you in ages, but I read your articles every day when my paper arrives. Your grandmother is so proud of you."

"Thank you, Miss Myra, and thanks for the phone call yesterday. As you know, I'm working on a story about the Blakes," she said.

"Oh my lands' sake. Such a horrible thing. Cassie was such a sweet woman. I can't imagine who would ever do that to her."

"What about Mr. Blake?"

"Dearie, I'd never speak ill of the dead. God rest his soul."

Victoria had never heard anyone criticize Mr. Blake, but then again, she only talked to people on his payroll, and his pockets ran deep. She sat looking puzzled for a few minutes as Miss Myra went on.

"When we were raising money for the memorial statue for the war veterans to go in the town square, that Mr. Blake was so stingy. He only wanted to give $100 for it. Can you imagine? Well, I talked to Cassie, and she fixed it. If we hadn't had their donation, we never would have been able to put that fine statue up in the square."

"I always heard he was extremely generous."

"He could be generous, but most of those gifts were hush money. Would you like some cookies?" Miss Myra said as she put a plate of freshly baked cookies in front of Victoria's face.

Victoria stared with her mouth open.

"No, thank you though," she said. "Hush money for what?"

"Well, I'm not one to gossip or speak ill of the dead, but Mr. Blake had his indulgences and improprieties. Before their housekeeper, Jessie died, God rest her soul, she would tell me stories! Jessie lived next door to me for all her days, and she came over to sit on the porch every night," said Miss Myra.

Victoria was scribbling furiously. She knew none of this would end up in her story, but she wanted to tuck these things away. Maybe she'd write a book someday.

"Well, there were all sorts of scandals involving the Blakes early on. Charles Blake was quite a Casanova in his day. There were all sorts of ladies to be paid off, and then there were the gambling debts. He loved to play the horses, and he had slot machines in the back of one of the restaurants he owned. He paid off a few deputies to cover that one. If the sheriff had known, he would have locked Charles Blake up without hesitation."

Victoria stared at Miss Myra who paused for a moment.

"Dear, are you going to put all of this in your story?" she asked.

"No, our publisher was really close to the Blakes."

"Dan Kennedy and Charles Blake close?" Miss Myra said and laughed.

Victoria was beginning to wonder if she was living in the same town as Miss Myra. Everything she thought she knew about Bennettsville and its residents was quickly unraveling before her eyes.

"Oh no. Cassie Blake and Dan Kennedy were in love at one time, but Charles Blake was Dan's rival. They fought over everything, especially Cassie. Dan joined the military to get his education and while he was overseas, Charles won."

"Wait a minute, you're telling me -"

"Victoria, dear, are you sure you don't want a cookie?" Miss Myra interrupted.

"No cookies, please," she said.

"Well, it was quite the scandal. Dan left Bennettsville for about 10 years and came back with a massive fortune and a movie-star-like bride. To this day, none of us knows what he did to make that money, but he bought the newspaper with it. Then, Charles really got messed up with his money. He almost lost Twin Oaks. He somehow got back into Dan's good graces so they could go into property development together. He needed Dan's money because there was so much debt because of an IRS scandal."

Miss Myra paused.

"I always thought Dan made his vast fortune as a way to get back at Cassie; you know a sort of revenge. She always loved him, and well, there were rumors about 28 years ago. How old is Allison?"

"Miss Myra, I need to go back to the newspaper building," Victoria said as her head spun with all of the stories Miss Myra had told.

"Oh yes, dear, won't you take some cookies with you? I made them this morning," she said.

"I'd love to, Miss Myra."

Miss Myra packed the cookies in plastic bags, and Victoria headed toward her car. Miss Myra had always been reliable in her information in the past, but she was talking crazy.

Victoria made it back to the newsroom in time to hear Ed bellow her last name. From the tone of "James," she knew it wasn't good.

"One of those cable news stations is reporting they've found the missing truck," he said.

"Deputy Hawes was supposed to contact me," she said pulling

her cell phone out of the pocket of her slacks. To her horror, she had three missed calls and several text messages. All were either from Ed or Jeff. She'd turned the ringer off her phone. The texts told her to ride out to Clarks' pond near the county line. The last text was about 30 minutes old, and it was going to take another 30 minutes at least

"Take a camera with you," said Ed as Victoria turned for the door.

The drive seemed to take forever. She drove as quickly as possible to Clarks' pond to find a slew of emergency vehicles. She had to park quite a distance from the scene, and with notebook and camera in hand, she ran to find the blue pickup truck being pulled out the pond. She began snapping photos when she heard a voice behind her.

"Well, look who's not paying attention to her cell phone. How is Miss Myra these days?" asked Jeff.

"Are you having me followed?" she asked without missing a shot.

"No, Ed told me where you were."

Victoria brought the camera down to turn and look at him.

"Yes, I got caught up on the back episodes of The Days of Bennettsville's Lives."

He grinned.

"Gotta love, Miss Myra. She's quite a character. Always has been. You'll have to enlighten me," he said.

"I don't think Miss Myra and I live in the same Bennettsville. It sounded like some freakish parallel universe that I'd been sucked into."

"That makes it sound even more interesting."

"So what's happening with the truck?" she asked.

"We'll take it back and check for evidence."

"Any more leads?"

"Not unless Miss Myra's stories pan out. Seriously, what she told me sounded like a soap opera. I can't use any of it. I've got a few other people to talk to. We're doing a huge front page centerpiece on Sunday about the legacy of Cassandra and Charles Blake. And it has to be positive because he was a close friend of our publisher, or maybe he wasn't. I don't know. It has to be positive is what I was told."

"Get anywhere with that business card?" he asked.

She raised her eyebrow.

"What do you mean?"

"I know you probably called it 7 or 8 times already."

"Ten, and it keeps going to voicemail, but who 's counting?" she asked.

Jeff grinned. Victoria turned away. That smile made her remember things she wanted to forget.

"I made some calls myself. It's a front for an escort service," he said.

Victoria narrowed her eyebrows.

"Why was that left on my doorstep?"

"We're going to find out," he said. "And I want to know what Miss Myra told you."

"I can do that. How's your family?"

When that came out, Victoria immediately wanted to pull it back in. Why did she even ask? She noticed his smile vanish instantly. Was it her imagination or did his eyes flash from blue to a steely gray?

"I've got an investigation to get back to," he said without answering her question.

Victoria wondered what that was about while she made a beeline to her car. All must not be well in the Hawes' household.

She needed to write a short piece on the truck and then get back to interviewing people for her centerpiece.

She rapped on Ed's door when she returned.

"I've got photos of the truck being pulled out of the pond," she said.

She heard a grunt and headed to her desk to make something available for the online edition. As soon as she finished, she went back to Ed's office.

"Hey, Ed," she peered around the partially opened door.

He looked up.

"I need to talk to you about these murders."

Ed waved her in. She sat down and poured out her story of the mysterious envelope and her conversation with Myra Evans.

"Sounds like a great movie script," he said.

"You don't think it's worth pursuing? I'm curious about this escort service, and Miss Myra's stories are -"

"Nothing we are going to follow up on," he said. "Even if she's telling the truth, we can't print it. Just hold on to it, and go find someone who will say nice things about the Blakes. We can't afford to make advertisers angry."

Victoria stood up.

"And Victoria, I've worked in towns a lot larger than this one, and when there's a high profile murder, all kinds of crazies and conspiracy theorists come out of the woodwork. I know Myra Evans is an upstanding and well-respected citizen, but it doesn't have any bearing on what you are reporting. Dan Kennedy would have my head over it."

He barely lifted his head and looked at her over the steel rims of his glasses.

"I have official statements from the mayor and some others that you can use. How about meeting with some of his board members?"

"You got it. In fact, I've got a meeting with two of them at his offices this afternoon."

4

Victoria couldn't stop thinking about the business card. Jeff said it was a front for an escort service. Why? She couldn't drive to Birmingham to find the answers though. She had interviews to conduct. Her first stop was Mr. Blake's employees and a couple of board members. At the Blake Enterprises' headquarters, she was greeted by Mr. Blake's assistant, Jennifer Campbell.

"Ms. James, please follow me," she said.

Tall and slender in her late 40s, wearing a tailored business suit and her hair in a perfectly coifed French twist, Jennifer Campbell could have easily passed as the owner of Blake Enterprises.

"I apologize that all of your interview subjects are running late. Mr. Blake's death has caused a panic, and that is off the record. They are all gathered in a board meeting. It should be wrapping up soon."

Victoria followed her down the corridor.

"If you'll wait here until they are finished, I'll send them in."

"That's not a problem," said Victoria. "Would you mind answering a few questions?"

"I can't meet with you long. I have a lot to attend to. What would you like to know?"

"How long did you work for the Blakes?"

She smiled.

"I started working for Blake Enterprises about 25 years ago. I had been working in New York, but home called me. One bad marriage later, I'm still here, and I owe it to Mr. Blake. He has always been a mentor to me..." Her voice trailed off; she seemed to be thinking of something else.

"Really?"

Jennifer looked at Victoria.

"It's not what you are thinking. My ex-husband was after my elderly aunt's money. We divorced long before she died at 102, two years ago. God rest her soul. She had a wicked sense of humor, and she lived just to spite my ex, I think. Anyway, Mr. Blake helped me with investments, and I was planning to startup own company by the year's end."

"Does his death change anything?"

"For me? Not really," she said. "I will miss them both. They were wonderful people. Now if you'll excuse me."

The rest of her interviews were much of the same. The Blakes were destined for sainthood if her interviews were truthful. At one point, Victoria was sure they had walked on water or fed the 5,000 with a few loaves and fish. They weren't nearly as interesting as her interview with Myra Evans. She had put her cell phone on silent and noticed two missed calls from Jeff.

"I'm sorry I missed you, Deputy," she said.

"We have a new development. There's a news conference in an hour," Jeff was curt and cut her off before she could ask any more questions.

"I guess I touched a nerve, " she said as she stared at her phone.

She headed straight to the police station from Blake Enterprise headquarters. It was only a 15-minute drive, but she had a hunch she might find out something else if she arrived early.

"Good morning, Victoria," said Jonathan Marlowe.

Not only did Jonathan and Victoria work together, but the two of them had known each other since elementary school. Journalism was not Jonathan's first career choice. He wanted to be a Shakespearean actor. He studied in New York and even lived in London while Victoria was in college, but it wasn't long before he was back in

Bennettsville. He was an outcast among the good old Georgia boys as a child and teen, but he excelled on stage. He was stunningly handsome with shoulder-length, wavy, jet black hair and green eyes, and if Victoria had anyone she'd call a best friend, it was Jonathan. There were pieces of his history that remained a mystery especially the whole story of his return to Bennettsville. He'd learned how to shed his thick Southern accent before he traveled to New York. He listened to English actors reciting Shakespeare and adopted a smooth, slight British accent as his own voice. He added more Queen's English to his speech patterns and phraseology. He knew how to diffuse hostile situations with just his voice. It was smooth and calming. Victoria would never admit it to him, but she found it extremely sexy. She enjoyed reading poetry and Shakespeare in her off-time, and she always imagined him reading it to her. She'd seen him perform in local community theater, and no one could interpret Shakespeare like he did. She knew he couldn't have failed at acting.

    He was always dressed immaculately. In his business reporter role, he wore tailored suits with vintage fedoras and silk handkerchiefs. On the weekends, he donned full-length duster coats. He was cultured and refined. And he was the opposite of Jeff, who had a thick Southern drawl and wore cowboy boots and a cowboy hat even when he was on duty. In Jeff's position, he wasn't required to wear a uniform.

    "They sent you, too?" she asked.

    "Apparently, all wasn't as it seems in the Blake kingdom."

    "I was getting tired of rainbows and unicorns. Tell me something real."

    "Rumors are the company was headed for bankruptcy. Charles might have wanted his beloved daughter to take over, but that's not happening. This morning at the board meeting, an attorney from an Atlanta-based law firm showed up representing an unnamed client who apparently owns 51 percent of Blake shares. Who knows what this means? Lots of people stand to lose their jobs, and investors stand to lose even more. It could be very bad for this town. Our entire economy rises and falls on the fortune of these people."

"He's not even in the ground yet."

"Greed doesn't have manners," Jonathan said and laughed. "Seriously though, is your résumé up to date? Most of the newspaper's advertising comes from a Blake-related company."

"Thanks for the warning. I guess this will burst Ed's bubble about only positive news on the Blakes."

"You and I will share the front page, but you'll get above the fold, I suppose. I'd hang on to the info Myra Evans gave you. It could be useful."

"How did you know about that? It's only worthy of a gossip column."

He winked.

"How did you know about Allison?" he asked.

She smiled and nodded.

"Ed doesn't have the final say," he said. "The publisher's family stands to lose a fortune. They were heavily invested in the Blakes. Dan Kennedy owns a fair share of that Blake stock. And since no one knows who is in control of Blake Enterprises, it could get very interesting. The suspect list keeps getting longer."

It wasn't long before the TV reporters arrived. There were other news media in town as well. No one as wealthy and connected as the Blakes could die and not have a swarm of journalists around them. When Jeff finally appeared, he flashed that smile that always made Victoria weak in the knees, but she could tell he was tired. He had dark circles under his eyes.

"Thank you, ladies and gentlemen for attending today's news conference. I will not open this up for questions at the end. Yesterday, at 8:14 a.m., we were called to investigate a disturbance at the Blake home. When we responded, we found two bodies. Both of the individuals were deceased at the time of our arrival. They have been identified as Charles and Cassandra Blake. Both victims were shot at close range with a shotgun. Mr. Blake's right hand was cut from the body after his death. Yesterday afternoon, we removed a blue pickup truck from Clarks' pond. It was registered to the deceased. Further investigation determined the weapon used to kill the victims was also registered to the deceased and was found inside the cab of the pickup truck we retrieved. We do have some persons of interest we are interviewing at this time. That's all I can release at the time. Thank you."

As he turned away, the reporters released a flurry of questions, but Jeff held up his hand and shook his head.

"Persons of interest?" Jonathan asked and raised an eyebrow. "The plot thickens. Well, I have a deadline."

"So do I," said Victoria as she looked at her phone. She had a text from Ed. "Write two stories," it said.

She rushed back to write her update and finish the color piece on the Blakes. She pressed the desire to solve the case into the back of her mind, but she knew there was more.

It was getting late. She was getting ready to head home when an email came in. There wasn't a name. It had "a friend" as the sender, and the subject line simply had the name of the escort service.

"I'm throwing you a bone. Aren't you curious? The Blakes aren't all that they seem."

She stared at the email. Yes, she was curious; more curious than she wanted to admit. She couldn't make a trip to Birmingham until after the funeral, and that was still a couple of days away. She had to cover that, and it would be front page material. She also needed to talk to Jeff. She'd left him several messages that he hadn't returned. It was nearly 10 p.m. Poor Auggie needed to be taken out.

Her cell phone rang. It was Jeff.

"Good evening, Detective," she said.

"Hey, Vic. These big city reporters don't understand when you tell them no questions."

She laughed.

"Neither do I. I wanted more info," she said.

"You've got all I'm allowed to give."

"Who found the bodies?"

"One of their employees," he said.
Tell me what you know about this escort service?"
"Why?"
"I just got an email from our informer."
She read it to him.
"I haven't even told Ed. He doesn't care about any dirt on the Blakes."
"I'll get someone on it."
"So I gave you my info. Do you have anything for me?"
"We think the Blakes knew whoever killed them," he said.
"Why?"
"No forced entry. Nothing out of place. No apparent robbery."
"Why kill them then?"
"That's what we are trying to find out."

Victoria knew Jeff was holding onto some information. She could tell. Despite what everyone had said to her, Victoria knew skeletons were getting ready to fly out of the Blakes' closets.

It had been a long day, and she knew the next few would be probably be longer.

Auggie was glad when Victoria finally arrived home, but he seemed agitated even after cuddling with her.

"What's the matter, boy?" she asked.

Auggie whimpered.

She looked around her apartment. Nothing seemed out of place. She heard the downstairs' door click. She ran to her apartment door. When she opened it, she saw another envelope. She felt numb. She ran back into her apartment to look through her window, but she wasn't fast enough to see the fleeing figure. She looked down at the envelope, and for the first time, she noticed her hands were shaking.

"Auggie, you're a good boy."

She sat down, and he jumped into her lap. She took a deep breath.

"Dear Ms. Award-Winning Journalist," the letter began mocking her from the start. "Stop writing this sugar-coated fantasy about the

Blakes. They weren't good people; and this town needs to know it. Stop believing the lies you are being fed. You haven't heard the last from me. Here's another bone."

There were a few newspaper clippings. They seemed random. One was an obituary from July 15, 1992 of a Blake employee who died in a car accident. Another clipping was about a sexual harassment lawsuit that the car wreck victim had been filed two weeks before her death. Another was a photocopy of a news article of an apparent suicide on the outskirts of town on March 13, 1994. The woman had jumped off a county bridge and drowned. Her body was found three weeks later. She had also filed a sexual harassment suit against Charles Blake.

She looked at her phone. It was after 11 p.m.

With her hands still shaking, she called Jeff.

"My mysterious visitor just left me another note."

"I'm still at the station. I'll be right there."

She watched from her window so she could let him in the building door. It didn't take him long to arrive. She buzzed him into the building, and he rushed up the stairs. She handed him the note and articles.

"Do you think this is from our killer or someone else?"

Jeff looked over the note.

"Anything is possible. I'll take this and check it for prints or anything else I can find."

"I know Bennettsville is a small town, but how does this person know where I live and have access to my building?"

"Who's your landlord?"

Victoria sat down still holding Auggie close. She shook her head and sighed.

"Blake Realty."

"Well, if it is the killer, you've just given me another clue," he said.

Jeff pulled up a chair and sat across from Victoria.

"Are you all right?" he asked.

"I'm fine."

"Vic, I told you I know when you're lying. Your hands were shaking when you handed me the letter."

She took a deep breath and looked at him.

"It's frightening to think a double murderer is stalking me."

"I'll have someone watch your apartment, but I don't want to completely scare them away. They could be the key to solving this case."

"Great. I'm bait now," she said.

"No, never. That's not what I meant. But while we have some people we are watching, we don't have many leads that are credible, and that, Ms. Reporter, is totally off the record," he said.

She nodded and tried to breathe.

"I appreciate you coming over here," she said.

"Vic, listen, if you need me, just call. It doesn't matter what time it is. If I can't answer it right then, I'll call you back."

Jeff walked to the door, where he paused. He looked into her eyes and started to say something. Instead, he broke the gaze and shook his head. She hadn't seen the depths of those eyes in many years. They looked sad; no, it was more than sadness. They looked tormented.

"Don't worry about anything, Vic. I won't let you get hurt."

She closed the door behind him.

"It's too late for that, Jeff," she whispered.

5

Despite her exhaustion, Victoria barely slept. She felt all sorts of emotions welling up inside of her. She was afraid of this person who kept breaking into her building, but that wasn't consuming her thoughts. It was Jeff. She had somersaulted into the depths of his blue eyes in that brief instant. He seemed to want to say something. It sent her thoughts and emotions into a tailspin. She remembered so many of the good times they had had together, and she remembered the last date they'd had before her senior year of college. They went on a picnic and spent the evening looking up at the stars talking after the Labor Day fireworks. They sketched out their lives together after she graduated. But that scared her. She wanted to break free from Bennettsville. What had happened? There was no fight, no real break-up? How did they drift apart? Or did she just not want to remember? She pulled a pillow over her head and screamed into it. Auggie put his paw on her arm and gently scratched her to get her attention. She looked at him from under the pillow.

"I'm sorry, Auggie," she said.

She pulled him close and began to cry in his soft fur. She knew she'd always love Thomas Jefferson Hawes. He still had her heart after all this time. He was her first love – her only love. At some point, she drifted off to sleep. Around 6 a.m., she had to get up.

She headed to Jake's for a cup of coffee and to listen in to the blue-haired ladies as they gossiped. She often heard the next day's headlines there, but sometimes, she only heard chatter and not words. She saw Jonathan at one of the tables. She and Jonathan had a unique relationship they couldn't explain to people. She loved him, but it had never been in a romantic way. They were very much alike, but yet worlds apart. He never liked Jeff though.

As she walked in, she noticed a couple of the ladies staring at her and whispering. She sat down with him. Jonathan smiled oddly like the proverbial cat who'd caught the canary.

"What is going on?"

"You, my dear, are the talk of Bennettsville. Coffee?"

"Me? What on earth for? Yes, black."

Jonathan waved for a cup of coffee.

"Something about a late night rendezvous with a handsome, married but soon to be single detective."

"Do these people not have lives of their own, and how on earth do they know these things?" She shook her head. "There's been a double murder of the town's most influential couple, and people want to talk about me?"

"Of course! Nothing sells like sex."

"It was nothing like that. It was all police-related."

"I believe you, my dear Victoria, but the Blakes are old news. They've been gossiped about for decades. And why was the handsome detective at your house? I don't care about the official business part. I want the other details."

"Jonathan, if we hadn't known each other since we were in the sandbox together, I'd -"

Jonathan cut her off as he laughed and waved his hand as if to shoo her away.

"Idle threats. I know you."

Victoria shook her head as she drank her coffee.

"So since you won't give me the juicy details, what kind of business has a handsome police officer running into a single woman's apartment without backup?" he asked.

"Someone keeps delivering cryptic messages and leaving them at my door."

"Cryptic, how?"

"Wanting me to investigate personal things that may or may not be related to the Blake murder," she said.

"And you haven't told Ed, have you? Heresay as he'd say, but it sounds like it could be juicy."

"Exactly. But the creepy part is they know where I live and have a key to the building."

"That would be scary, especially if it's the Bennettsville serial killer. So what kind of salacious tidbits are they leaving for you."

"So far, there's been a business card for an escort service in Birmingham and a couple of notes fussing at me for not investigating the escort service. They left some newspaper clippings last night."

Victoria stopped and looked puzzled.

"So, Mr. Busybody, what did I hear you say about a 'married-but-soon-to-be-single detective?'"

Jonathan laughed.

"Wow, you really didn't sleep last night. I was wondering if those dark circles under your eyes were the latest in eye makeup trends. It took you long enough to get back to that - way too long. I saw the way you looked at him yesterday. I felt like I was the jilted eight grade dance date all over again."

"Jonathan, you weren't jilted. And stop changing the subject."

"Fine. Rumor is the lovely Mrs. Hawes fled to Atlanta with their daughter in tow a few months back. And you've been pining away for how long now? And all the while, you could have had me? What does he have that I don't have?"

"How long has she been gone?"

"Supposedly she went to visit friends about three or four months ago and never returned. She's already filed papers. And you are completely ignoring my question."

"Yes, I am, Jonathan. No one is pining, and you and me? You are joking on that right? Didn't we discuss this when we were like 12, and you wanted me to marry you? We were smart enough then to know it would never work. And how is it everyone knows about my personal life, but they don't know who killed Bennettsville's power couple?"

"They probably know more than they are letting on, but no one has asked them yet. And you are pining. When's the last time you went on a date?"

"They don't usually need to be asked, and I don't have time to date."

"True on the first part, but there's always time to date."

"Jonathan, I've only got my heart set on one man, and his name is Auggie. Besides I have some great books I need to read. So am I the only topic this morning?"

"Oh no, the Blake daughters are high on the list. Lots of rumors are swirling about them. Something about a knock-down, drag out fight on the lawn a couple of nights away. And my story has caused a stir."

"And mine?"

"You know as well as I do that no one talks evil of the dead - in public and in print in the South. Your stories and the phrase 'God rest their souls' has been mentioned in the same breath several times. Do you still have to write the 'what would Bennettsville have done without the Blakes' story?"

"Of course. I think there's a special commemorative section coming out. There may even be a glossy magazine at this rate as well as bumper stickers."

He laughed, and his eyes darted toward the door.

"Well, well, the blue hairs are about to get some more to talk about."

"Why?"

"The married but soon-to-be single detective is coming this way."

Victoria's heart skipped a beat. She took a deep breath.

"Oh, you have it worse than I thought. You, my dear, are blushing."

"Shut up, Jonathan," she said punctuating each syllable through clenched teeth.

"Marlowe, do you mind if I talk to Vic?"

"Not at all. Join us. Don't mind me. We were just talking about you."

He smiled and winked at Victoria.

Victoria glared at Jonathan as Jeff slid next to her in the booth.

"You are up early this morning," she said.

"I haven't been to sleep. This case is a top priority," Jeff said. "I checked your mysterious letter. There are no prints, no saliva or DNA. Nothing to identify the sender. The person seems to be well-educated, judging by the grammar and punctuation. No errors. But that's not much to go on.'"

"How is it possible you have results back already? You just got it a few hours ago."

"When I say it's a top priority, I mean it's top," Jeff said. "We're checking into the email; again there are no identifying signatures, but they were sent from Bennettsville Public Library."

"Is there any way to track who used computers there at a certain time?"

"I checked, and there's a gap in the security records for 30 minutes.

"You really haven't slept, have you?" she asked.

"Someone has really thought this out," he said. "It's frustrating. There will be someone patrolling the building tonight. I'm headed back to the station. We are expecting the autopsy results at any time, and I've got to prepare security for the funeral. The governor and several congressmen are expected - as if I didn't already have enough nightmares."

"Goodbye, Detective," said Jonathan.

"See you later, Jeff." she said.

Victoria noticed the blue hairs averting their eyes from her direction as they chattered excitedly.

"See! You are the talk of the town. I'd love to drive with you to Birmingham."

"It will have to wait until after the funeral. I'll see you in the office."

She stopped at Ed's office on her way in.

"I heard about the deputy's late night visit," he said without missing a beat.

"Yes, apparently the entire town knows about that but can't find a double murderer."

Ed looked over the top of his glasses at her and stared silently.

"It's true," she said.

"I want to know everything. I don't care what time of day it is. And having a relationship with a spokesman for the sheriff's department is an ethics' violation. Don't do it."

"I'm not having a relationship with him," she said. "Do you have time now? I've got a lot of stuff."

"I'm all ears," he said as she sat down and told him everything.

About 30 minutes later, she made her way to her desk to find a thick brown envelope on her desk with her name on it.

She picked it up and stared at it.

"Jonathan."

He glanced up from his desk.

"Where did this come from?" she asked.

"I have no idea. I think someone from the mail room brought it up. What is it?"

"This wasn't mailed. It's the same type of envelope the other info has been in, and the address label is the same."

"Don't you think you should open it rather than analyzing it to death?"

She stared at it and slowly sat down. She felt her hands shaking as she opened the envelope. Jonathan walked around to her cubicle.

"What is it this time?"

"Well, there's a note. It says 'Calling the police? Not a wise decision. Here's another softball for you. Don't make me do your job for you,'" she read.

She looked through a stack of papers.

"I don't know what all this is. It looks like something up your alley, Jonathan. There are charts and graphs in here. And there are all kinds of legal-looking documents."

"Let me see those."

Jonathan took some of the pages and began reading through them. She tried to stop shaking as she watched Jonathan skimming through the pages.

"I need a close look at this, but if what I'm seeing is true, Blake had been lying about his assets and businesses for a while. The bankruptcy rumors weren't just rumors."

"We need to tell Ed."

"Tell Ed what?" said a voice behind them.

"Victoria just had a care package delivered," said Jonathan. "It's going to take some time to go through it all."

He shoved some of the papers into Ed's hands.

Ed glanced over them.

"You may have something. Once you make heads or tails of this, then let's talk and get it in the paper. Hide those for now. We have a visitor, Marlowe. It's the former board chair of Blake Enterprises. James, you may want to sit in on this."

Ed turned to Jonathan.

"He's not happy, but then you would know that," Ed said.

"Oh, I know that all too well." Jonathan smiled. "Let me handle this."

Jonathan entered the conference room with confidence.

"Bill, fantastic to see you!" Jonathan grabbed the hand of William Davies and attempted to turn on his charm. Bill was holding the morning edition.

"You know why I'm here. This story on the front page -" Bill said hitting the page with each word he uttered.

"Is completely factual and well-documented," Jonathan interjected.

"That's not the point. Do you know how many people this impacts? We have not had time to process this."

"My job is to present the facts, not interpret them or speculate what they mean. I'm not an analyst."

"We are still reeling from Mr. Blake's death, and now this," Mr. Davies paused. "All this uncertainty. Mr. Blake was getting ready to announce his retirement and hand over the reins."

Jonathan tilted his head and raised an eyebrow. Victoria and Ed sat quietly. Victoria took a few random notes and glanced at Ed.

"Really? Go on," Jonathan said.

"Yesterday's meeting had been already been scheduled. Allison was going to be named president of Blake Enterprises."

Jonathan glanced at Victoria and smiled.

"And how did the board feel about that?" Jonathan asked.

"There was a lot of division on the matter," Mr. Davies said.

"What do you mean by division?"

"There were many angry words at the last board meeting. Allison is inexperienced and has a lot to learn. We felt there were plenty of others more qualified than she was."

"Anyone angry enough to kill them?" asked Victoria.

Mr. Davies turned to look at her.

"Ms. James, when there are millions of dollars on the line, anyone can get angry enough to kill someone. She could cost this town everything. There are jobs on the line and investors' dollars," he said.

"What would your role have been in the reconstructed Blake Enterprises?" she asked.

"I'm still an investor with a voice," he said.

"No titles or positions?" she asked.

"Ms. James, what you are insinuating?" he said and glared at her.

"I'm just asking questions. You declined to let me interview you on my retrospective. As a former board chairman, I'm sure you have plenty to say about the Blakes," she said.

"I've known Charles Blake since we were kids. We went hunting together often. Don't make accusations, or I will call the police," he said as he gritted his teeth.

Jonathan stepped in.

"Any clue as to the identity of this unnamed holding company and who has taken over the company?" Jonathan asked.

"None. It was totally unexpected. Apparently, someone had been purchasing the stocks from small investors for a long time," Mr. Davies said. "It's all mysterious. I can't help but think the murders and takeover are somehow related."

"How many people knew this?" asked Victoria.

"Only a handful," Mr. Davies answered. "Are you writing a story on this?"

"Ms. James and Mr. Marlowe are writing lots of stories right now," Ed said.

"Why was Charles Blake going to retire?" asked Jonathan. "I spoke to him about six months ago, and he told me that he'd operate his holdings until the day he died. It was prophetic, wasn't it?"

"No one knew. He never answered."

"Have you heard from the new mystery owner?"

"Not a word. What's going in tomorrow's paper? We have panicked investors and a workforce on edge."

"We will be previewing the funeral. We'd love an investor reaction story. Would you like to be quoted?" Ed asked.

"I don't want anything I said in tomorrow's paper except to say we are all still in shock, and we are grieving the Blake family," said Mr. Davies. "I've known you for a long time, Jonathan. Please respect that."

"I do," Jonathan said.

"It's not a problem," Ed said.

Jonathan shook Mr. Davies' hand.

"I'll walk out with you," Jonathan said.

As they walked out of the conference room, Ed turned to Victoria.

"He certainly had motive, and he was a friend of the family. Deputy Hawes said whoever killed them was close to them," she said.

Jonathan peeked into the conference room.

"Do you still need me?" he asked.

"Find out what you can on this retirement and shakeup. Also find out the face behind this mystery corporation," Ed said. "If you knew this was going on already, why didn't we have something on it?"

"Victoria had already told me about the plan to put Allison Blake in. So far, Mr. Davies' comments were the most I've gotten out of anyone. No one on the board is talking. Besides, I thought you weren't going to print that?"

"Probably not tomorrow, but it may come in handy. Oh and find out what's in that stack of papers. James, have you finished the retrospective yet?"

She shook her head.

"Finish it ASAP and help him with that file."

"Marlowe, I need a story."

Ed left the conference room.

"I swear that man hates me. Well, it's going to be a long day," Jonathan said. "Where's that coffee?"

Victoria spent the next two hours finishing the retrospective. Once it was in, she rejoined Jonathan in the conference room.

"Anything interesting?" she asked.

"Lots," he said. "Whoever gave you this hates the Blakes and is well-connected. There are lots of reasons for Sissy Blake to have a good attorney."

"Why?"

"Looks like she would never get more than a small allowance from her father. He practically disowned her. But I can't verify any of this. It could be made up. Who's going to go on record for this? I've got several phone calls into the Blakes' attorneys. They're not calling me back. "

Jonathan leaned back in his chair and ran his fingers through his hair.

"You haven't called your deputy yet?"

"He's not my deputy."

"Whatever you say," he said.

She tried his cell, but no answer.

"Jeff, it's Vic. Give me a call."

She turned to Jonathan.

"In all the excitement this morning, I forgot to call security to find out who delivered our package this morning," she said.

"I did. It was dropped in the mail slot overnight, and there aren't any security cameras where it was dropped."

"This is exhausting."

"So he didn't tell you his wife left him?" Jonathan asked.

Victoria stared at him. At first, she was confused. Then she realized what he was talking about.

"We are working."

"Yes but this is much more interesting. I'm currently in between romances and quite bored with the fish in Bennettsville's pond. And you still aren't biting. This has the taste of forbidden love, and I can trade this info on the black market for breakfast tomorrow. The blue hairs would love this," he said and laughed.

She picked up the file folder and hit him on the arm.

"The lady doth become violent."

"You haven't seen me violent."

"Actually, there was the time in seventh grade." Jonathan was laughing harder.

"You'd better stop now," said Victoria. She couldn't help herself. She was laughing too.

"We've been reading graphs and charts all day. We can't get anyone to answer our calls. We might as well lighten up a little," he said.

She stood up and walked around the conference room.

"You're right. It seems no one wants to talk about the Blakes unless it's to tell us how wonderful they were."

"The funeral is tomorrow. We should crash the wake. It should be about time for it. We've gotten nowhere with these papers all day."

"Jonathan, you're a party animal."

"Please don't ruin my image. This is strictly business. And we should probably walk. There won't be anywhere to park at the funeral home."

"True."

It was a 15-minute walk to the Hodges and Sons Funeral Home. There was a line outside the funeral home as the entire town plus some residents of surrounding counties seemed to have come to pay their respects to the family. Victoria wondered if there were any deputies on duty in Bennettsville. All of them were either directing traffic or standing guard. The extended Blake clan was in attendance as well as Cassandra Blake's two sisters and their families. Blake Enterprises' board members, the city officials including the mayor and members of the city council were also in attendance. There was barely any room to stand inside the funeral home. Despite the large crowd in the funeral home, there was a surreal hush. It was hard to believe that many people could gather with little noise.

Victoria was aware of the eyes on her and Jonathan. As members of the press, she wasn't sure they were entirely welcome.

"I feel like a party crasher who's getting ready to be escorted off in cuffs," she whispered to Jonathan.

"I know what you mean."

Despite the glances in the duo's direction, no one asked them to leave.

Miss Myra stopped as she departed the funeral home. She grabbed Victoria's hand and looked into her eyes.

"This time, dearie, take care of the detective," she said as she patted Victoria's hand. "I always thought you and he were destined to be together. I never liked that girl and her Atlanta ways. She didn't belong in Bennettsville."

"Miss Myra, there's nothing between the detective and me. He's married," she said.

"Yes, dearie. He's a good man. Good parents. I've known him since he was a little boy. I've known you, too. You let him get away the first time. Don't do it this time."

Miss Myra kept moving to the door and acted as though she didn't hear a word Victoria said.

"I tell you she knows who killed the Blakes. She just wants the deputy to ask her," said Jonathan.

"The people in this town are unbelievable," Victoria said, ignoring Jonathan's statement. "She's already got me married to him."

For most of the evening, they watched as Allison and Sissy shook the hands and accepted the condolences of hundreds of people all with a pleasant smile on their faces. Victoria wondered what was going on in their minds.

She was lost in her thoughts when she heard a familiar voice.

"Working?" Jeff asked.

She had been looking for him in the crowd, but she was still surprised when he walked up behind her. She tried to hide the smile when she heard her voice.

"We could ask you the same thing, Deputy Hawes," said Jonathan. "We are merely observers."

"Anything new, Jeff?" Victoria asked.

"You'll be the first person I call."

"Our friendly informant has struck again, but this time, he or she, as the case might be, came by the office," she said.

"Lots of interesting charts and graphs. It could give you a few more suspects to add to the list," said Jonathan.

"More suspects are the last thing we need. We need to find the killer, and we are working around the clock to do that. Trust me," Jeff said.

"So who's at the top of the suspect list?" Victoria asked.

Jeff smiled.

"I'll let you know when we have something concrete. We don't need any more rumors either. I have enough fires to put out," he said.

"I'm telling you Myra Evans knows who the killer is or possibly the ladies who drink coffee and play canasta at Jake's every day. They seem to know everything else going on in this town," said Victoria. "I see them over there if you'd like to interview any of them."

"Thanks, Vic, and I'll see those papers?"

"Could you give a dog a bone, Deputy Hawes?"

"We could negotiate," Jeff smiled and walked away.

"So why are you feeding him information again? Is it that one dimple when he smiles at you?"

"Knock it off, Jonathan. Headlines, front pages, Pulitzer Prize, maybe?"

"Award-winning smile I think, or is it the blue eyes?"

"That's ancient history. He's still married. There's a ring on his finger, and I don't play those types of games. This is strictly professional. Besides, play nice with the cops, and they'll play nicely with you. Is there any other reason to stick around here?"

Jonathan laughed.

"What was it that Shakespeare said - the lady doth protest too much?" he asked. "You have to be the world's worst liar."

Victoria didn't answer.

"Give it another few minutes. I think it will get interesting before too much longer," he said. "The line is almost finished, and Allison Blake has looked over this way numerous times."

"I've seen the way she's been looking. She wants your head on a platter for that story about the Blake Enterprises' coup."

As they chatted, Jennifer Campbell approached Victoria. She smiled.

"You've written glowing pieces on the Blakes. I know they would be pleased."

"Thank you, Ms. Campbell. So what's next for you?"

"I'll be fine. Remember, I had a wealthy spinster aunt who left me a nice nest egg. I guess this will be the time for me to start that new project I was telling you about."

"I smell a business story," said Jonathan.

"Possibly, Mr. Marlowe. You should call me," she said and excused herself before leaving.

Jonathan's prediction came true about 15 minutes later after Allison Blake shook the last hand and hugged the last neck. She made a direct line to them. She spoke to Victoria first.

"I want to thank you for the kind coverage on my parents, Ms. James. You've shown them to be the wonderful people they are," she paused. "They were, I mean. I can't believe they are gone."

As she turned to talk to Jonathan, her demeanor changed.

"I know you are only doing your job, Mr. Marlowe, but you could have waited with your salacious headlines," she said to Jonathan coldly.

"I'm sorry you feel that way, Ms. Blake, but I don't write headlines. I write stories about things that will affect many people. These stories are important, and the timing of them was of the utmost."

She glared at him.

"Should I be warned of anything going into tomorrow's paper?"

"No warnings. There's more Blake legacy stories to come, and you have Ms. James to thank on that one."

"Rumors are terrible things, and there are plenty. I hope the paper doesn't become a gossip rag."

"No. We don't print gossip. We aren't a tabloid," he replied.

"I understand Bill Davies ran away at the mouth. I expect that won't be in the paper tomorrow. I've spoken to Mr. Kennedy," she said.

"Not at all, Ms. Blake."

She nodded and turned away.

"Don't you love it when they tell you what to print and drop the publisher's name in the same sentence?" Jonathan asked sarcastically.

"I think we're done here," said Victoria.

She and Jonathan left the funeral home. In her oversized hobo purse, she carried the package left by mysterious informant. Jonathan walked Victoria toward her apartment building. She paused at the corner of the block. She noticed a car patrolling. He slowed down as she approached the building, and she could see him nodding at her.

"Jonathan, you go on. I'll be fine. There's the patrol car," she said.

"Are you sure? I can go in with you," he said.

"No, I'm a big girl. I've got a patrol car, and Auggie will protect me."

"Oh yes, Auggie is such a ferocious beast."

"I'm sure, Jonathan. Go get your car and go home," she said.

He hesitated, but he turned and walked away. She let out a deep sigh. She wanted to ask Jonathan to go with her, but she had this independent streak that needed to have its way at times. Her mysterious visitor had definitely left her anxious. Was this informant the killer? Did this person just hate the Blakes or was there more to it? She wondered if she was in danger too. She hadn't done anything with what was left in the envelopes. Until after the funeral, there was no way she could make it to Birmingham to check out the enigmatic business card.

When she arrived at her building, she had her key ready to put in the exterior door's lock, but it was ajar. That was odd; it was so heavy it usually closed on its own. The lock appeared to be broken. She wondered if she should flag the deputy down, but his patrol car had disappeared. And Jonathan was already out of sight. She pulled her cell phone out just in case and walked slowly up the stairs. She heard a door open and stopped on the staircase.

"Hello, Victoria," her next door neighbor called out. "I called the landlord about the lock. Someone is coming out in the morning."

She jogged up the rest of the stairs.

"What happened?"

"Not sure," said Becky, her neighbor, who was peeking out of her door. "Looks like someone tried to break in."

Victoria's heart began to race. Becky came out into the hallway holding a box.

"I noticed this outside your door. I picked it up with the door broken and all. I didn't know if it was valuable or not."

"Thanks," she said, taking a box wrapped in brown paper away from her. Victoria's hands began to shake.

"Your apartment looks fine."

"Thanks Becky," she said.

A knot formed in the pit of her stomach. She knew who it was from. The other packages had been left without breaking and entering the building. When she arrived at her apartment, she stared at the door. She wasn't sure she wanted to go in, and she was afraid to open the box. Should she call Jeff? She didn't want to feed the rumor mill anymore. She could hear Auggie on the other side of the door. He must have heard her voice. His yapping bark meant he had missed her. She needed the comfort she found in his sweet furry snuggles.

She opened the door, and he jumped into her arms.

"Come on, Auggie. Are you hungry, boy?"

She picked him up, and he excitedly licked her face.

"I've missed you, too. Mommy gets a day off soon, and you and I are going for a ride."

Victoria stared at the box. She was afraid to open it. Where was the deputy who was patrolling the area? How did anyone break in? She opened it slowly. There was a lot of tissue in the box and a note atop the tissues. She pulled out the note without disturbing the contents of the box.

"Silly little girl. I'll give you time to sort through all the documents I left you. I'm sure someone will be able to help you decipher them – maybe the nice detective you've decided to call to help you out. That was a very bad decision, by the way. My other clues were more to the point. Don't you think it's more than a coincidence that two beautiful, young women died so soon after filing lawsuits against Charles Blake? Don't these things show you how horrible that man was? He was evil, and all you keep doing is printing fluffy, happy stories about him. There's a new one every few hours on the internet. You should just be a good girl and print these stories I'm sending your way. You could be a famous writer. They'd probably offer you a book deal or a movie contract. If you know what's good for you, you will print my stories. There are other ways for people to end up on the front page of the paper besides having their byline there."

Victoria's hands were shaking, and she'd gone numb. Her heart was pounding fiercely as she tried to pull back the tissue. Inside the box was a finger. She would have screamed, but her gag reflexes got the better of her. She rushed into her bathroom to throw up. Auggie came in to comfort her, but she was throwing up and crying at the same time. He whimpered beside her.

Her phone. What had she done with her phone? She couldn't think. Where was Jeff's number? She couldn't remember her own name much less his at the moment. What did she call him in her phone? She'd called so many people during the day that he was not in her history anywhere.

She finally remembered how to look up his number. He didn't answer. She couldn't get anything out to leave a message. She jumped up and ran to her door, locking the deadbolt chain and sliding bolt. She leaned against the door and slid down to the floor. She couldn't stand. Why was this person tormenting her? Her phone began to ring. She answered it, but she couldn't say anything. She felt as though something had its hands around her throat. She tried to utter words, but they stuck in her mouth.

"Vic, Vic. Are you there?" it was Jeff.

Nothing came out of her mouth.

"Vic, what's wrong? Where are you?"

She managed a weak whisper.

"Help" was all she could get out.

"Stay where you are and don't hang up. Where are you? Don't hang up. Do you hear me?"

Jeff sounded frantic.

"I'm coming to you. Just hang on."

"Home," she said as she tried to regain the strength in her voice. "I'm home."

Within a few minutes, she could hear footsteps up the staircase and soon, Jeff was banging on the door. She tried to stand; she couldn't reach the locks. Her legs felt like cooked noodles. She had no strength. She opened the locks and threw herself into his arms before he got across the threshold. Although he was stunned by her action, he wrapped his arms around her and held her close. He whispered that everything would be all right now that he was there. She felt safe resting against his chest as she sobbed out of fear. As the shock of the package began to wear off, she realized what she'd done, and those buried feelings began to rise to the surface. She pulled away from him.

"I'm sorry," she said.

"What's wrong? You look like you've seen a ghost," he said.

Victoria turned and pointed to the box on the table.

Jeff moved toward the table. He saw the finger and the letter.

"It's not safe for you to stay here. Do you have someplace you can go?"

Victoria tried to think.

"You look pale. Are you all right?"

Victoria shook her head.

Jeff pulled out a glass from the cabinet and put some cold water in it.

"Drink this," he said.

She thought she heard him make a phone call. She wasn't sure. She felt as though she was in a cave. His voice sounded distant and garbled. She sat down on the floor and tried to breathe. She felt dizzy, but as she took a few sips of the water, she began to calm down.

"Can you stand?" Jeff asked.

"I don't know."

He picked up Auggie and her purse as she stood in a dazed state. She noticed a couple of other deputies in her apartment. They were dusting for prints and taking photos of the box. Did she take a photo of the finger? She thought she did. She couldn't remember anything.

Jeff held her arm to steady her as she walked down the stairs.

"Where are we going?" she asked.

"I'm taking you to the station for now. Come on."

"What's the matter?" her neighbor noticed all the commotion. The glow of blue lights from the cars outside flooded the hallway through the window storefront.

"Go talk to the deputies in Vic's apartment. They will have a few questions for you."

"Sure," Becky replied.

"Am I going to the station in a patrol car?" Victoria asked.

"No. I am technically not on duty right now," he said. "Would you rather go to your parents' house?"

"No, take me to the station. What time is it anyway? I don't want them to worry. My mother will freak out. I can't deal with that. Where's my phone? I need to call Ed."

They got in Jeff's truck.

"I hate to tell you this, Vic, but you are now part of this investigation. And I can't release details of this investigation to the press," he said.

"But I have to work. I have to cover the funerals tomorrow."

"I realize that, but I need to see those files the killer left for you."

"This can't be happening."

Her phone vibrated.

"It's Jonathan," she said. "And it looks like he's tried to call me several times."

"You can talk to him, but you cannot talk about what happened tonight," he said.

She nodded.

"Victoria, what's going on?" Jonathan sounded concerned. "You didn't answer the phone so I'm at your apartment where there are two deputy cars with blue lights flashing. No one will talk to me. Where are you?"

"I'm fine," she said. Her voice was strained. "I'm with Deputy Hawes, and he said I'm not allowed to talk with anyone about what happened. He's taking me to the station. Auggie and I are going to need a place to stay for a few days, if you can think of anyone. I'll see you in the morning."

"Victoria, I know you aren't all right," he said.

"I'm afraid I'll be skipping breakfast at Jake's. Don't believe anything the blue hairs tell you," she said trying to make light of the situation. "I've got to go."

"Call me as soon as you can," he said.

She hung up as they pulled into the parking lot. Jeff turned to her.

"First, I need a statement from you. Another deputy will handle that. I'm calling Ed, and I will be in there to talk to both of you at the same time."

She nodded. She held Auggie close to her as she walked into the building. She could feel him shaking too. He always knew when she was upset. He licked her hand a couple of times to try to reassure her.

Someone gave her some ice water; she wasn't sure where it came from as she sat down at a desk with a female deputy.

Victoria heard words coming out of her mouth. She really wasn't sure what she was saying. She tried to separate herself from her testimony. She wanted to look at it objectively in the third person, but she found it difficult. She was still in shock. She'd had some angry readers in the past, but she'd never had her life threatened. The dismembered finger was proof the threats had come from someone who'd murdered two others in cold blood, and this made the situation even more frightening to her.

She must have finished her statement because the words stopped coming. She stared blankly at the deputy. She wasn't sure what she was going to do next. She couldn't go to her apartment, and she didn't want to call her parents. She wondered what time it was.

She felt Auggie lick her hand again. She was in the middle of wondering what might happen to him if something happened to her when Ed and Jeff entered the room together.

"Victoria, are you all right?" asked Ed.

He never called her by her first name, and he seemed concerned. She was confused, but she nodded.

Jeff leaned across the desk.

"Nothing leaves this room. If any of this comes out, I will personally come and arrest you both," he said.

"I understand," said Ed.

"Victoria James is now part of this murder investigation, and this information cannot be leaked to the public. It could jeopardize our case."

"Does that mean you know something?" asked Ed.

"I know a lot, but for now, let's say that Vic's safety is at risk if any of this is printed."

Victoria came out of her stupor.

"Apparently, it's the not printing of certain things that puts me at risk," she said with her voice raised. "That's why I'm a target."

"Vic" started Jeff.

"Don't 'Vic' me, Jefferson Hawes."

Auggie's ears stood up as he looked at Victoria. He barked.

"That's right, Auggie, you tell him," she said. "I'm a target now. I've given both of you some great material to work with, but I'm getting the raw end of this deal. Fine, we can't print what happened tonight. I understand that, but this investigation needs to go somewhere. Why is it that the town gossips already have Jeff and me married when he's still married to someone else – all because he showed up at my apartment when this lunatic broke into my building to plant an envelope outside my door?"

Victoria's voice rose.

"And you people can't solve a double murder? What is wrong with this picture? Well, you know what? I'm going to solve this crime because you aren't moving fast enough. No one has threatened your life."

Victoria's hands were shaking.

"I got a text from Liz. I'm crashing over there tonight. She's coming to pick me up now and will make sure I make it to the funeral. If I'm not a suspect, I'm leaving," she said.

She got up and walked out of the building.

Liz was the education reporter. She was single and had a small cottage on the outskirts of town. She also had a Doberman.

Victoria got into her car.

"I'm under a gag order," she said. "I wish I could tell you, but I can't so don't even ask."

"You look awful, and Auggie looks stressed," Liz said.

"Thanks. He needs some food and water. I had just gotten home when everything I'm not supposed to talk about happened. I just need a shower, and I have no clothes with me or anything. What am I supposed to wear to this funeral?"

"Can you go back to your place in the morning?"

"I'm not sure."

"Well, I have my single black suit that I wear to the important meetings. You and I are the same size."

"Thanks Liz. Maybe one day, I can tell you what's going on."

6

Cassie and Charles Blake's double funeral was scheduled for noon, but Victoria knew she needed to be there early. The First Baptist Church of Bennettsville was the town's largest, both in its membership and in its sanctuary's seating capacity. With so many dignitaries coming from all over the state and beyond, there would be more people in attendance than for the church's annual Christmas cantata, which always packed the church. An overflow crowd was expected. Additional seats were available and a live video feed would take place in the chapel, as well as the church fellowship hall.

Victoria wore Liz's suit to the event, and even though, she arrived more than an hour early, she barely squeezed into one of the packed pews. It was going to be a long day, she thought as she sat between two elderly ladies who kept staring at each other and nodding as though Victoria wasn't even present. They seemed to be having their own conversation through stares and raised eyebrows. Victoria barely slept the night before. She kept having visions of the severed digit. It almost looked like a fake. There wasn't any blood on it. She hoped she could pay attention and actually hear what the speakers were saying. She didn't use a recorder often especially for an event that would take so long and be so time-consuming to replay, but she knew she wouldn't be able to concentrate. She looked through the throng of people. The Blakes' murderer was likely right under her nose. Even though she'd interviewed so many people who said glowing things about the couple, there was someone who hated them, and from what Miss Myra said there were probably more. She wondered though what really took place on that night less than a week ago. Was it both of the Blakes the killer hated or was it just him? Was Cassie Blake collateral damage? And it was someone known by the family? But most of the state of Georgia was at the funeral or had been at the wake so that didn't help in narrowing down the playing field any.

Until the previous night, Victoria was more interested in writing about the story as the case played out, but Jeff told her she was now part of the investigation. After writing her funeral story, she was going to do what she wanted to do for days. She was driving to Birmingham. The timing couldn't be better. She needed a break. She needed to be away from her apartment, and she didn't have any place to stay. She couldn't see what she'd do after that, but maybe she could find a clue, a needle in a haystack? She knew it could possibly mean her going to jail or something, but she had to risk it. It would also give her a chance to go through the papers the killer had left in her office. In her stupor the night before, she'd forgotten to hand them over, and Jeff was too sidetracked to ask.

She hoped her recorder was picking everything up. Even with the air-conditioning cranked up, the sanctuary was huge, and it gets hot in Georgia in July. Liz's suit was not the best choice of attire, and Victoria was sweating buckets. There were several speakers to honor both Cassandra and Charles Blake. They seemed to drone on endlessly. Just when she didn't think she could take the heat and monotony any longer, the last hymn was sung, and the two caskets were taken out of the church.

Back at the news building, Victoria felt sarcasm bursting in her veins after yet another glowing treatise on the virtuous Blakes. She couldn't stomach the saccharine any longer. She thought she might throw up as she put the finishing touches on the Blake story.

She said her goodbyes and headed back to her apartment to grab a suitcase and a few items for her and Auggie. Even though the sun was still shining, she felt anxious as she walked up the stairs inside her building. She took a deep breath as she put her key in the lock. There were no boxes or envelopes in front of the door. She looked around her apartment. There were no signs the police had been there. She had seen Jeff at the funeral in the distance. She could think of no reason to talk to him, and she certainly wasn't telling him where she was going. She still felt as though she wanted to cry. Her job could be stressful at times, but it had never been this bad. Death threats weren't discussed in any of the journalism classes she'd taken.

Before she left the apartment, she had one more thing she needed to take with her. She hadn't turned over everything to Deputy Hawes. She had it taped in an envelope behind the headboard of her bed. It was the photo of Charles Blake and the young woman. From the newspaper clippings the killer had left, she could only assume this was another young woman he'd taken up with. There wasn't anything written on the back of the photo, and there were no special markings on it.

She wondered what was up with it. Too many questions, no answers.

"Come on, Auggie, let's blow this place!"

Auggie's ears perked up, and he barked in agreement. When she picked him up, he licked her face. She locked the door and headed out of her apartment. She ran into Jeff as she left her building.

"Going somewhere?"

"Detective Hawes, whatever gave you that idea?"

"Suitcase?"

Auggie whimpered.

"You wouldn't happen to be going to Birmingham, would you?"

"Am I a suspect?"

"Not at all, but you need to leave the investigating to us. Now, stop changing the subject. You were supposed to give me something."

"Fine."

She and Jeff walked back into her apartment, and she put Auggie on the floor.

"You are going to have to stop showing up like this. The blue-haired ladies kept eyeing me and raising their eyebrows throughout the funeral today. Jonathan told me what rumors they've been spreading."

She pulled the envelope with the financial data out of her overnight bag. As he reached for it, she held onto it.

"What about the finger?"

"DNA matches Charles Blake," he said. "No prints on the box. Very clean cut. Do you want details?"

She shook her head.

"Where's his hand?" she asked.

"Find the killer, and we'll know," he said. "Our killer is not only a hunter but judging from the gift you received, this person may have some taxidermy experience or could be a surgeon. What did you write for tomorrow's paper?"

"Most of it has already been posted on the internet. It will be a front page spread. Sideline stories inside of more reaction. More of the stuff the killer hates."

"Sounds like our killer is not going to be happy," he said. "Where are you going, Vic?"

"I don't know but away from here."

"I could have you arrested."

"On what grounds?" she asked raising her voice. Auggie whimpered again. He put his paws on Victoria's leg.

"Obstruction of justice, Ms. James," he said.

"I have cooperated with everything you've asked."

"Not if you go to Birmingham. If you do, you are crossing a line."

He took a step forward and was uncomfortably close to her. She could feel his breath on her face.

"Remember what I do for a living, Ms. James. I can tell when someone is lying," he said. His stern look softened as he got even closer. "Especially you. I used to know you pretty well, and the corner of the left side of your lip used to curl slightly before you said something that wasn't completely true. I don't think you've learned how to control that."

She backed up and moved to place her small table between them.

"I have a couple of days off. There's someone threatening me so I can't stay here. The stories tomorrow are going to make this person mad. If I stay here, I'm a sitting duck. Your deputy didn't prevent that maniac from leaving a finger at my door. I can't tell anyone what's going on, and as you said, I'm a bad liar so I can't go to my parents because my mother will know something is wrong. What sort of lie can I make up that she won't see straight through? I'm stressed out, and I need to get away. So you tell me what I'm supposed to do."

She folded her arms and stared directly at him.

"That deputy has been placed on leave – indefinitely," he said "Stay with Liz a couple of days."

"For how long, Jeff? Do you have any leads on this killer?"

"Yes, we do."

"But you can't tell me or give me anything printable?" Victoria's voice began rising again. Auggie scratched on her leg. He could tell she was agitated.

"No, I can't."

She let out a deep sigh and shook her head.

"Deputy Hawes, I gave you the information you requested. Please leave now," she said

He hesitated before he turned and left.

Victoria sat down and tried to figure her next move. She looked at Auggie.

"Obstruction of justice, Deputy Hawes. We'll see about that."

She called Jonathan.

"Can I borrow your car for a few days?"

"Is something wrong with yours?"

"I had another visit from our friendly detective."

"Well, from the sounds of things it wasn't all that friendly."

"No, it wasn't. I was going to follow that lead in Birmingham. I need to get away. I can't tell anyone what happened last night. I can't stay at my apartment because I don't feel safe."

"You can't tell me about last night, but what if I guess?"

"I'm not playing 20 questions with you, and that's not why I called. Help me figure out how to ditch the deputies? With you and your cloak-and-dagger personality, haven't you ever tried to figure something like this out?"

Jonathan laughed.

"Many times, and I have just the plan."

Victoria hoped the plan would work. She took her suitcase and from underneath her bed, she pulled out the accordion file of copies of the items the killer had left and put them in her purse. She headed back to the newspaper building. Liz met her outside the news building, and she handed Auggie and her suitcase off to Liz while she went inside. She hoped the deputy saw the hand-off. Liz drove away. The plan was for Victoria to work on another story until dark and leave through the back exit into Jonathan's waiting vehicle. Jonathan insisted on driving her and Auggie to Birmingham.

While she sat at her desk, her office phone rang.

"This is Victoria James."

"I thought you were off," it was Jeff.

"Seems I've been grounded, Deputy. At least, there's security in the news building. I feel semi-safe here, and I really don't want to see the inside of a jail cell although I might be safer there than at my apartment. I do have other stories to work on. The news business never sleeps, and you know I work late. Goodnight, Deputy Hawes."

"Goodnight, Ms. James."

She turned off her cell phone and opened the desk drawer.

"This is probably a bad idea. I'm sure you'll be blowing up by the end of the weekend," she said as she dropped it inside and closed the drawer.

Before she sneaked out the back, Victoria changed her clothes in the ladies room and stuffed her hair under a baseball cap. Jonathan was watching outside. When the security guard left his post, Jonathan called. She slipped out the back door. She got into the backseat of his car and lay across the seats. Auggie jumped into the back and rested next to her.

"I think I could fall asleep," she said. "Do you think anyone is going to buy this?"

"Well if we make it out of the county without being pulled over, I'll take that as a good sign."

"Thanks for driving me. Birmingham is a long trip."

"I wouldn't have missed this for the world. This is much more exciting than Bennettsville."

"Jonathan, why did you come back to Bennettsville anyway?"

He paused so long that she didn't think he was going to answer.

"That, my dear, is for another day," he said breaking the silence.

He didn't say much, and Victoria fell asleep on the back seat of his car as he drove. She didn't wake up until the car stopped.

"Sleeping beauty, we're here," Jonathan said as they pulled into the parking lot of a hotel.

"Jonathan, why didn't you wake me up?"

"You've had quite a week. I didn't want to wake you. Besides, I was hoping you were one to talk in your sleep. I wanted to find out all about your police visit last night, but sadly, you don't."

"Jonathan, where are we?"

This was not the hotel she'd chosen. Her choice was clean and pet-friendly, but it wasn't exactly five stars.

"Atlanta. I cancelled your reservation," he said as they walked to the hotel "I have one suite. It has a separate bedroom with two beds, but I'll gladly take the foldout couch if you prefer. The room is in my name. You and I are spending the weekend in Atlanta. Let's get checked in then we can talk."

She nodded. She was too exhausted to argue with anyone; besides he'd booked a much better looking hotel than she had. Once inside the room, Jonathan started asking questions.

"So Sherlock Holmes, what's your plan now?

Victoria collapsed face forward on one of the beds while Jonathan sat in a chair next to a desk.

"I don't know if I have a plan. Why are we in Atlanta? I need to go to Birmingham."

She sat up, and Auggie curled up in her lap.

"Birmingham is only about two hours from here on I-20. When your detective asks where you've been, you don't have to tell a complete lie. I have tickets to tomorrow afternoon's baseball game, and a play on Saturday evening, and we can go to a museum Sunday to further pad it. There's a lot of museums to choose from or the aquarium if you prefer."

She smiled.

"You've got this covered, don't you?" she asked.

He nodded.

"I am officially your alibi."

She pulled out the photograph of the woman with Charles Blake.

"This is our mystery lady in Birmingham," she said.

"She's pretty."

"Jeff told me her business was a front for an escort service."

"Interesting."

She stared at the photo for a few minutes.

"What happened last night?" Jonathan broke the silence.

"I'm not sup-" she started.

"I know you aren't, but how long have we known each other? We were friends long before you fell for the dreamy detective, and you know there are secrets of yours that I haven't told a soul. In our job, we have to keep confidences."

She stared at him.

"He threatened to arrest me if I said anything."

"We had a blood oath in the sixth grade," he said as he held up his right hand, pointing to a faint scar.

She wrinkled her nose.

"Really? Do you have to pull that one?"

"Spill it, Victoria. You know me."

"The killer left me a threatening note and Charles Blake's finger."

Jonathan wrinkled his brow.

'That explains why you were so upset," he said. "No wonder you don't want to stay at your apartment."

"I actually took a picture of it with my phone when I stopped throwing up," she said. "But my phone is in my desk, and I'm sure I'll hear about that on Monday – from a variety of sources. I can't have it in jail anyway."

"You aren't breaking the law. You aren't in Birmingham," he said. "A missing finger from the missing hand. When they said the hand was removed from the body, they never said if they found it, did they?"

"No, they didn't. And I barely got that detail in the paper. It was only because I overhead the feuding sisters. They weren't going to release it. I guess it was a trophy. Our killer is a hunter with taxidermy experience who is close to the Blakes so that would make sense. Sissy Blake hated her sister and father, but they were chummy hunting companions. Bill Davies hunted with him and had motive. How much money would he have stood to lose? I think almost every member of Blake Enterprises' Board of Directors was also a member of the Bennettsville Hunting Club."

She stopped.

"Why kill them, Jonathan? If the plan was to stop Allison from taking over the company, why kill them?"

"It wasn't about Allison. Whoever did this hated the Blakes. It was a personal vendetta. All the rest is icing on the cake."

"And only two people have said negative things about the Blakes - Miss Myra and the killer."

"Well, I can't see Miss Myra killing them," he said with a laugh.

"I don't want to think about this anymore. I just want this to end and for Bennettsville to go back to the same boring place it's been for decades. Then, I don't have to see Jeff much anymore."

"Don't lie," he said.

She raised an eyebrow.

"We both know Bennettsville is boring and should stay that way," she said.

"The Jeff part?"

"He's taken. He's still wearing that ring. I know because I've seen him a lot lately. Let's change the subject. Since it's truth time, you have to tell me what brought you back to Bennettsville."

"Let's just say, I have a detective story of my own."

"You could have at least said that, but knowing you, I'm sure that's not all of it."

He tried to smile, but she could see something in his eyes.

"Still hurts after all this time," he said. "It's something I don't like to think about, but I do on a daily basis."

She looked at him and smiled.

"Yeah, it does. Whoever said time heals all wounds was a liar. It just gets covered over."

"Enough of this cheerful talk," he said. "I'm going to sleep."

"I'm awake now. I'm going into the other room to read these papers."

"I'll help you with that later."

"I'm going to see if we missed something."

They'd already spent hours looking through them. Jeff had said whoever killed the Blakes probably knew them, and from all the information, the person knew them well. She wondered what made the killer think he or she wouldn't get caught. Some of this information seemed illegal. There were tax documents along with supporting information that could have put the Blakes in jail for fraud and tax evasion. Documents appeared to have been forged. Why go to all this trouble to smear his name? And why kill them? Why not just send him to jail? Who could have that much hate?

Maybe it wasn't about destroying Charles Blake's name. Maybe there was something personal against Cassie. So far, the only dirt on the Blakes was about Charles. Had Cassie been hiding something, too?

Victoria fell asleep on the couch with the papers strewn all over the floor.

"Good morning, Victoria my dear, are you ready to break the law now?"

"Five more minutes," she said as she tried to roll over on the couch. Auggie began licking her ears to rouse her.

"Go away, Auggie," she moaned.

"What time did you finally go to sleep?"

"3 o'clock maybe? What time is it now?"

"7 a.m. on the nose."

"On a Saturday? You are evil, Jonathan."

"We have a two-hour drive."

"Fine."

There wasn't much conversation between the two of them on the ride. She was trying to figure out what she'd even say to this woman if they met. Somehow, "Hi, I'm Victoria James. I understand you run an escort service out of this office, and how is that related to the Blake murders?" didn't seem like the right thing to say. And what would she gain from this trip anyway? She couldn't print any of it. Maybe it was just a good excuse to get out of Bennettsville.

The drive passed quickly. The Davenport Travel Agency was in a small red brick building with a green awning over the door. A sign in the window indicated it was open for business.

She looked at Jonathan and Auggie.

"Did we ever come up with a plan?" she asked weakly.

He smiled.

"My drama training has come in handy on more than one occasion in my life. Never underestimate the power of improv class. We'll think of something. You've been torturing yourself over this for a while. Besides, women love men wearing hats."

He winked at her as he placed his fedora on his head at an angle. Victoria tried to smile, but she felt a lump in her throat and a knot in the pit of her stomach. They'd come a long way for her to chicken out now. She took a deep breath. Auggie looked at her. He seemed to be smiling at her.

"It's now or never. The quicker we do this the quicker we can work on our alibi," he said.

She nodded.

They walked to the door and went inside.

"Hello?" Victoria called out.

There didn't seem to be anyone in the office. It looked like half-travel agency, half taxidermy shop. There were photographs on the walls of Paris and London right next to deer heads and fish. She noticed some photographs of the woman in her picture. In these, she was dressed in hunting gear, and she was with Charles Blake. As they stood in the office, they heard another door open. Victoria turned around still thinking of something to say. She wasn't officially working for the paper; she was just Victoria James.

"Can I help you?" it was the woman from the photograph.

"I'm Victoria, and this is my friend, Jonathan," she said. Auggie barked. "And this is Auggie."

"Hi, I'm Amy," she said. "Where do you want to travel to?"

"No, it's not that. We live in Bennettsville, Ga."

Amy's smile vanished.

"Do you know Charles Blake?" Victoria asked.

"Are you with the police?" she sounded defensive.

"No, it's not like that at all. We wanted some information," said Jonathan in a soothing tone he used when he read Shakespearean sonnets for a literary event at the Bennettsville Library.

"You knew him?" Victoria asked again.

"Of course, I knew him. He was my father," she said. Tears began streaming down her face.

She sat down, and Victoria grabbed some tissues to hand to her.

"This is the first day I've come to work in more than a week," she said.

It wasn't long before Amy was telling them her whole life story.

"My mother met Charles Blake in college, and his family didn't like it much. He told her he would marry her and break with his family's wishes. But his family won. He took care of us until she found a really nice man to marry her. My stepfather was about 20 years older than she was. He was a good man. They had 20 happy years until he died of a stroke. My mother died a couple of years ago of a heart attack. My stepfather wouldn't accept any of Charles Blake's money, but my father put money in a trust account for me. He would visit, but his wife didn't like the idea of me very much. Let's just say I was not a welcomed guest at Thanksgiving and Christmas."

"Cassie knew about you?" Victoria asked. The words came out in a jerky fashion.

"A lot of them knew, but you know how things are in the South. People don't talk about things except in whispers. It's like if they don't say anything, they'll go away. My mother would have me write letters to him when I was little. At first, she sent them to the house, but those were returned. Then, she started sending them to his office. He got them there. I remember one time he came to visit on my birthday. I was eight. It was right before my mother met Bob, my stepfather, and Cassie had followed him. He gave me the most beautiful teddy bear, which she destroyed in front of me. She called my mother horrible names. I'd never seen my mother cry so much. She was so mean to my mother and me. She always seemed to find out when he was going to see me. She showed up so many times and made awful scenes. She was not a nice woman."

Victoria sat and listened to Amy. This was the first she'd heard anyone say anything bad about Cassie.

"When I got older, he would tell Cassie he was going on a business trip. He'd take me hunting and fishing. He was great with my daughter, Ava. Then, two weeks ago, I got this official-looking letter in the mail. I opened it, and the secret account he'd opened for my little girl had been emptied and closed. I'm a single mom."

She pulled out a photograph of a little blonde with curls.

"Then that hateful woman called me to make sure I got the letter, and she rubbed it in. She said they were changing his will, too," she said. "I'm glad she's gone. Now, I've got to work double time to try to at least stay afloat. I haven't been able to work the past few weeks. I went to the funeral in Bennettsville. I was in one of the overflow rooms. No one knew me there."

"You haven't been able to go to work?" Victoria asked.

"Ava's been sick, and then this," she said.

"We're so sorry for your losses, Ms. - " Jonathan started, but he didn't know her last name.

"It's Blake," she said.

He handed her a few more tissues and shook her hand.

The two of them left as Amy Blake continued to wipe her eyes.

Despite the bombshell they'd just experienced, one thought came into Victoria's mind.

"Why did Jeff lie to me?" she asked right after they got into the car. "Jeff told me that was an escort service. He lied. She's not running anything illegal there."

"You're worried about Jeff lying. Did you listen to Amy? Motive and a mysterious two-week absence from her business."

"Yes, she's suspicious, and she admitted to being in Bennettsville. It's not like I can hand that over to the Bennettsville Sheriff's Department."

"True. Let's make an honest woman of you," he said pulling out a baseball cap from the glove compartment and handing it to her.

"You hate sports, Jonathan," she said.

"But I love the theater so I'll suffer through the afternoon game to enjoy the traveling Broadway show tonight. I have friends who got us great tickets to both. Our bases are covered."

She shook her head and groaned.

"You really should be a copy editor and put those bad puns to use," she said. "Thanks for being my friend."

"And since you conveniently left your phone, we'll take photos at every place we go for further proof," he said.

Victoria laughed.

"We can't post them on social media or we could lose our jobs. But pictures would be handy. I'm sure it will all even out. I don't have anything appropriate to wear to the theater. I guess we'll have to go shopping, too," she said and smiled.

7

It was good for Victoria to be out of Bennettsville even if it was for less than two days. She tried to purge Bennettsville and everything associated with it out of her mind during her time in Atlanta. She enjoyed spending the time with Jonathan. She laughed a lot; however, on the ride home, everything kept spilling back in. She held Auggie close as Jonathan drove.

"I give our friendly deputy about 10 minutes, 15 minutes max to show up after I get home so would you mind staying until he arrives? You have the photos to back me up," she said.

"I'm your alibi," he said. "I won't leave you."

When they arrived outside her apartment building, she paused. She wondered what might be lurking inside the building.

"Why don't I go in first?" he asked pushing past her and heading up the stairs. There wasn't anything in front of her apartment door, and no neighbor with packages. She tried to unlock her own door, but her hands were trembling.

"I don't know what's wrong with me," she said to Jonathan.

"Let me," he said taking the keys from her and opening the door.

He walked around her apartment.

"All clear," he said.

She smiled.

"You aren't alone, and the deputy on his white steed or actually his pickup truck will be here soon," he said.

"I'm afraid of that, too. He won't be coming to save me. He's not going to be happy with me. He might even cart me off to jail."

"Five minutes," Jonathan said and glanced at his watch. He took his fedora off and put it on the table.

She tried to smile.

"I don't think I'll look good in orange," she said.

"You aren't going to jail. That's why I'm here."

After about 15 minutes, there was a knock at her door.

"He's not as punctual as we thought," she said as she went to answer to the door.

Jeff didn't look happy as she let him in. He scowled at her and stared down Jonathan.

"Where have you been?"

"Good evening to you too, Deputy Hawes," said Jonathan. He walked up behind Victoria, startling her when he put his arms around her waist. He pulled her toward him and kissed the back of her neck.

"Jonathan and I went to Atlanta," she said, trying to sound nonchalant when her heart was racing.

"We had quite the weekend. Theater, baseball and the museum," Jonathan said with his smooth, seductive voice. His tone hinted at so much more than he was saying. "I have the ticket stubs if you want to see them and photographs as well. We would post them on social media, but we have to keep things quiet."

"That doesn't account for the entire weekend," Jeff said.

"Some things aren't appropriate for this conversation," Jonathan shot back in wicked tone; Victoria elbowed him.

"So sorry, my dear," he said.

"So the two of you –" Jeff started.

Victoria raised her eyebrows.

"Is there a problem with that?" she asked. Her voice reflected her agitation and growing anger with the whole scenario. She wasn't sure which male in the room was angering her more at this point.

"No, no. I just thought he was -" he paused.

"Oh, Deputy Hawes, there's so much you've gotten wrong about me in the past. You know nothing about me. Besides, Victoria and I have to keep things quiet since we work together. The newspaper frowns on workplace romances," said Jonathan.

Victoria could tell Jonathan was enjoying getting his jabs in at Jeff.

Jeff nodded as his scowl deepened.

"Atlanta?" he asked.

"Yes, Atlanta. Baseball, museums, theater. Tickets, hotels photos," Victoria said.

"I'll be going now."

"Yes, Jeff, you need to be going," she said.

As soon as she closed the door behind Jeff, she turned around and pushed Jonathan in the center of the chest. She was angry, but she didn't want to raise her voice and have it carry for Jeff to hear her.

"What is wrong with you?" Victoria asked in an angry whisper.

Jonathan tilted his head back and was laughing.

"You are laughing, and he thinks we're dating," she said.

Jonathan tried to talk, but he was laughing too hard. That only fueled Victoria's anger. She stood there dumbfounded as he continued to laugh. After a couple of minutes, he was able to compose himself a little.

"While you were busy being mad at me, you couldn't see the priceless look on his face. He is beyond jealous. This weekend was so worth it. You've paid me back 1,000 times for all the favors I've ever done for you, and I will forever be in your debt. I've always wanted to wipe that smug look off his face."

He continued to laugh.

"If only I'd had a camera," he said almost to himself.

"Why do you think this is funny?"

She grabbed her pillow and hit him with it several times. Soon she began to laugh too.

"You should be thanking me instead of being angry," he said. "He's so jealous right now. And since you obviously are so observant, Ms. Sherlock Holmes, you didn't notice the ring is missing."

She stopped laughing.

"Don't tell me that. I don't want him breaking my heart again."

"Your new boyfriend will protect you," he said and winked at her.

She hit him with the pillow again.

"I'm going to walk to the newspaper and get my phone. Send me the photos? I think I'll change my relationship status online, but I won't put with whom," she said with sarcasm.

She paused and realized how grateful she should be to him.

"And thanks for all the trouble. Don't I owe you something for all the tickets?"

"I called in some favors on that. I didn't pay for any of those tickets. I have friends and press badges. Besides, the idea that Jefferson Hawes is jealous of me – I couldn't put a price tag on that - ever. This one incident has done more for me than years of therapy. Oh, what he put me through when we were kids because I didn't play football or baseball. His words cut deep, but this - priceless."

He continued to smile.

"Mind if I walk with you? I haven't been the breakfast topic at Jake's in months. The blue hairs' tongues will be wagging tomorrow. I'm sure this news will travel fast."

"Great. I've been the daily special lately. Let's give them more to talk about. Who knows what they'll come up with now?"

Auggie followed her to the door.

"Auggie, you stay here. I'm going to check my email, and then, I'll be back. I promise."

She waved as she passed the deputy in the car outside. He nodded. Jonathan smiled during their short journey to the news building.

"I'll see you in the morning," he said.

"Rushing away so soon?"

"I have a date later."

"Cheating on me already?"

"My love - Angelica - will be upset I've been gone so long, and you know how she feels about Auggie. She will ignore me all evening

I'm sure."

Angelica was Jonathan's Persian cat.

"Have fun and thanks."

In true Jonathan form, he bowed and tipped his fedora to her, then he reached for her hand and kissed it.

The newsroom was quiet on a Sunday evening. She sat at her desk and stared at her cell phone before deciding to turn it on. As she'd anticipated, there were several texts from Jeff. Nothing really stood out. He was aggravated that she wasn't responding, and he did ask if she was in Birmingham. She was surprised there were no newspaper calls or texts.

She was apprehensive about opening her email. She knew there had to be something in there from the killer, and she knew the killer would be angry. There were several emails that she immediately recognized as being from the killer. She opened the oldest one first. It chastised her for the funeral coverage. Everything was sugar-coated and canned. Where were the real stories? it asked. All of them said the same thing, but they got angrier each time.

The newest one had only been sent a few minutes before.

She felt ill as she opened it. There was a photo of Auggie.

"What a beautiful dog," the email read. "It would be such a shame for something to happen to him. Auggie is his name, isn't it? If you want to see your dog again, I'll give you something to print, and this time you'd better do it. Meet me alone at 225 Cedar Lane. The key word is 'alone.' No deputies and no other reporters."

If anything happened to Auggie, she couldn't bear it.

225 Cedar Lane. Did she even know where that was? She was having problems thinking straight. She pulled it up on her phone and stared at the map. She knew exactly where it was even though the address wasn't familiar. It was an abandoned textile mill on the river. She ran out of the news building toward her apartment building. Her car was parked nearby. How could someone have gotten Auggie? As she passed the deputy's car in front of the building, she found him slumped over the wheel. There was blood trickling out of his temple.

She dialed Jeff's number. It went to voicemail.

"Jeff, your deputy in front of my apartment – I think he's dead. I don't know," her voice broke. She could feel the fear rising up, and she held back the urge to cry. This person had killed at least two people, maybe three. Now, the killer had her dog. All she could think of was Auggie.

She ran into the building. The front lock had been replaced from where the killer had broken in, and there was no sign of damage this time. Her apartment door was open, and Auggie was gone. Her mind was swirling with all of the facts as she ran to her car and raced out toward the mill.

It was almost sunset by the time she reached the mill. She didn't see another car anywhere. She parked outside the main gate. The mill had closed about 20 years before. There were several buildings along with abandoned warehouses. Most of the gates were padlocked except for one around back. The chains had been severed with a bolt cutter and were cast away on the ground. Through that gate, she entered the complex. She wasn't sure where to go. She walked around checking the doors until she finally found one that was open.

The owners of the company had simply closed it and walked away leaving all the equipment behind. The expansive room held the industrial-sized looms. Vandals and vagrants had broken into the building over time. There were remains of fires; equipment had been destroyed; windows shattered. The setting sunlight streamed in from the second story windows.

Victoria called out.

"Hello. Is anyone here?"

From behind her she heard Auggie's familiar yip and a woman's voice.

"You have been a bad girl, Ms. James. You don't follow instruction well."

Out from between the looms stepped Jennifer Campbell, Mr. Blake's secretary. Victoria could see that Auggie was in a small kennel on one of the loom mechanisms.

And she was holding a gun.

"Don't worry about him. He'll be fine as long as you cooperate. And I know you will cooperate."

"What do you want from me?"

"I want you to print the truth not all of these lies about the Blakes," she said as she walked toward Victoria with the gun pointed at her. She wore a black blazer with black pencil skirt. Her hair was slicked back and into a bun. Her black stilettos tapped as she walked closer to Victoria. Jennifer's usual calm voice rose with anger.

"And you are going to write what I tell you here tonight, and then you are going to make sure this winds up on the paper's website, or I will kill you and your dog," she continued.

"Why are you doing this? I thought you were happy working for Mr. Blake."

"Happy? What would make you say that? I'm happy now since I'm the new owner of Blake Enterprises, but I'll be the happiest when you help me destroy their name forever," she said.

"You are the new owner of Blake Enterprises?"

Jennifer laughed.

"Sissy and Allison – what insipid brats! He was going to give Allison the company? Please," she paused and laughed. "All they will have is a house full of antiques and a huge tax bill."

"That's your new business venture you told Jonathan and me about?"

"Oh yes, I've spent years planning this. I take it you met Amy? You did at least follow one of my leads. Lovely girl. I felt sorry for her, especially when her stepmother cut off her little nest egg. She had great motive, but your stupid detective doesn't take hints well either."

"You aren't going to get away with this."

"My dear, if you have enough money, you can get away with anything including murder. My private jet is waiting to take me to the Bahamas. The airfield is less than a mile from here. When you cooperate and post this online, then I will be out of the country before anyone knows."

She heard Auggie whimper.

"What do you want me to write?"

"You really are thick, aren't you? Charles Blake was a liar and cheat. He was always the womanizer. Amy was the only proof of that because he made sure to cover his mistakes the older he got. He spotted me not long after I started working for his company. I quickly became his 'assistant' so I could go on trips with him. Very convenient, don't you think? And then there were the others that he saw when he was supposed to be seeing me. He drove one to jump to her death, and that car accident was no accident. Believe me. I was working for him at the time. "

Jennifer turned her face away, and Victoria could see the anger as she clenched her jaw.

"Our relationship lasted a long time. When I found out I was pregnant, well, he couldn't have another Amy running around so he drugged me and took me to Atlanta, where I woke up the next day - not pregnant. He arranged for a trip to Aruba to make up for it. I 'recovered' there. He splurged and doted on me. What he didn't know is I started plotting my revenge there. I've spent more than 20 years working on this. I kept working for him to gain his trust and his stock options. He never knew what he was signing. He never read the papers I put in front of him; he just signed things over to me. Then, Cassie found out that money was missing. He let her get involved. I'm not sure if it was out of a guilty conscience or what. When I found out he was going to put that idiot Allison in charge, I knew it was time. That never would have worked. So on the night of the murders, I went to try to talk things out with them. Cassie was angry about the money, and the stock options. She began to accuse the both of us."

She stared at Victoria.

"Why did you kill them? Why not just humiliate them or send them to jail? You had enough evidence on him to put him away forever."

"Cassie didn't seem to care about the women or the forced

abortion. He told her I was lying on the anniversary of our child's death. I don't think she believed him, but I was too angry at both of them. They were arguing with each other like I wasn't even there. They really shouldn't have turned their backs on me and ignored me."

Jennifer looked like she might cry when she talked about the pregnancy. She refused to release the tears, instead the lines of rage etched in her face became deeper.

"His gun was on the wall, and it was loaded. I knew that. I'm so glad he taught me to shoot all those years ago. Two shots, and it was done. They never knew what hit them – literally."

She laughed.

"So you are going to write the story about the cheater because he did cheat on everything – not just his wife. I gave you the documents."

"I needed to double check them."

"No double checking needed. Now you will need to write. Turn around."

She walked closer to Victoria.

"I have a nice spot and a laptop for you to use."

"I don't think so. I think you are headed to jail," Jeff called out and startled Jennifer. She fired the gun, but she didn't take aim. The bullet hit Victoria's left arm. As Jennifer tried to turn and fire at Jeff, he fired, hitting her in the shoulder. She dropped to the ground and two other deputies raced to her to arrest her.

Jeff headed toward Victoria who sat on the floor slumped in pain. She looked up to see Jeff kneeling over her. Their eyes locked briefly. He wasn't smiling; his face was marked with a serious stare. Was that fear she saw in his eyes as he examined her arm? He didn't say anything as he touched her. She looked at his left hand. Jonathan was right – no ring. She looked up at him again. It was hard not to get lost in his eyes. For that instant, she didn't feel her arm.

"It looks like she only grazed you."

"It doesn't feel like she only grazed me," she said and winced as she came out of her trance and realized he was touching her arm.

"We need to get you to the hospital."

"Where's Auggie?" she asked.

Jeff waved his hand and one of the deputies brought her her dog. He was shaking, but he was so glad to see her. He licked her faced.

"Wait a minute. How did you know I was here?" she asked.

"The deputy came to as you were calling me. He called me back and tailed you here," he said.

"Came to? I thought he was dead. He was bleeding and not moving."

"She sprayed pepper spray in his eyes and hit him really hard in the head. It knocked him out and caused him to bleed some."

He paused.

"I know I told you to leave the detective work to us, but if it wasn't for you, it would have taken longer to solve this. She was careful until the end."

He smiled.

"I recorded her confession."

"You mean you've been listening and waiting that whole time?"

Jeff nodded.

"Look up," he said.

In the rafters of the cavernous room, there was a metal catwalk, and when she looked up, she saw two deputies with rifles.

"We haven't given them the all-clear. They were there much of the time, and you didn't even know it."

"How did they get up there?"

Jeff laughed.

"Well she still shot me even if they were up there," she said.

"Just sit tight; there's an ambulance on the way."

She reached into her pocket.

"I need to make a call."

His smile dropped.

"What? I'm sitting on a front page story here. This could be national news. I need a photo of them taking her away."

8

"Good work James and Marlowe," said Ed as he tossed the front page of the paper onto Victoria's desk. "Picture is a little grainy, but it worked."

It had been a long time since she'd stayed at the newspaper until the first edition was printed, but she wanted to see the final copy. Jeff wanted her to go to the hospital, but while the paramedics were patching her up, she had called Jonathan to get his help in writing the story. She dictated it to him from the scene and had Jeff take her to the news building.

She stared at the front page and its bold headline - "Blake Killer Arrested."

"So do I get an extra day off?" she asked Ed.

"So you and Marlowe can go goofing off in Atlanta? You know what the paper says about that sort of thing," he responded.

She and Jonathan looked at each other for a minute.

"You can have the day off to get your arm checked out," Ed said. "And no crime solving at the hospital. Marlowe, you will be busy with the Blake Enterprise follow-ups. This could be messy. I'm going home."

"What time is it anyway?" she asked Jonathan.

"You don't want to know, Detective James."

She smiled and shook her head.

"Oh no. I'm not a detective. I'm hanging up my magnifying glass and Sherlock Holmes' hat. No more crime investigations for me. I'm just going to report them."

"Never say never, my dear," he said and smiled. "Never say never."

MURDER AT THE MASQUERADE

A Victoria James Mystery

DIAMOND KEY PRESS

1

Labor Day weekend might signal the end of summer in some communities, but in Bennettsville, it is the highlight of the social calendar. Not only does it mean the first home game for the Bennettsville Bulldogs' high school football team on Friday, but it's also the weekend of the annual Bennettsville Masquerade Ball.

Victoria James often wondered why anyone would have a fancy dress-up ball the first weekend of September in south Georgia when the temperatures could still tip the mercury in the 90s. But it was a longstanding tradition dating back to the 1940s, and no one messed with tradition and football in the South – no one. At the Bennettsville Masquerade Ball, the Bennettsville Business Exchange Club honored the person who'd made the biggest impact in the city's economy during the past year.

It was a high priority story for the newspaper since the publisher was a former president of the Bennettsville Business Exchange Club. Victoria had only covered it once because the previous business writer was conveniently ill that night. She didn't have much of a choice. But now she was off the hook because Jonathan Marlowe, the current business writer, loved the Bennettsville Masquerade Ball. It was an occasion for him to wear his tuxedo with tails, and it provided that air of drama he thrived on.

Despite the deaths of Charles and Cassie Blake earlier in the summer, the Bennettsville Business Exchange Club decided the event should continue. A new scholarship was being set up in the names of Charles and Cassie Blake.

In Jake's Diner where Victoria had breakfast on most mornings, she could overhear the chatter about the event. Those who weren't on the guest list were still interested in it because of the rumors of who might be attending. Usually there were outlandish guesses of celebrities who never showed up, but people still liked to speculate. Once it was rumored that royalty might show up. It turned out to be some reigning beauty queen in her sparkly tiara. And fashion was on the tongues of those in town. The Herald even published photos of the best dressed at the ball.

Victoria sat and listened while she drank her sweet tea and ate cheese grits and bacon. By Labor Day weekend, the succulent homegrown tomatoes were usually gone; bacon and tomato sandwiches, her standard fare for the summer months, just didn't taste the same after August.

"Good morning Cinderella, do you have your dress for the ball?" Jonathan sat down across from her. He was dressed in his full-length duster coat and was wearing a fedora.

"Good Lord, Jonathan, it's 150 degrees outside at 8 a.m. Why are you wearing that?"

"It's never too hot to look your best, my dear," he answered. "And I happen to look amazing in whatever I wear."

He said and winked.

Victoria giggled.

"Well, you definitely look hot, and you are making me sweat. Don't let it go to your head though, it's not for the reasons you think," she said. "Besides, I'm not going to the ball. Auggie and I have a hot date planned with a new romance novel."

"Sounds steamy," he said as he grabbed a slice of bacon from her plate. "Reading with a Yorkie in your lap."

"Get your own. What on earth makes you think I want to be part of that dog-and-pony show anyway? You're covering it. It only requires one reporter who can take photos."

"They haven't contacted you yet?"

"What are you talking about?"

Jonathan laughed.

"Priceless. You are going to be honored at the ball because of your work in helping solve the Blake murders."

Victoria's jaw dropped, and she slowly shook her head.

"Oh no. Where did you hear that?"

"I have my sources. You should have gotten some sort of official something. When was the last time you checked your mailbox at work?"

"People still send mail?"

"You'd better look. They will be calling you today."

"How do you know this?"

"I have fallen into the good graces of Allison Blake," he said. "It was her idea especially since you might have gotten killed had your valiant detective not been there to save you. How is your detective anyway? You're going to need a date to the ball."

"He's not my detective. He has called to check on my arm a couple of times, but nothing else. We have a professional relationship. I can't date the spokesman for the Bennettsville Sheriff's Department. Besides, he still thinks you and I are an item because of your convenient public display of affection."

"It wasn't in public. We were in your apartment, and we needed that to validate your alibi. Remember?" he said. "Oh by the way, his divorce should be final in a couple of weeks."

His breakfast arrived. She tried not to look excited about that statement and grabbed a piece of bacon off his plate.

"Are you sure you are the business writer? I didn't know the paper had a gossip column."

Jonathan laughed.

"You are so good at trying to change the subject. I saw that look Victoria, my dear. You know you've been waiting to hear those words for how many years now?"

"I don't know what you are talking about," she said without

looking at him.

He laughed. He could always tell when she was lying.

"Speak of the devil," he said looking at the door. Victoria sat in the booth with her back to the door. "And he's heading this way."

"Good morning, Vic," said Deputy Hawes as he paused at their table.

"Good morning, Jeff," said Jonathan.

"Marlowe," Jeff said coldly without looking at him.

Jonathan winked at her.

"Hi, Jeff," she said.

"How's your arm?"

"I'll have a scar, but it seems to have healed otherwise. It was just a flesh wound. Thanks for asking."

There was an awkward pause. Jeff seemed to want to say something, but he hesitated too long.

"It's good to see you, Victoria," Jeff said.

She smiled.

"Yes, the past few weeks have been quiet and uneventful so I haven't seen you much. I have a story to work on. I'll see the two of you later," Victoria said as she slid out of the booth and headed to the newspaper.

Victoria wasn't up to anymore of Jonathan's teasing about Jeff. She knew Jonathan was harmless, but it bothered her that she was so obvious she still had feelings for Jeff. Those acting lessons in college hadn't helped her. She hoped Jonathan was wrong about having to attend the ball and receive an award. Victoria didn't like the spotlight. She was a behind-the-scenes type of person even though her job forced her to mingle with the public. She'd had enough of Bennettsville's high society in all her stories about the Blakes' double murder. The Blakes were Bennettsville's old money with their hands in most of the business and social ventures in town. A vengeful secretary named Jennifer Campbell killed the couple and sought revenge on them by trying to use Victoria to print about his many misdeeds. She'd obtained enough stock options to take over Blake

Enterprises, but Allison Blake submitted a lawsuit alleging that some of the shares were obtained by Jennifer forging Charles Blake's signature. It didn't take long for a judge to award the company back to Allison, where she was acting as its chief executive officer and president.

Victoria thought it was suspicious with the speed at which the reversal happened, but as Jennifer Campbell stated, "if you have enough money, you can get away with anything." Unfortunately for Jennifer, she forgot another rule. "It's not what you know, but who you know," especially in Bennettsville, and the judge was a longtime crony of Charles Blake.

Victoria was surprised Allison Blake would want to honor her in any way because some of Jennifer's confession and the sordid details of why she killed the Blakes made it into the paper, giving the gossipmongers something to talk about for several days.

When she arrived in the newsroom, it was quiet. She checked her mailbox, and she found an envelope with her name written in calligraphy. It didn't have a postmark so it had apparently been hand-delivered.

She opened it at her desk.

"Miss James," it began.

"The annual Bennettsville Masquerade Ball was the highlight of the season for my parents, Charles and Cassandra Blake. They put a lot of energy and money into it each year. Because of your involvement in bringing their murderer to justice, the committee and my family would like to recognize you at the ball, and we are requesting your attendance."

It was signed by Allison Blake.

She felt a knot form in her stomach. As she sat at her desk, she felt someone walk up behind her. It was Ed Grady, the managing editor. She wondered what horrible thing she'd done. Usually he bellowed her last name when he needed her. He didn't walk to her desk.

"Victoria, I need you to come with me," he said.

I'm being fired; he called me by my first name, she thought as she stood up.

She followed him, but they weren't going to his office. Her uneasiness grew even more as they got into the elevator and headed to the second floor executive suite. She was glad she had worn a dress to work as they walked toward the rich mahogany double doors which were a stark contrast to the white bland cubicles in the newsroom.

Ed didn't even try to make small talk.

He paused outside the office and mentioned to the receptionist they were there to see Dan Kennedy, the publisher.

"He's expecting you," she said. "He said to go in as soon as you arrived."

"Mr. Kennedy, I have Victoria James for you," Ed said he dropped Victoria off at Mr. Kennedy's office.

Mr. Kennedy had left for Europe hours before the story of the Blake murders broke and had just returned so he wasn't there for all of the summer's drama. Jennifer Campbell had lured Victoria to an abandoned warehouse in an effort to force her to write a negative article on the Blakes. She had been feeding Victoria information about them in the week after the murders. While the information had been incriminating to the Blakes, Victoria was unable to corroborate any of it so it hadn't made it into papers. This angered the killer who wanted to destroy the Blakes' name and reputation even after killing them. Jeff had followed Victoria to the warehouse and heard Jennifer Campbell's confession. Before they arrested Jennifer, she shot Victoria in the arm. While Victoria managed to get the front page story in the paper the next day, she had a wound that required her to take a few days from work

"Ms. James," Mr. Kennedy came forward to shake her hand. In his late 50s, he was tall with salt and pepper hair.

"It's nice to have a hero in the newsroom," he said.

"I'm not sure I'd call myself a hero. I was more concerned with my dog, Auggie, and I was just doing my job."

"That's what all true heroes say."

"Thanks," she said.

"I spoke with Allison Blake when I got back into town. She told me about the honor at the ball."

Victoria didn't know what to say.

"You probably don't understand fully the role you played in saving this town. Blake Enterprises has its hand in most of the major and minor businesses here. Without solid leadership, those businesses could have folded having a devastating impact on the community and its economy. The newspaper depends on those businesses for the advertising revenues. So you protected the newspaper's assets as well."

She nodded.

"I also wanted to congratulate you on being named employee of the month for July while covering the Blake murders and the funeral. I read all of the stories online, and the papers were waiting when I got back. You did a fine job."

"Thank you," she said quietly.

She wondered where all this was going.

"As you know, the Bennettsville Masquerade Ball is the most prestigious event in town. It attracts a lot of attention from around the state. While you will be recognized at the event, you will be representing the newspaper as well. Your photograph will appear in other papers and on the internet. We know there are expenses related to this. The employee of the month typically receives a small bonus, but the reasons you received the award go far beyond what a normal employee does. Hazard pay doesn't come with this job," he said and laughed.

Victoria returned his laugh nervously.

Mr. Kennedy handed her an envelope.

"Please take this small token of our appreciation," he said.

"Thank you," she said.

"I'll see you in a few weeks. This will be a fine day for the paper and for you," he said.

As she walked out of his office, she wondered what had just happened. She opened the envelope, and there was a check in it. Her jaw dropped. She thought that was a hint for her to buy something appropriate to wear for the ball.

"James," she heard the bellow as soon as she entered the newsroom and walked blindly to Ed's office, still in a fog.

"Why is this so important?" she asked.

"I don't know, but Mr. Kennedy definitely wants you to attend the ball."

"So I gathered."

"Call Ms. Blake."

She nodded.

"I think I'm supposed to buy a dress and look presentable," she said waving the envelope. "Can he do this?"

"I think he just did, but then, he owns this company and does a lot of things I can't say I condone. I just need to put a few more years in here before I can retire. And take Marlowe shopping with you," he said without looking up.

2

Victoria went into journalism mainly because she enjoyed writing. An introvert at heart, she didn't realize all of the social interaction her job would require. She learned that being a reporter was simply a role she played. She could be social for a few hours at a time, but she enjoyed being able to remove the reporter mask at the end of the day. When she'd covered the gala a few years before, she was able to slip into the event quietly. She talked to those she needed to get her information from and left the hobnobbing to the others. She didn't have to dress up for the event. She did what she needed and then got out of the way. Victoria was a beautiful woman, but she didn't spend a lot of time on her appearance. At 30, she had shoulder-length brown hair with a soft curls. She wasn't a bodybuilder, but she did like to take her Yorkshire terrier, Auggie, for walks near the river and around town as much as possible. She enjoyed the quieter side of life. She had soft hazel eyes, but she hated her nose and wished she had higher cheekbones.

There was only one place in Bennettsville to shop for formals – Peggy's House of the Bride. With the gala only a week away, Victoria knew she couldn't put off getting a dress any longer. The bridal boutique was located in a restored historic Queen Anne-style home a few blocks from the Bennettsville business district.

"Good morning," a perky blonde in her early 30s greeted Victoria as she entered the foyer.

"Hi. I need a dress for the Bennettsville Masquerade Ball. Do you have anything available?" she asked.

There were no dresses in the front waiting room for Victoria to see.

"Of course, we do, Hon. Everyone got their dresses months ago. Plus, we made a few. We do that too, you know," she said with a thick Southern accent.

She stood back and examined Victoria for a few minutes.

"Size 8," she stated it with no questions and smiled. "I have the perfect thing."

She quickly disappeared into another room, leaving Victoria standing awkwardly. Victoria peered through the door and saw the bridal room with its antique crystal chandelier and numerous wedding gowns. One corner of the room was devoted to an array of full-length mirrors positioned around a raised dais in the center for brides to get a better picture of themselves.

Several minutes passed. There was an antique, velvet-covered settee in the room so Victoria sat down and waited there. Just when she thought she'd been forgotten, the woman reappeared with a red strapless evening gown.

Victoria stood up and looked at the dress.

"Oh no. I can't wear red," she said and shook her head.

"I think you look stunning in red," said a smooth voice behind her.

She turned to see Jonathan.

"I'm not as over-the-top as you, Jonathan, and how did you know I was here?"

"Since I'm the most well-dressed male in all of the newsroom, I was tasked with making sure you looked your absolute best at the gala. We have to keep up appearances," he said and smiled.

She laughed.

"Someone is thinking highly of himself today," she said.

"Naturally," he said and winked. "I met with our lovely friend, Ashley, and told her to call me the minute you arrived. I'd been waiting for the call. I figured it would be today since Saturday is your day off, and the ball is a week from today. Now, go try this on."

"I should have known it was a set up," she said.

She followed Ashley into the dressing room and reluctantly tried it on. The dress fit as though it was tailored just for her, but she felt self-conscious as she stared at her reflection. It was strapless and fit smoothly along the hips and waist before flaring at the bottom. She could see the reminder of the gunshot wound on her arm.

"Jonathan was right, Hon. This dress is perfect for you," said Ashley. "And with your hair up and a sparkly necklace, you'll be gorgeous. I think you should keep the curls. Everyone is doing the straight-haired thing now, but it's not you."

"Victoria, you can come out now," Jonathan called from the other room.

Ashley led her to the dais for her to get the full view. He smiled as he walked up behind her.

"If I'm not careful, you might turn more heads than I do at the gala," he said with a laugh. "This should definitely catch your deputy's eye."

"He's not -" she started.

"Yes, I know he's not your deputy. You keep saying that. You could date me, you know."

"A few people already think we are," she said.

"You've done nothing to stop those rumors, and our morning breakfasts together at Jake's only fuel it."

"True. I don't even care anymore. You can't tell people the truth in this town; they believe what they want. Just add them to all those other rumors about you," she said.

He held out his hand to help her off the dais and held her hand as he responded.

"I'm aware of them all, Victoria. Despite the ones you are talking about, I very much enjoy the pleasure of a woman's company," he said in his velvety voice as he seductively gazed in her eyes. She felt strangely vulnerable.

He turned her to the mirrors and gently nudged her to look at herself. He stood behind her and whispered in her ear.

"I'm especially drawn to the ones who are as intelligent as they are beautiful. I won't be forced into anyone's mold just because people see me as flamboyant and dramatic. I enjoy being the enigma, and I'm comfortable in who I am. You should know me well enough by now."

She couldn't help but read between his lines. He'd always made her aware he wanted more than friendship with her. The closer Jeff came to finalizing his divorce the more she became aware of his desire. But Victoria never saw Jonathan as the marrying kind. And for Victoria, marriage was an important part of the picture. She still had that white picket fence idea somewhere, and he just didn't seem to fit it. He had brief romances which she didn't ask too much about. He kept some things extremely private. Even though she'd rebuffed his romantic advances for as long as she could remember, they still enjoyed each other's company and had developed a strong friendship. He definitely was an enigma, even to her at times. He seemed to enjoy tension and their odd game of cat and mouse. What was different now? For some reason, his words were getting under her skin as they stood in the bridal shop together. She tried to think of something to say.

"And you're happy to live here?"

"My dear Victoria, I have big plans for my life. I won't be a reporter and editor all of my days. I may have Ed's job. Who knows, I could end up running the company one day or even owning it. It's not what you know; it's who, and right now, I'm working on my list of 'who,'" he said.

There was a glint in his eyes as he smiled.

"And that's why I love being around you," she said.

"You don't need to try on another dress. That's the one," he said. "And you will be the most beautiful woman at the ball. I'll pick you up at 6 o'clock. You need to be there before the festivities begin."

"Somehow, I feel there's more to this 'date' than meets the eye. Are they paying you extra to make sure I go?"

He laughed.
"I'm going to enjoy the evening. Don't worry about that," he said.

3

As much as she dreaded being center stage, Victoria decided to play her role to its fullest and went for a morning of pampering on the day of the ball. The stylist piled all her curls on top of her head in a soft, romantic coif and gave her a manicure. She even decided have her makeup done. Of course, in the swelter of a Georgia September, she wasn't sure how long it would all last.

She heard Jonathan ring the bell outside her apartment building. She buzzed him in and opened the door to her apartment. He was a little earlier than she thought. She wasn't quite ready for him.

Auggie had never seen her this dressed up. The inquisitive Yorkie wanted to go with her and brought her his leash.

"I'm sorry, Auggie, you can't go with me," she said as she bent down to pet him. He sat down and placed a paw in her hand and tilted his head. "Tomorrow, you and I will have the whole day together."

She stood up and saw Jonathan in his white tie with black jacket and tails. He was wearing white gloves and holding a single-stemmed red rose. He smiled.

"A rose for a rose," he said handing it to her.

He moved a little closer to her.

"Victoria, you look stunning."

There was something about his eyes. She couldn't break away from his gaze. He had the most beautiful green eyes. How had she never noticed?

Where did that thought come from? she thought.

He kissed her hand.

"Sadly, however, we have to hide some of your beauty behind this," he said as he pulled out a gold Venetian mask.

"I have to wear this?" she asked.

"It's a masquerade ball," he said. "You have to wear it until you receive your award, but I'm sure your deputy will recognize you instantly."

She took a deep breath.

Victoria's family wasn't part of Bennettsville's high society. Her mother was a schoolteacher, and her father worked in one of the many Blake subsidiaries as a paper pusher. Her lack of social standing was one of the main reasons she avoided events like the Bennettsville Masquerade Ball. In a town like Bennettsville, who your parents were was of the utmost importance. Jonathan somehow managed to rise above it. He had a single mother; Victoria could never remember him talking about his father, and his mother died when he was in New York about 10 years before.

For more than 25 years, the ball had been held at Twin Oaks. The antebellum plantation home had a huge ballroom, and two additional rooms which opened into one another. There was also a huge solarium in the back of the lower level. Despite her parents' death in the front parlor less than two months before, Allison Blake was determined to honor her parents' wishes and have the ball in the house. The room where they were killed had been sealed to prying eyes.

Victoria had been in Twin Oaks a few times. The party would take place inside the home as well as on the back terraces, which led into perfectly kept lush gardens.

"The fun of this little party is to wear the masks for about an hour or so and try to guess who people are. If you know them well, it's not hard, but it can get tricky if you're only acquaintances. Then, the novelty wears off, and it's down to business. Just be ready when they call you," Jonathan said and turned to walk away.

"Where are you going? You are just leaving me here?"

"Victoria, pretend you're working. You and I are a lot alike. Observe, take mental notes. I will see you soon enough." He smiled. "Besides, you need me to leave you alone so your handsome deputy can find you. His divorce should be final very soon. I haven't checked the records recently."

She watched Jonathan walk away and mingled with other guests.

It was hard to pretend she was working. She decided to walk around the house. She loved architecture and the gardens. The terrace had several levels overlooking a lake on the back of the property. She hoped to get lost out there and miss the presentation. Plus, now she was dealing with conflicting thoughts. Her long-buried feelings for Jeff were rising to the surface, and she couldn't process what she felt for Jonathan. She felt her pulse race when he presented the rose to her and his hand brushed hers, and she'd gotten lost in his eyes.

Most of the guests stayed inside. It was still hot especially wearing all the finery. It was fine with Victoria. She wanted to escape from them anyway. It was peaceful outside. The sun was beginning its descent into the horizon. She took out her phone and snapped several photographs. She was hypnotized by the beauty of the moment, but she soon realized she wasn't alone. She heard footsteps behind her and turned to see Jeff standing there. He was dressed in a tuxedo and left his cowboy hat and boots at home. She could tell he was uncomfortable, but he looked so handsome even behind his mask.

"Vic? I guess I shouldn't call you that. Tonight, you look more like a 'Victoria.'"

"Not many people call me 'Vic' anymore," she said.

He took his mask off.

"I really hate these things."

She followed his lead.

"So do I," she replied.

"You look beautiful."

She smiled.

"Thank you. Apparently, I'm supposed to get some kind of recognition tonight. I wouldn't be here otherwise."

"Your arm is looking much better."

"Yeah, I have this scarf to cover it and me. I'm still a little self-conscious in this dress."

"That dress is incredible on you."

She felt her cheeks flush and turned toward the granite railing.

"How did you know where I was or that I was even here?" she asked.

"I knew about the award, too. I know you don't like crowds, and I know your silhouette," he said.

She looked at the setting sun on the water. She needed to change the subject.

"The lake is beautiful tonight. I've only been here a couple of times, and it's always been on business. I've never gotten to see this."

He moved closer to her.

"Vic, I was wondering if you'd like to have dinner with me some time? I really want to talk to you."

"Well, I -" she started.

"Is it Marlowe? Are the two of you serious? I completely understand."

"No, it's not that at all. Jonathan will never settle down. He's a free spirit."

He started to say something, but there was a blood-curdling scream from the house. Victoria had heard that scream before. It was on this same lawn a few weeks before. It was Allison Blake. Jeff glanced at her briefly before bolting up the stairs and back to the house. Victoria followed, but her high heels wouldn't let her move as fast as he did. Maybe this meant the moment she was dreading wasn't going to happen. When she walked into the home, the guests stood frozen in horror as the Bennettsville Sheriff's deputies prevented them from leaving. They were pointing and whispering among themselves. A few women stood close to their male companions, clutching them with fearful looks. Victoria kept walking. She saw Jeff holding a hysterical Allison Blake.

"Where's Marlowe?" Jeff asked her.

She shook her head.

"I haven't seen him since we arrived. Why?"

"Dan Kennedy's been shot. He's dead, and the last person seen coming into this room was Marlowe or at least a man with shoulder-length, dark, wavy hair. He was wearing a mask, and he seems to have left from through a side door."

Jonathan? He was a lot of things, but a murderer wasn't one of them.

Several people immediately corroborated the story.

No. It couldn't be true.

She pushed passed the crowd into the solarium to see Dan Kennedy lying on his stomach. His head turned sideways, and his face frozen. There was a pool of blood around his chest and abdomen. His eyes remained open, staring blankly. While Jeff called in other deputies, she took photographs on her phone. She had to work fast. She noticed several papers in Mr. Kennedy's hand. They were blood-spattered, but his hand was far enough from the pool that the papers were untouched. It looked like he was going to give a speech, but on what? She tried not to look at his face while she took the photos. She put her phone away when she heard Jeff barking orders and coming back into the room.

"Vic, this is a crime scene. What are you doing in here?"

"This is my boss, and you are implicating the wrong person."

"Why do you say Marlowe is the wrong person? Because you are sleeping with him?"

Jonathan was right about the jealousy, she thought.

"So what if I am? Is that a crime? Do you want to arrest me?" her voice rose in anger. "Jonathan is a lot of things, but he's not a murderer."

"Get out of my crime scene, Vic."

She pulled out her press badge from the small purse she carried.

"I have a right to this information especially when it concerns the publisher of the paper I work for and one of the most respected journalists in this town."

"Fine. Stay out of my way," he said through gritted teeth as he glared back at her. "No one is to leave this house."

It wasn't long before more of Bennettsville's finest had flooded the mansion, to begin interviewing witnesses and survey the crime scene.

She nervously called Ed. He didn't usually work on a Saturday evening, but she knew he'd want to hear about this as soon as possible. Where was Jonathan? She couldn't reach Ed on his home phone. She called his cell instead.

"Ed, there's been a murder at the Bennettsville Masquerade Gala," she said. She could tell Ed wasn't at home. She could hear lots of voices in the background.

"Where's Marlowe? Why isn't he calling me?"

"The victim is Dan Kennedy, and they think Jonathan did it. I haven't seen him since we arrived. I can't leave. The good Deputy Hawes has us on lockdown."

"I'm heading to the paper. I'll call you, and you dictate your story to me. James, put those new found detective skills to work."

"I'm on it," she said.

Victoria wondered why anyone would want to kill Mr. Kennedy, and what was that speech he was planning on delivering?

Allison and Sissy Blake initially seemed distraught; a third murder in their home in less than two months. Victoria wondered if she could get close to them and ask them questions based on her guest of honor distinction. She couldn't stop wondering where Jonathan was.

She found Allison seated in the study and huddled in a deep conversation with Tom Snider, the newly appointed chairman of Blake Enterprises' board of directors. Snider held a law degree and had practiced at one time. He was still in good standing with the Georgia Bar, and he provided Blake Enterprises with legal counsel. Allison looked up as Victoria approached, and Mr. Snider whispered something into her ear. She nodded and then tried to smile.

"Victoria," she stood up. "I wanted to thank you for everything you did to help find my parents' killer. I'm sorry I won't get to publicly do it tonight."

Victoria nodded. She was amazed at how quickly Allison had gotten over her histrionics. She looked like she'd completely redone her makeup too; there was not a smudge of mascara to be seen. She was flawless.

"What else was on the agenda?" Victoria asked.

"They were going to name the person of the year," Allison said. "And then, there was your award."

"Was Mr. Kennedy scheduled to do something?"

Allison seemed surprised.

"No, I don't think so."

Victoria smiled and nodded.

"We do have a lovely plaque for you," Allison said.

Victoria glanced at Mr. Snider. She couldn't read him. His face was blank. There was no smile or frown. She smiled at him, but he didn't respond.

She said "thank you" and turned to walk away. As she did, Martin Anderson, the president of the newspaper's board approached her. She hadn't seen him earlier.

"Ms. James. Are you covering this for us now?"

"Yes, sir. I am. Technology is a wonderful thing," she said holding up her cell phone.

"I can't believe one of our own would do this," he said in a deadpan voice.

"Innocent until proven guilty, sir. Jonathan had nothing to gain from Mr. Kennedy's death," she said.

"Don't let your obvious bias influence your writing," he said.

"Was Mr. Kennedy scheduled to do anything tonight?" she asked ignoring his comment.

Mr. Anderson returned an icy stare.

"Nothing at all," he said.

Victoria had the feeling he was lying. If Mr. Kennedy was making an announcement, surely Mr. Anderson would have known. She knew a speech when she saw one. As she stood there pondering, she heard a rumble of chatter spread though the Blake mansion. She moved to the corridor to see two deputies – one holding each of Jonathan's arms. He was a mess. His once immaculate shirt was covered in mud, and his coat was missing. His hair was disheveled. He looked dazed. He snapped out of it enough to catch Victoria's glance. He shook his head and mouthed "I'm innocent" as he passed her.

She knew that. She nodded and offered a weak smile. She marched to the back of the house where Jeff was. They'd cordoned off the area so none of the guests could gawk.

"Deputy Hawes, could I have a minute of your time?" she asked in as professional a manner as she could.

Dan Kennedy's body had not been removed from the crime scene. Something looked different, but she wasn't sure what. Without making a scene, she surreptitiously took a photo. There was no flash so no one seemed to notice. She hoped it turned out.

Jeff turned in her direction.

"So we're not on a first name basis any longer?" he asked.

"I have a job to do, and I don't want to play any games," she said. "I want to be able to work with you on this. It means a lot, and I can't let feelings get in the way. What can you tell me about this case? And what's going on with Jonathan Marlowe?" Victoria had put on her reporter façade.

Her concern for Jonathan and anger at Jeff were balancing out the fact that she'd just seen her employer dead on the floor. The sight of a dead body hadn't ruffled her; maybe she was in shock, and it would hit her later.

"Jonathan Marlowe is being held in connection with the death of Dan Kennedy. He was found on the lawn with what we believe to be the murder weapon lying next to him?"

"What do you mean found on the lawn with the murder weapon next to him?"

"He was passed out."

"That's not strange?"

"We'll be running toxicology reports."

"Maybe, he was knocked unconscious," she said.

"We will check out all of the scenarios," he said. He looked skeptical.

"What about Mr. Kennedy?"

"He was shot at close range with a small handgun. Looks like a couple of bullet wounds to his chest; not sure how many. An autopsy will be performed."

"When will the guests be free to leave?"

"Not for a while. We have a lot of people to interview including you."

"Jeff, I was with you earlier."

"I don't expect the killer to feed you clues on this one, but if you hear anything– "

"You're on my speed dial, Jeff," she said. "But I'm telling you that you have the wrong man. Test his fingers for those residues or whatever they are. You won't find anything."

"Standard procedure. You seem pretty positive."

"I'd be willing to stake my life on it. And have them check Jonathan for a bump on the head or something. He must have been hit and knocked out. Someone here is lying, and I'm going to find out why."

It was a long night as the deputies interviewed people one by one. Victoria tried to eavesdrop on as many witness statements as she possibly could. By the end of the night, it sounded as though everyone had seen a masked man fitting Jonathan's description, jumping out through the solarium window, which was impossible since the window wasn't broken, and it was locked. It seems the power of suggestion and alcohol played into some of the responses.

It was getting close to dawn before the deputies finished their questioning. Victoria stayed to the bitter end. She wasn't sure how she was getting home since she rode in Jonathan's car.

"Vic, why are you still here?" Jeff asked.

"I rode with Jonathan," she said. "And I'm not walking all the way into town in this dress and these shoes."

"Come on," he said.

Jeff drove a white pickup truck. She stood next to it trying to contemplate how she was supposed to maneuver in a skin-tight dress and heels.

"Need some help?"

"It's been a long night. I forgot what you drove when you said you'd take me home."

In one quick motion, he picked her up and placed her on the front seat. His touch sent a pulse of electricity through her. She remembered being in his arms, but she couldn't focus on that. She felt extremely vulnerable, and she didn't need him to know it. She didn't say much after he got into the vehicle. Her mind was darting in hundreds of directions as she thought of Jonathan sitting in jail. He would be wearing an orange jumpsuit. She knew he'd hate that. She couldn't think of anything to say to Jeff. She wanted to look at the pictures she had of the crime scene. She wondered if she could make out anything on that speech that no one seemed to know Mr. Kennedy was making. Why was it so important for her to be at the event?

"Vic, I know it was a hard night. I know you and Jonathan have always been friends, and whatever is going on with the two of you now will taint your opinion," he said.

"I believe in him, Jeff. His quirkiness, his faults. He's a good man. I know it."

"I didn't mean to make things awkward since you and he –"

"He and I are friends, but everyone wants to draw a conclusion about my life. Half the town has me dating you while the other half has me dating him. I wouldn't be surprised if there are a few fence-sitters who have me dating you both. The truth is I'm not dating anyone. I sleep with my dog, Auggie. He's the only man in my life."

"Then why didn't you say something?"

"Why should I have to? Besides, the last time I checked you were married, and I don't play games like that," she said.

He pulled up in front of her building as the sun started to rise. He lifted her out of the vehicle and placed her feet on the ground. He held her there for a few minutes. She tried to avoid his eyes.

"Thank you for bringing me home."

"No problem, ma'am," he said in his thickest Georgia drawl.

Before she headed inside, she grabbed a newspaper out of the box on the street corner. The front page had Dan Kennedy's murder story on it, but as she looked at it, she realized it was not what she'd dictated to Ed over the phone. She rushed upstairs to see an excited Auggie and took off the expensive and uncomfortable dress for a pair of shorts and tank top.

She dialed Ed's cell. No answer.

She only thought she was angry before; now, she was really ticked off.

4

She spent most of Sunday morning trying to reach Ed. He didn't pick up his desk or cell phone. She waited until lunchtime before heading to the newspaper because no one would be there. She was still going in a little early. She tried to get a little sleep in first. With the sunlight streaming and Auggie wanting to play, it was impossible. She changed into a pair of jeans and put a button-up shirt over her tank top.

She noticed Ed's car in the lot when she arrived. She rushed in and headed straight for the newsroom. She found Ed in his office.

"Where have you been? I've been trying to reach you," she said.

"I run 10 miles on Sunday. I thought you knew that," he said.

"Why is my story not in the paper?" she demanded. "What is this thing you printed instead?"

"I was hijacked last night by Martin Anderson. He came in and stopped production. He made us print the story in the paper."

"It's not even a news article. It's opinion and heresay. Put my article in. I'll go and talk to Jonathan," she said. "I've got information from Jeff, too."

"James, you're too close to it, and you aren't covering it."

Her mouth dropped in amazement, and she stared at him for a minute.

"What?" she said.. She couldn't believe her ears. "You can't do that. I'm practically an eyewitness." Her voice began to get louder, and the pitch became elevated.

"Anderson doesn't want you on it, and you can't be objective as close as you are to Marlowe."

She put her hands on her hips and shook her head.

"I can't believe what I'm hearing," she said. "And you are going to sit back and do nothing? I've given my life to this paper and for what? So has Jonathan."

"One more word, James. Anderson said I could suspend you if there was an outburst," he said.

She paused. She took a deep breath and tried to think, but she couldn't think straight.

"Why? So you can retire in five years because you toed the line. Whatever happened to the fourth estate? The media printing truth? Are we a tabloid now?" she said with her voice raised and her hands on her hips.

"James - get out and don't come back for a week."

She threw her press badges onto his desk.

"I know people in the other media outlets in town. You haven't heard the last of this. I will not let Jonathan Marlowe go down. Something else was going on last night, and I intend to find out what is was."

Victoria headed home. On her short walk, she called Liz. She was in church like most of Bennettsville so she left Liz a message to meet her at Jake's when she got finished. Victoria hadn't looked at the photos on her phone. She decided to upload them to her laptop, but she backed them on a flash drive for safekeeping. After her reaction to the special delivery of Charles Blake's finger during the last murder, she was surprised at how well she handled seeing a dead body. It must have been from the adrenaline rush.

She looked at the first crime scene photo and began to feel a little sick to her stomach. She hadn't looked at Dan Kennedy's face. Something wasn't right when she went back. She'd gotten very close to the body and took a close up of the speech in his hand. She couldn't see much except that it was typed.

She looked at the second set of photos. The paper was gone. She did a double take. It was missing. Her first photo was taken before the crime scene was investigated. She remembered that much, but so much of the previous night was a blur due to lack of sleep and the sheer stress of it. She had more photos on her phone, but she needed to walk to Jake's. She wasn't sure she could trust anyone now, and her thoughts went to Jonathan in jail. Her heart ached. He did not belong there.

She tucked her hair under a baseball cap. It was a mess of curls and hairspray from the night before, and she headed to the back of Jake's and passed the blue hairs. She often wondered why they never talked to her just about her. As she passed them, she could hear their whispers.

Liz showed up in her Sunday best.

"We missed you this morning."

"I know. It was a very late night, and I still haven't slept," she said.

Victoria told Liz about the murder and the story. She also told her about her week suspension.

"What?" Liz was incredulous. "I can't believe he'd do that, and he changed your story."

Victoria had the paper in front of her. She passed it to Liz.

"He didn't change it. He wrote something completely different. This is not what I wrote."

Liz shook her head.

"And Martin Anderson is in on it too?" Liz asked.

"Yes. Seems so," she said. "Ed's so concerned with losing his retirement. I mean it can't be that much money."

"I think it's more than that."

"Probably. Jonathan told me that he thought Ed hated him."

Liz laughed.

"Ed hates us all," she said.

Victoria nodded.

"Will you keep me updated? Be my eyes and ears."

"You know I will," Liz said. "Get Jonathan out of jail soon. He's so beautiful to look at, and that voice of his is to die for."

Victoria smiled and shook her head.

"I'll do what I can."

"I've got to run. Lunch at the parents since it's Sunday and all."

"Yes, I knew last night would be late so I gave my excuses early. My mother is freaking out about Jonathan, but I can't deal with it right now."

"I understand," she said as she hurried out the door.

Victoria didn't know what else to do. She did have a couple of friends at the nearby television stations. She wondered if she should call them. She couldn't be without a job for long. While she'd ordered a cup of black coffee she hadn't drunk any of it; she absent-mindedly stirred it, staring at the back wall.

She was surprised when Jeff slid into the booth across the table from her. She smiled.

"Vic. I've been trying to call you," he said.

She looked at her phone. She had four missed calls. She hadn't even noticed. She didn't feel the phone vibrate.

"I'm sorry. I feel like I've been sucked into an alternate universe where nothing makes any sense," she said.

"I'm there with you. There's something strange going on with his case," he said. "Marlowe has already been arraigned, and he's being held on $1 million bond."

"What? It's been less than 24 hours since Dan Kennedy's death, and who gets arraigned in this town on a Sunday during a holiday weekend?"

"Exactly. Your friend ticked the wrong person off," he said. "I just don't know who that person is yet."

"Can I see him?"

"Probably not."

"I can't believe any of this is happening," she said. "Yesterday, I could do no wrong, and now, I can't even write about this."

"What?"

"I told you freaky, alternative universe. I've been pulled off this story. I've been pulled off every story. Martin Anderson has taken over the newspaper. Ed suspended me."

"What? That's crazy, Vic."

"I know," she said.

Victoria pulled the baseball cap over her face as she leaned forward in the cushioned booth seat. She closed her eyes for a minute. She wanted to trust Jeff, but she already knew he was biased against Jonathan. She wanted to show him those photos, but he lied to her when she thought she was helping him on the Blake case. That sounded like two strikes. And she didn't know how wise it would be to tell him she'd gone to Birmingham to follow a lead on the Blake case when he'd threatened to arrest her if she did, but she had to help Jonathan. The newspaper had turned against him and her. Who would be on his side?

"I don't know if I can trust you, Jeff," she said after a few minutes.

"Why would you say that?"

"Because you lied to me. You told me that Davenport Travel Agency in Birmingham was a front for an escort service."

"I knew it. You lied to me. You told me you didn't go to Birmingham."

She smiled.

"Technically, I didn't lie. I just didn't tell you the whole truth. We went to Atlanta, and that was the truth. I spent almost the entire weekend in Atlanta with Jonathan. We just made a side trip to Birmingham. You thought what you wanted to think. Don't argue with a writer on semantics. I still don't know why you lied, though."

"Look, Vic. I had a hunch that whoever killed the Blakes was the one who sent you the information. I didn't want you to get hurt. I wasn't sure what game the killer was playing. Plus, you aren't a trained investigator. I didn't need you doing my job," he said.

He paused and leaned across the table. He lowered his voice.

"I think there's a leak or something worse in the department. Someone is pulling strings, but I'm not going to see an innocent man go to jail for something he didn't do."

She looked up at Jeff and smiled.

"Jeff, you really believe Jonathan is innocent?"

She stared into his deep blue eyes to see if she could uncover the truth. His right eye twitched slightly when he wasn't telling the truth, but she couldn't see his eyes on that day when he told her about the Davenport Travel Agency.

He nodded.

"Too many things don't add up. He's being railroaded," he said.

"Then, I need to show you something, but if I do, you can't shut me out of this investigation. I can help you."

"You are a civilian."

"Oh, good lord, Jeff. Give me a break. Without me, Jennifer Campbell would be in the Bahamas sipping fruity drinks with umbrellas in them right now instead of in jail where my friend doesn't need to be. I've even been wounded in the line of duty. That should count for something. Plus, I can't sit around and twiddle my thumbs for a week."

He pursed his lips and thought for a minute.

"What do you have?"

"Come on. I'll show you."

When she arrived at her apartment, she noticed the door was slightly ajar. Jeff pulled out his gun and moved in front of her. He pushed it and saw Auggie peek his head out from under her bed. Victoria grabbed Auggie. He was shaking.

"It's okay, baby," she said.

Jeff looked at her.

"Is anything missing?"

She looked around.

"Not exactly. Look," she said. She walked over to the pieces of what was once her computer and knelt down in front of it. Someone had deliberately smashed it.

"Are excessive break-ins and stalkers grounds to get out of a lease?" she asked sarcastically.

"Well at least you're keeping your sense of humor about

everything."

Jeff picked up the shattered pieces while she grabbed a piece of paper and wrote on it. He was taking it as evidence.

"Where can we go safe to talk? I need a computer," she wrote. She had become paranoid to wonder if there was a listening device in the room.

He nodded.

She had the flash drive as well as the phone with her. She was afraid something like this might happen.

"Well, I think you're right about a leak in your department," she said as they walked out of the building toward his car. "Whoever was in my apartment had been watching me. They're probably watching us now."

"I'll take you to the station later, but I know how to find out if someone is watching us," he said. "Hang on."

Traffic wasn't heavy on the lazy Sunday afternoon of a holiday weekend. He watched out his rearview mirror as he made a few sharp turns and then did a u-turn in the middle of the street.

"Deputy Hawes, I don't think that was legal," she said catching her breath.

"No, but there wasn't anyone following. They probably got spooked when I went to your apartment."

"Yeah, well, I'm moving to a different place. I'm spooked now."

Jeff laughed.

"Might not be a bad idea," he said.

"I'll file a police report when I go to the station."

Within a few minutes, they were out of Bennettsville's town limits. She had an idea of where Jeff might be headed. She closed her eyes for a few minutes not realizing how exhausted she was from the night before.

"Hey, sleepyhead. We're here," she heard Jeff's voice and opened her eyes to see the lake in front of her. She'd spent a lot of summer days on this lake. Jeff's family had a log cabin there, about 20 minutes from Bennettsville.

"We should be safe here to talk," he said.

She let Auggie out. He loved the outdoors, and here, he could roam freely with no leash. He was a good dog and wouldn't wander far from her anyway. She watched him for a few minutes. He played in the grass and chased a yellow butterfly.

Butterflies, she thought. The place gave her butterflies. It was the place where Jeff gave her her first kiss, and it was where they spent their last night together after the Bennettsville Labor Day picnic. That was a thought she needed to get out of her mind really fast.

"Your dad kept the place, huh?" she said as she walked up the steps of the porch.

He opened the door to let her in. It was a simple cabin with an open kitchen and living space and a bedroom with adjoining bathroom.

"Yeah, and I'm glad he did. Before Lacy moved back to Atlanta, she kicked me out. I stayed out here several months. I come out on the weekends some, but our, I mean, my house is closer to the station so I'm back there for now."

He walked over to the table. There was an desktop computer on it.

"So, show me why they destroyed your computer?" he asked her.

She reached into her jeans' pocket and pulled out the flash drive.

"I guess I wasn't being as inconspicuous as I thought last night," she said, handing it to him. "When Allison screamed, we both ran to the house. I guess I've gotten over my squeamishness a little. I pulled out my phone and took some photos."

He sat down and loaded the photos while Victoria stood behind him. She leaned over his shoulder while he looked at them.

"If you look at that one, you can see there is something in Mr. Kennedy's hand," she said. "I'm glad I stood my ground and refused to leave. Later, after your team arrived and began sweeping the crime scene, I thought something was off. I couldn't tell at the time what it was so I took several photos. Look at this one and the first one side by side."

He clicked on the two photos.

"Someone removed those papers," Jeff said.

She sat down and looked directly at him.

"I spoke to Allison Blake and Mr. Anderson last night. I asked both of them if Mr. Kennedy was on the agenda. They both told me 'no.' Another odd thing from last night was the fact that Mr. Kennedy had insisted that I attend that ball. The paper paid for my dress. There was some type of announcement Mr. Kennedy wanted to make last night. There were a couple of other writers from out of town at last night's event. He wanted those people to know about the announcement."

She could tell he was trying to process everything she was saying.

"I need to talk to Jonathan, and I need to get back into that house," she said. "And someone needs to get to Mr. Kennedy's computer before it's too late."

Jeff's cell phone rang.

"Hawes, here," he said.

She strained to hear the other side of the conversation. Jeff just said "yeah" a lot.

"That was about your gun residue. You were right. There was none found on him or the cuffs of his tuxedo shirt," he said to Victoria after hanging up. "And there appeared to be a slight bump on the back of his head. He was complaining about being knocked out. They checked him for a possible concussion."

"And if you were looking at him last night, you would have seen no blood on his shirt. It was stained with mud. There was no blood spatter. You said it was done at a close range. Would some have gotten on him?"

Victoria felt a mix of anger and helplessness arising in her.

"I even took a photo of him as he walked by me."

Jeff found it. Jeff reached out with his left hand and touched her hand to reassure her. She felt her pulse begin to race.

"Vic, I believe you. You're preaching to the choir at this point. There are too many other things about this murder that don't add up.

I need to get back to the station. I don't know if I can arrange for you to see him or not, but I'm going to talk to him," he said.

He saved the photos onto another drive and handed hers back.

"Keep these safe. I need to get back to the station," he said as he headed back outside.

"Where are you going to stay tonight?" he asked once inside his truck.

"I don't have any idea. My mother is still freaked out over the whole Blake murder and being threatened by the killer. She's been calling my phone all day. I'm sure she's calling about Jonathan. I'd rather not go there, but I will if I have no other choice."

"My sister, Margie, has a room over her garage. My nephew lived in it until he went to college. She might let you stay there."

She remembered Margie. Jeff was the youngest of the Hawes clan, born about a decade after his two older siblings. Victoria had always liked Margie. His other sister, Debbie, lived in Savannah.

"I don't want to cause any problems."

Jeff pulled another cell phone out from underneath his seat.

"This is the family line. Only a few people have or use this number. I'm going to give it to you before we get back into town."

He called his sister and within minutes, Jeff had it set for her to stay with Margie. Victoria felt awkward about the whole situation, but she didn't have too many alternatives.

"You have five minutes to get what you need, and I'll follow you to Margie's place to make sure no one follows you. I'll check on Marlowe and let you know what I find."

"Thank you, Jeff."

Victoria grabbed an overnight bag and shoved a couple of changes of clothes and other necessities in it. Auggie was acting strangely. She noticed something shiny on the floor under the table She called for Jeff to come back. It looked like a button, but she didn't want to touch it.

She wondered why they hadn't seen it before. Did someone come back?

"This is off the sleeve of a deputy uniform," he said. "It must have rolled under the table when whoever it was smashed your computer."

"Sounds like your theory of something in the department was correct."

Jeff stared at it a few minutes before looking back at Victoria.

"There was information leaked during the Blake investigation, but there wasn't any wrong-doing."

The drive to Margie's was a short one. Jeff followed her in his truck to ensure no one else was watching. He got out and gave his sister a quick hug.

"Take care of her, Margie, and call me if you need me. Vic, I've got a lot to do. I'll update you when I can."

5

As much as she wanted to rush out and start her own investigation, she knew she had to follow the Southern pleasantries and catch up the last decade of their lives. And you aren't a really good Southerner unless the pleasantries come with food so Margie had prepared a lot of food. Victoria had always liked Margie because she made her feel part of the family years ago.

Margie's home was a quaint century-old cottage with a porch and a swing. It had three bedrooms and the vacant space over the single car garage. Margie's husband worked shifts about an hour away at a chemical plant. He was on nights this month so he wouldn't be home for a while. While he spent the years as the breadwinner, she'd raised their kids, and now their youngest was off to college.

Margie's living room was a cozy mix of antiques and newer pieces, and she had framed photographs everywhere. On the mantle, there were pictures of her two children from infancy to graduation. A baby grand piano had become a photo display with numerous wedding photos. She noticed a few from Jeff's wedding – minus the bride. There was a photo of him and his family. He looked so handsome in his white tuxedo. She always imagined him at the end of an aisle in a white tux.

Stop it, Victoria, she thought.

Her walk around the room was like a stroll down memory lane. The Hawes' family was a huge part of her life for several years. She walked over to the bookcase and saw a batch of older photos. She thought she recognized one. She reached back behind the mass of photos. Yes, she was right – it was her and Jeff at senior prom. He was so handsome with his light brown hair and that smile. She wasn't as impressed with her photo. She heard Margie coming down the hall and tried to put the photo back into its place, but it was crammed in with all the others. She knocked a couple of them on the floor. Fortunately, none of them broke when they fell onto the hardwoods.

"Oh dear, let me help you," said Margie. "I can't tell you how many times I've pushed these over when dusting them. They do collect the dust."

She noticed the prom picture and picked it up.

"I remember that night," she said. "The two of you looked so happy together."

Victoria looked away.

"It was a long time ago," she said softly.

"Yes, some things change, but sometimes, they don't."

Victoria looked at Margie.

"You have a sweet dog. I bet he's hungry, too. I don't have any dog food, but I might have some chicken," she said.

"I brought some for him. He's had a rough night."

"I heard."

There was an awkward silence as Victoria handed the frames to Margie, and she put them back in their places.

"I think he's always loved you, Vicki," Margie said as she looked at the photo of the two of them. "Maybe that's why it didn't work out with Lacy."

She smiled while Victoria remained silent.

"I'm not going to meddle," Margie said.

There was no more talk about Jeff and Lacy. Victoria tried to make small talk with Margie, but her thoughts kept going to Jonathan in jail. She wondered if there was some clue at the Blake house; something police might have missed - like the missing speech. They wouldn't have known to look for it.

"Are you all right, dear"? she asked, breaking into Victoria's reverie.

"No, I'm sorry. You've been so sweet to let me stay here, and I am being rude. I'm exhausted, but I have so many things on my mind. I need to take a drive. Could Auggie stay with you?

"He won't be any trouble at all. I miss having a puppy around. Go clear your head," she said.

Despite all of the events of the afternoon, it wasn't that late. The sun hadn't set yet. She could hear Jeff in her head telling her to leave the investigating to him, but she couldn't do that when her best friend could face the death penalty unless he was proven innocent. And the only way to do that was to find out who really killed Dan Kennedy.

She was trying to think of some kind of lie as she pulled into the driveway at the Blake mansion. She took a deep breath. She got out of the vehicle and walked to the doors. She had seen Jonathan's car on the road next to the house when she pulled up. She was surprised they hadn't impounded it yet.

She knocked on the door, and Allison Blake answered within a few minutes.

"Hi," said Victoria. "I am so sorry to bother you, but in all the confusion last night, I must have lost one of my earrings. My grandmother wore them on her wedding day, and they have such a sentimental value. I crashed this morning, and I didn't realize I didn't have them. I looked several places at home, and I checked Detective Hawes' truck. Do you mind if I retrace my steps? I hate to be a bother, but I thought it would be easier to find before the dust settled from last night."

"Of course, the sheriff's department was here earlier, and they told me not to have the cleaning crew come yet," said Allison. "I can't go in the front parlor and now I can't go in the solarium."

Allison's face was gray; she began to cry.

"I'm sorry," Allison said as she wiped her eyes.

"No, it's understandable. You just lost your parents, and now this. I can't imagine how horrible all of this must be for you."

"If I didn't have my Daddy's businesses to look after, I think I'd lose my mind," she said as the tears began to flow. "The masquerade ball always meant so much to them. For some strange reason, I feel like it's my fault that there was a murder here last night. Crazy thought, I know."

Victoria often thought her job as a reporter was part therapist at times. People opened up to her and spilled out their secrets.

"You aren't writing about this for the paper, are you?" Allison asked.

"No, I just need to look for my earring. My mother would never let me live it down if she knew I lost my grandmother's jewelry. She's always telling me what a klutz I am."

"You go and look wherever you want."

"Thank you."

"And I'll get the plaque we were going to give you last night. I forgot it in all the uproar."

Victoria nodded. She wasn't sure what she was looking for, but she could retrace every step she took in hopes of finding something. Of course, if she did find anything she wasn't sure what she'd do.

She started in some of the front rooms, but her ultimate goal was the murder scene, and she wanted to take a look outside. She tried to make small talk hoping Allison would get bored with her and give her access, but she didn't think that was going to happen.

She got on her hands and knees to look under chairs and tables. She looked around one of the formal living rooms. It had a fireplace. It was still summer; surely, there wasn't a fire blazing last night, not in the heat of September.

Think, Victoria, was there a fire for ambiance?

She tried not to be too obvious as she looked into the fireplace, but she thought she saw partially burned papers.

"I walked outside for a little while to look at the amazing sunset over the water."

"Go ahead," said Allison. "I'll pass on going outside. It's still too hot out there. Just knock when you are ready to come back in, and

I'll let you through."

She went to the spot on the lower terrace, where she was talking to Jeff and turned around to the house. She studied the layout and tried to replay the sequence of events as they might have taken place. The murder occurred in the solarium, which was to the far right of the home from her current vantage point, and Victoria had been taking photos before Jeff came up to her. Could she have something else on her phone that she didn't see? She'd have to come back to that thought.

There was another set of stairs and a porch outside the solarium. Jonathan had mud on him.

Where was mud?

She walked up the granite staircase to the side of the home to find the mud.

Just then, Jeff called. She thought about ignoring it for a minute, but she figured he would call again.

"Hi. Jeff, how are you?" she said in her most innocent Southern drawl, knowing she'd been busted.

"Where are you, Vic? I just talked to Margie, and she said you took a drive without Auggie so I know you are up to something you shouldn't be," he sounded aggravated.

"Oh, you know, just out, clearing my head."

"Vic, don't lie."

"Fine. I'm at Twin Oaks," she said.

"I'll be there in 15 minutes."

He wasn't happy. She could tell. She needed to move fast.

There was a mud puddle. That must have been where they found him. There were several azalea bushes and holly. She saw something sticking in one of the holly bushes.

She knew she didn't have long before Jeff showed up. She pushed into the bushes and found a black wig.

Whoever it was impersonating Jonathan had worn a wig. That would make sense. They must have tossed it, hoping to come back later for it.

She made her way to the crime scene. She'd have to go in through the French doors. To her surprise, the doors weren't locked. She opened them and walked in. The solarium was an expansive room. There was a grand piano in the corner of the room. If someone wanted to hide something to pick up later, where would they hide it? She looked through the cushions of couches and under the ottoman. Nothing. Piano bench? There was also a music stand. Great hiding places. Allison said the sheriff's department hadn't been gone long so the killer wouldn't have had time to remove the speech if they'd left t in the room. She heard the front bell ring.

Jeff was there. It seemed like a fast 15 minutes for Victoria.

She bolted out of the French doors and down the staircase. She made it down to the lower landing in the nick of time. She was out of breath, but she figured she could regain her composure by the time he made it to the bottom of the stairs.

"Detective Hawes, I'm still looking for that lost earring I told you about earlier," she yelled up to him.

Allison still wasn't interested in venturing out of doors. It wasn't long before she was out of earshot.

"What are you doing here?" he asked, and he wasn't smiling.

"Here, here is proof that Jonathan didn't do it," she said, holding out the wig. "Get the DNA. Do something. I found it in the holly bushes near the French doors of the solarium. How did your deputies miss this?"

"You aren't ever going to listen to me when I tell you not to investigate, are you?" he asked.

She took a deep breath and smiled.

"Not at all, Deputy Hawes," she said. "I'm pretty good at this."

"Don't let it go to your head," he said.

"I didn't get to look around the solarium too long, but there are a lot of places to hide things. Go check it for Mr. Kennedy's speech."

"Yes, ma'am," he said sarcastically with an eyebrow raised.

"You go back to Margie's now, and I'll be there within the hour unless I find something."

"Fine," she said. "How's Jonathan?"

She watched as he clenched his jaw and the vein bulged from his temple in anger. "I don't know. He's already been transferred to another facility."

"What? No, that's not supposed to happen."

Being in the small Bennettsville jail was one thing. There weren't too many violent felons in Bennettsville, but the thought of Jonathan being sent to another institution caused Victoria to panic.

"Vic, calm down. I'll give you the details when I know them. Go to Margie's house and call your mother. Your mother has my work cell phone now. She's called four times."

"Really? Maybe you should hire her, too."

"Go, Vic," he said.

"One day, you'll appreciate my help."

"Now."

"I'm going," she said.

She was beyond exhausted, but her adrenaline was pumping. As she'd learned from the Blake murders, Bennettsville was full of secrets. Dan Kennedy was going to make some sort of announcement that neither Allison Blake nor Martin Anderson wanted him to make. Myra Evans, one of the town's busybodies had fed her some interesting gossip about her publisher. What was worth murdering him over? And why use Jonathan as the fall guy? She thought about his comment that he wouldn't be a reporter all of his days. Did he know what was going on and not tell her?

She was already in enough trouble for one night so she figured she couldn't do much more damage. Her next stop was Jonathan's apartment. She had a key to it because she fed his cat, a white Persian named Angelica, for him if he was gone for the weekend. Who knew how long he might be gone this time? She wondered if there was some clue to his involvement in all of this in his apartment.

She let herself in. Angelica was not amused. She slowly moved her tail to express her disapproval. Her bowls were empty. Victoria filled her empty crystal dishes and looked around his apartment. It was spotless and modern. All of the furniture was white so Angelica's fur didn't show up. Jonathan kept spare lint brushes in his desk at work and in the glove compartment of his car just in case.

She knew a few of his secrets. He had one laptop in the second bedroom of his apartment, which he used as an office. He sometimes wrote freelance articles. She knew something other people, like the deputies searching his place, wouldn't; he had another computer in a secret drawer in his armoire.

Victoria had brought in her oversized purse and put the laptop in it. She figured it wouldn't be long before her favorite deputy had arrived at his sister's house and would discover she wasn't there. She looked around the apartment to see if she was missing anything.

As she was getting into her vehicle, her phone began to ring.

"Well, I'll be. If it isn't Jefferson Hawes. I didn't expect to be getting a call from you," she said once again trying to feign innocence.

"Your sarcasm isn't humorous, Victoria."

"Ouch, you just called me 'Victoria.' I'm on the way."

"You'd better be," he said and hung up.

"Nice chatting with you, too, Jeff," she said as she stared at her phone.

She kept one eye on the rearview mirror at all times as she drove back to Margie's house. She had developed a paranoia over the past couple of months. She didn't see anyone behind her, but taking a page from a self-defense class she took once, she made some sharp turns and zigzagged across town. She felt like a teenager who'd missed curfew when she saw Jeff waiting on Margie's front porch for her. He was leaning against one of the pillars and had his arms folded. She decided now was not the time for him to find out about Jonathan's second computer. She didn't know if there was anything on it or not so she slid it under the seat of her car.

"Vic," he said as she approached the porch.

"I had to feed Jonathan's cat. I had forgotten about her, and she wasn't happy. See, I've even got cat hair on me. So what did you find out?" she asked.

"Come on in."

His face looked grim as they walked inside the house. He made his way to Margie's kitchen table. He sat down and folded his hands on the table.

"Jonathan is okay, but he has been transferred. When I looked into the paperwork to find out who authorized the transfer, it's missing."

"I need to see him," she said.

"You can't right now. He can't have any visitors. I'm going to get there as soon as I can."

"What did you find at the Blake residence?"

"I checked the bushes again and found a pair of white men's dress gloves. They're in my truck, and I'm taking them to the station when I leave here. I couldn't find the speech though. There wasn't anything in the solarium. We need to find out what he was going to announce."

He reached into his shirt pocket and pulled something out.

"And I did find this," he said giving her her earring.

"Well, I had to make it credible," she said. "What about the button?"

"It's from the cuff of a long-sleeve deputy uniform shirt. I couldn't get a full print off of it – only partials. I'm checking it for DNA; that will take a few days."

He started to stand.

"Rushing off already, Jeff?" asked Margie.

"I need to get back to work."

She gave him a peck on the cheek and handed him a bag.

"I made you a sandwich," she said. "And Jeff, you need to get some sleep."

"Thanks."

"And you, no more missing earrings or feeding cats," he said, pointing at Victoria.

"I have barely slept in two days. I'm going to bed," she said.

"Thanks, Margie."

Victoria walked out onto the porch and followed him to his truck. She needed to get the computer out of the car, but she wanted to wait until Jeff was out of sight. He couldn't see it yet - not until she knew what was on it.

"I'll talk to you again, soon," he said.

"Night, Jeff."

Once inside the garage room, Victoria opened Jonathan computer and curled up with Auggie on the bed. Auggie put his paw on her arm.

"I'm not lying, Auggie. I said I was going to bed. I said nothing about sleeping."

Everything in this computer was passcode protected. She could see the names of files, but she couldn't get into them. He had financial information on the laptop. She didn't think she needed that. Despite all of his eccentric behaviors, Jonathan was an astute businessman. He parlayed his business contacts into some lucrative business deals. He didn't make a lot of money in his writing for the paper, but he'd made some wise investments that had paid off for him. He was learning from those he hung around.

As she scrolled his documents, one caught her eye; the file was called "Victoria – in honor of our weekend together."

It was password protected too. She knew the weekend he was talking about. The password had something to do with their time in Birmingham or Atlanta when he was helping her create an alibi. Neither Birmingham nor Atlanta worked. She tried other words associated with their trip.

"Auggie, I don't know," she said. "I'm so tired."

She closed her eyes to try and clear her mind, but exhaustion won out.

6

She awoke to Auggie licking her face. The laptop was still open next to her.

She closed it and wondered where she could put it for safe keeping.

She walked down to see Margie, but she couldn't find her. She noticed the newspaper lying on the kitchen table. She read the front page. She couldn't believe what she was seeing. Her blood began to boil. Martin Anderson had written a column slamming Jonathan and making crazy accusations. It was done as an opinion piece, but so much for innocent until proven guilty. They'd gone past an assumption of guilt. He's already been convicted in her own newspaper, and she had to prove him innocent. And when she did, she would help Jonathan on his libel lawsuit against the paper.

Maybe it's time for a career change, she thought as she balled up the newspaper and threw it. It was Labor Day, and Victoria didn't know what to do with herself. She thought about going to Jake's. Most of the blue hairs would be at the campground for the annual Bennettsville Labor Day Barbecue, an event Victoria always covered. She couldn't remember the last Labor Day she had off.

Labor Day held too many memories especially the evening hours. She usually worked during the day and closed herself in her apartment at night. She could hear the fireworks in her apartment, so she'd put on music to shut the world and the memories out.

She didn't know what to do and slumped down at the table. In that moment, she just wanted to cry. She was exhausted and had too many emotions she was dealing with. She had bottled up anger inside her and the thought of Jonathan in jail combined with this vindictive spirit from the paper added a profound sense of hopelessness and despair. And she totally avoided thinking about the fact that she had feelings not only for Jeff, but Jonathan too. She wondered what was wrong with her.

"God help me," she said as she tried to fight back the tears.

She took a deep breath and stood up with a new resolve to help Jonathan. She headed to the store to get some poster board and adhesive notes. She was going to make an outline to figure out what pieces of the puzzle she had and what was missing.

Fortunately there was a blank wall in the garage apartment. She wrote down all the clues on the adhesive notes and placed them on the poster board. She felt like she was playing pin the tail on the donkey as she blindly placed the notes on the board. She just couldn't see the connections between Allison Blake, Jonathan Marlowe, Martin Anderson, and Dan Kennedy.

What was on Jonathan's computer? And why did it all have to happen on a stupid holiday?

She knew who she needed to talk to, but she couldn't do it until the next business day, or did she have another lead? As she stared at the wall, Jeff called from the family phone.

"So what leads do you have on my case?" he asked.

"And a good morning to you, Deputy Hawes."

"I'm running the wig and gloves for DNA," he said. "It seems obvious someone dressed up as Marlowe to make witnesses think he did it. I hope to have answers soon. I'm not sharing my information with too many people."

"I have confidence that you will find answers, Jeff."

"But you totally avoided my question."

"Because I know you don't want my help. But trust me, when I find something, I'll call you."

"You sound pretty confident."

"Oh I am," she said and hung up.

She stared at the crudely made flow chart. She knew where she had to go. Fortunately, Myra Evans didn't mind guests just dropping in unannounced. Miss Myra, the town busybody and retired librarian, lived in a cottage only a few blocks from Margie.

"Victoria, so good to see you," she said when she came to her screen door. "Come in, dear."

"I'm sorry I didn't call before coming."

"You are just fine. I was expecting a visit from you," she said. "Would you like some lemonade and cookies?"

"Thank you."

Victoria made her way into the parlor filled with its wingback chairs and tables covered in lace doilies. Faded antique Persian rugs covered the heart pine floors. Dust particles floated on the stream of September sunbeams which flooded in the room through the yellowing lace curtains. She loved the ambiance of the room - musty smell and all.

"You aren't at the picnic today, dear?" she asked as she returned with a crystal pitcher of lemonade and plate of freshly baked sugar cookies.

"No, I'm actually off today."

"I know why you're here, dear, and Jonathan is innocent," Miss Myra said and smiled. "He was always such a sweet boy – perfect manners. He loved to come to the library when he was a boy. We spent a lot of time together on afternoons before his mother got off work. She was a good woman. We had long talks about literature and his desire to write. He loved Shakespeare."

"I've got to help him. I don't understand what's going on."

Miss Myra smiled and nodded.

"What do Martin Anderson, Allison Blake, Dan Kennedy, and Jonathan Marlowe have in common?" Victoria asked.

"You've lived in Bennettsville all your life and don't know connections? I'm surprised at you, Victoria."

"No, I don't," she said and sighed.

"Well, it goes back to the love triangle between Charles, Cassie, and Dan, which I told you about on our last visit."

Victoria nodded as Miss Myra continued.

"Allison Blake is not Charles' daughter. She's Dan's daughter."

"How do you know these things?"

Miss Myra just smiled.

"Everyone knew including Charles and Dan. Charles was only interested in Cassie for her family's money. Charles was just plain greedy. There was never enough for him. The more he got; the more he wanted. A divorce would have cost both of them a lot and would have been very messy."

"And this isn't messy?"

"Charles' plan all along was to hurt Dan. I don't know where their rivalry began, but what Dan had done was an affront to Charles' pride. He spent most of his life trying to find ways to instill hatred in Allison for 'Uncle Dan.' And he made himself a hero in her eyes, giving her everything she wanted. All's fair in love and business."

"So where does Martin Anderson fit in, and why pin a murder on Jonathan?"

"Martin is Cassie's nephew. He's the son of Cassie's sister who lives in Atlanta. She was a black sheep of Bennettsville. He's a weasel. He's a confused individual who wants to destroy the Blakes and Kennedys for his own purposes. There's more than meets the eye, dear."

"And Jonathan?"

"I can think of four people who know the answer to that. One's dead, one's your killer, and two are in jail," she said.

"I was afraid of that."

Miss Myra patted Victoria's hands.

"You'll find the answer."

"Are you sure you don't have them all?" she asked.

Miss Myra smiled and shook her head.

Back at the garage apartment, Victoria added Miss Myra's

information to her suspect board. A few missing links were filled in, but she only opened more questions. That would have to wait. Miss Myra was right. There were only a handful of people who knew what was going on. The two in jail were Jonathan and Jennifer Campbell; she couldn't get to Jonathan. She wasn't sure she'd be able to see Jennifer either, and even if she did, what would Jennifer gain by talking to her? Victoria had no leverage at all.

7

Victoria sat on the floor of the garage apartment with her back against the bed and the suspect board on the floor in front of her. She thought about Jonathan's computer and the need to find the missing password. She felt like her brain was turning to mush as scenarios and passwords flew through her brain. She tried not to concentrate on hacking into Jonathan's computer too much. She was frustrated she couldn't come up with an answer. It was probably an obvious one. She was so deep in her thoughts she didn't hear the knock on the door.

"Vic," Jeff stuck his head into the room.

She quickly scrambled from her spot on the floor and tried to hide her papers. It didn't work. He just smiled and noticed her poster board on the wall. He didn't say anything at first.

"I've been trying to call you," he said. "I called Margie, and she told me you were still here."

"I'm sorry. I'm just thinking."

"Any leads?" he asked.

She felt he was making fun of her.

"I'm working on it," she said.

"Listen, there's still entertainment for a couple of more hours and then the fireworks at the Bennettsville picnic. Would you be interested in heading that way?"

"I don't know if that's such a good idea," she said. "Besides, watching Betty Sue Higgins' cloggers and hearing Bubba Edwards and Grandpa Hinson with their banjos is not what I consider entertaining."

She tried to come up with any reason not to go to the Labor Day event with him because the last one she'd went with him to was as vivid as if it had only happened last week.

"It's not a social event. I need a second pair of eyes."

"Really? What about Auggie?"

Auggie's ears perked up, and he began to wag his tail.

"Do you have your camera gear?"

"Yes. Sorry, Auggie, this sounds like work," she scratched his ears. He barked as if to express his disapproval.

Margie was standing at the bottom of the stairs and smiling when the two of them came down. He stopped and gave her a peck on the cheek.

"It's not what you're thinking."

"You don't know I'm thinking, Jefferson Hawes."

"Oh, yes, I do, big sister; you are an open book."

They got into Jeff's pickup truck and headed to the fairgrounds.

"So what am I looking for?"

"I want you to watch Martin Anderson and Allison Blake."

"Why? I'm not exactly on Martin Anderson's favorites' list."

"The paper is sponsoring the kids' scholarship program, and the top prize winner will be announced at 8 p.m., right before the high school band begins its concert. You should know he's announcing the winner, and she's presenting an added savings bond in honor of her parents. I want you to watch them both. We won't be together most of the time. I have someone else I'm watching."

"I thought you didn't want me in your investigation?"

"I trust you, Vic, but I'm not sure about some of my deputies. I've seen some disturbing things in the past few days, and I know it doesn't stop with them. I want you to take photos of anything suspicious. You've got good instincts, and you have a couple of killer lenses."

She laughed.

"You only want me for my lenses. I'll remember that."

As soon as they arrived at the fairgrounds, Jeff headed in one direction while she went near the stage. She didn't see Martin or Allison. Neither of them arrived until a few minutes before the presentation. And they didn't look happy about it. Not that Victoria blamed them. It was still hot and humid out. She hoped Martin was catching a lot of grief for the stories he was publishing.

Where were the newspaper's board members?

He'd gotten out of hand.

She followed them with her high-powered lens, glad that she could stay out of the crowd and out of sight of Mr. Anderson.

Boring speech. Blah, blah, blah was all Victoria could hear.

Shut up and give out the checks already.

She was getting impatient.

She wasn't sure what she was looking for, but after the check presentation, she noticed Allison and Martin huddled together. She started snapping photos. Was this what Jeff wanted? After a few minutes of deep conversation, she saw Allison pass him an envelope. Victoria couldn't tell what that was about. She followed Martin as he headed into the crowd. He talked to a few people before one of Bennettsville's deputies approached him. They seemed to be arguing.

That's interesting, she thought as she snapped several more photos. She couldn't tell what they were doing, but she was hoping she was capturing something on her memory card. She wished she could hear what they were saying, but she didn't have a high-powered microphone.

She sent a text to Jeff. She was ready to leave; she wanted to be gone before dark. He told her to meet him back at his truck. When she got there, he was standing outside and talking on the phone. She got into the truck when he stuck his head through the open window.

"Do you want to watch the fireworks? Out here is as good a place as any," he said. "Margie sent a blanket."

She really did not want to stay. She got out of the cab and

hesitated while he spread the blanket out in the back of the pickup. He sat down, and she followed.

"Did you get any interesting photos?"

"Oh yes, I did," she said. "What made you think something was going to happen here?"

"Just a hunch. I've spent the last day trying to figure out who my leak is. And then I found one deputy who insisted on working the picnic. I thought it was odd. Usually, everyone is begging to have today off because it's such a pain to deal with the drunken idiots. Then there are the ones who don't want to obey the traffic flow. It's a huge hassle."

She handed her camera to him. He flipped through the images.

"Looks like Allison Blake and Martin Anderson are chummy," he said, handing it back.

"Do you want the memory card?" she asked.

He nodded.

As she handed it to him, he touched her hand.

"I've wanted to talk to you," he said, holding her hand and looking into her eyes. "I'm sorry I hurt you."

She felt her heart begin to race.

"There's nothing to apologize for. It happened a long time ago," she said as she removed her hand from his. "I went away to school and got busy with things. I didn't come home on the weekends like we'd talked about."

"But I didn't come to see you either."

"We drifted apart. It wasn't anyone's fault."

"Vic, Lacy and I were all wrong for each other," he said. "It was a crazy, whirlwind romance that was doomed from the start. I think I was angry at you and wanted to make you jealous at first. Then, it got totally out of control. I think we both woke up on our honeymoon realizing it, but we had too much pride to admit it. Our families didn't approve, and we were going to prove them wrong. When we found out she was pregnant, we decided to stick it out for our daughter. But it's been over for a really long time. She made a lot of trips to Atlanta, and I think there was someone else. In that time, I thought a lot about the mistakes I'd made, and the biggest one I made was not going after you. You said 'yes' to me then you ran. Now, it's officially over with her. It's final. I have the paperwork to prove it."

He was saying everything she'd wanted to hear for so long. Her heart was pounding. She didn't want him to know she still had feelings for him although she was sure he knew. She didn't want him to hurt her again, and if she did get her job back at the paper, there were ethical reasons not to be involved with him especially in her position as crime reporter. And then there was Jonathan. Her head was swimming.

"It was young love with us." she said, trying to break his gaze.

"Do you remember the last time we saw each other?"

"Besides today?" she asked and tried to laugh nervously.

"Our last date? It was Labor Day. The day I proposed to you?" he said as he tilted her chin toward his face. He kissed her softly, and the tears began to fall.

And that was exactly what she was trying to forget. That was what she always tried to forget every Labor Day. That Labor Day had started with the all-day picnic. At one point, they decided to sneak away from the Labor Day festivities and headed back to his parents' cabin at the lake. There, he proposed, and they talked about their future while lying on a blanket watching the stars. How could she forget that day? It scared her though. She'd always thought she wanted to leave Bennettsville and see the world. She had thought she wanted to move to New York. When she finally came back after graduation, it was too late.

As he kissed her, the fireworks' show began.

"Corny, isn't it?" he said as the lights flashed in the sky.

Victoria hadn't noticed the fireworks. She was lost in the kiss. She was expecting it, but she was surprised at the same time. She didn't know what to do. She jumped out of the back of the truck while the fireworks still went off overhead. The floodgates of all those emotions were now opened, the excitement and the pain. She wondered where all of this was leading. What exactly was he up to? She remembered all the nights spent crying and dreaming of being in his arms again. This is what she thought she wanted. Why didn't she stay there with him? And then, there were thoughts of Jonathan sneaking into her mind.

He got out of the truck too.

"I'm sorry," he said. "I should have handled that better."

"You're fine," she said without looking at him. "We're not getting out of this parking lot for a while; I'm going to take a walk."

She heard Jeff kick the side of his truck and curse as she walked away.

8

When the crowd dissipated, she made her way back to Jeff's pickup. The ride back to Margie's was quiet. Neither of them knew what to say. Victoria got out of the truck as quickly as she could and bolted up the stairs.

She held Auggie close and silently cried as she drifted off to sleep. She hoped she would rest, but in between dreams of Jeff and waking up every two hours, she got little sleep.

She was up before dawn. She'd forgotten to feed Jonathan's cat so her first plan of action was to visit Angelica. Victoria decided she needed to take another look around. She had been rushing on the night she found his computer. Maybe he left some hint as to what his password might be. He was such a neat freak; everything seemed to be in order. There wasn't a speck of dust in sight. She stared at Angelica.

"How does he keep your hair off everything?" she asked.

Angelica turned away from her and walked over to her crystal dish.

Victoria looked in his bedroom and walked into his office. She couldn't fathom how anyone could be so perfect. There wasn't anything on his desk except a movie. That was definitely out of place. She walked over and picked it up. She smiled. The name of the film was Atlanta Alibi. She knew that had to be the password for the file in Jonathan's computer.

She rushed back to Margie's house and prayed that it would work. She pulled out Jonathan's computer from its hiding place. She knew he'd probably add a special character or number.

She tried several unsuccessful combinations before she typed "Atlanta$Alibi."

It worked.

"Yes," she said and clapped loudly, frightening Auggie in the process.

Jonathan had written her a letter.

"My dearest Victoria,

"First, I must commend you on your detective skills. Maybe you are in the wrong profession after all. If you are reading this, then something has gone awry with Mr. Kennedy's plan. He had been receiving threats several weeks before the Blake murders; from whom, neither of us knew. He has a business deal he intends to announce at the Bennettsville Masquerade Ball. Your dress is perfect, by the way.

"His plan is to spin off from the newspaper into several additional digital printing companies. He sees the future in ebooks and other forms of communication in addition to a search engine that would rival the biggest ones; however, he could make waves within Blake Enterprises as well as Kennedy Holdings by doing this. He's heavily invested in Blake Enterprises, and there could be scared investors in both the Blake and Kennedy camps from this speculative enterprise on one hand. On the other hand, he's been consulting outside of Bennettsville, which would make the infrastructure nervous and feel slighted because they aren't included. He can't win for losing, I'm afraid. He's been consulting with me over the past several months, and I've been doing a lot of the ground work and research. He intends to make me chief executive officer and president of this new venture. He wants new blood, so to speak. This stands to be a problem for the Herald, which will likely be absorbed into the new business if it takes off as planned. There are people in the Herald who've been there a long time who will no longer have jobs.

"Also, it stands to hurt Blake Enterprises because Mr. Kennedy intended on pulling out of some of Blake's ventures and selling some shares. He wanted to do it slowly over time to cause less damage, but there would be damage.

"I know you are probably mad at me by this point, but I was sworn to secrecy by Mr. Kennedy. I have a job for you if you ever want one and a lovely title to go with it. In the event that Mr. Kennedy's computer can't be accessed, I've saved all important files on this computer as well as emails.

"I can't imagine Martin Anderson and Allison Blake are happy about any of this. Both of them would lose a great deal. I know there are others right under our noses, but I can't point you in the right direction. I hope this helps you."

Victoria stared at the letter. She needed Jeff to see this. At least she knew why Dan Kennedy had been killed, and it certainly pointed suspicion several different ways.

Who else could have known about the business arrangement and who it would affect?

She hesitated before calling Jeff. She didn't really know what to say to him after the previous night. She called his work phone, but he didn't answer. She sent a text.

"Hey, Jeff, I have some information you might be interested in."

She wondered if he was upset with her. She couldn't blame him if he was.

She called the family phone number. No answer there either. Myra Evans and Jonathan had given her her next clue. She needed some help from Liz. She called her on her cell.

"What's going on down there?" she asked Liz.

"I'm at home right now, but the paper is totally out of control. I hear they are talking to the newspaper's lawyers behind Anderson's back. He's out of control. How's your information search going?" Liz asked.

"I've got several leads, but one I'm going to need some help with."

"What can I do?'

"I need to get in to see Jennifer Campbell."

"Jennifer Campbell, as in the one who just tried to kill you, Jennifer Campbell?" Liz sounded confused.

"I don't think she really meant to kill me, and I didn't press charges. But, yes, that one."

"Let me make a few calls. Someone around here must have a contact who could help you get in. I'll be discreet."

"I'm not going anywhere although I would really love to see her today."

"I'll see what I can do," she said.

She stared at her poster board for a while. Too many dots and not enough connections.

No return text. She tried Jeff again on his work cell. It went straight to voicemail. She tried on the family line. No answer. She looked at the time. It had been more than an hour since her first call. She was starting to panic.

"Something's not right, Auggie. He's not that mad at me," she said

She folded up the computer and put it in her hobo bag. She went downstairs to see Margie and knocked on the side door. When Margie came to the door, her face was as white as a sheet.

"Margie, what's wrong?" Victoria reached out and touched her shoulder. Her instinct immediately told her it was Jeff.

"I was coming to get you."

"Why?"

"Jeff's been shot," was the answer, but it didn't come from Margie. It was Jeff's father, Benjamin Franklin Hawes, who had retired as Bennettsville's sheriff about a year before. He was in the room behind Margie. Victoria felt a knot form in the pit of her stomach. She felt a stab of guilt after the night before. What if she'd lost her second chance with him? Who would shoot Jeff?

"Is he okay? What happened?" she said as she began to panic.

"He's at the hospital now. He was shot in the shoulder. He called me right before he drove himself to the hospital. He got your messages," the elder Hawes was gruff when he spoke. Even though he'd retired, people around town still called Ben Hawes "sheriff" out of respect because he served as sheriff for more than 20 years.

The man she knew as Jeff's dad from when she and Jeff dated was different from the sheriff who didn't like her nosing around in police business. In a lot of ways, Jeff and his father were alike, but the longer she worked at the paper, the more she sensed Sheriff Hawes' dislike of her. He didn't have a department spokesman. He was the spokesman; he was the department iron fist, and if you wanted something when he was sheriff, you had to go through him. It was like easier to break a prisoner out of jail than it was to get information out of Sheriff Hawes if he didn't want you to know. Sometimes, he scared her, and she was sure he didn't like the fact that Jeff had brought her to Margie's house.

"Drove himself to the hospital with a gunshot wound? Why does that not surprise me?" Victoria tried to lighten the mood and get Sheriff Hawes off her scent.

Margie's face was pale. She nervously tried to make some food in the kitchen. It was her way of dealing with stress.

"Did he see who did it?"

"Whoever it was was wearing a mask? Are you writing a story?" he said as he narrowed his eyes at her.

"I could be," she said. He riled her, and she felt the hair on the back of her neck stand up.

Sheriff Hawes glared at her, and she backed down only because she didn't want to cause any backlash for when Jeff got out of the hospital.

"I am concerned about him especially with all the violence in Bennettsville lately. They got his shoulder?" Victoria asked, trying to mask her true feelings. Sometimes, the training from the drama classes came in handy. She was hoping this was one of those times.

"Shoulder. They weren't intending on killing him. Someone wants him conveniently out of the way so he can't finish this investigation," Sheriff Hawes said. "Margie, are you coming with me?"

"I'll be outside in a minute, Daddy," she said. "You go ahead."

Victoria looked at her phone. She had a text from Liz to call her right away. He nodded and walked to the car. As soon as he was out of range, Margie spoke.

"There's a lot more going on there than meets the eye. Jeff will get your friend out of jail even if he has to do it from his hospital bed, but all he's going to do is kill a roach or two. He's not going to get to the root of this. It runs deep. Daddy curbed it for several years, but as soon as he left the department, it was like a vacuum needing to be filled. The pockets of corruption have exploded. Jeff thinks he can do it, but he's not powerful enough yet. I just pray he doesn't get killed."

Victoria reached out to hug Margie. Victoria didn't want Margie to see the tears she was trying to fight back, and the hug was as much for Victoria as it was for Margie.

"Margie, ever since I started working for the Herald, your dad hasn't liked me very much. I want to go to the hospital, but I don't feel welcomed around him. I'm trying to track down a lead on this case. I may have something today."

"I know Jeff will act like he's mad, but he wants your help. Just don't tell him I said that. He has that headstrong, macho thing. He inherited it from Daddy," she said. "Take care of yourself, Hon. I always wanted you for my sister-in-law."

"Thanks, Margie," she said and smiled.

Margie made her way to the vehicle.

Once they pulled out of sight, Victoria took a deep breath and frantically called Liz.

"Deputy Hawes has been shot, Liz," she said.

"I'm on it, and I got you in to see Jennifer Campbell this afternoon at 2:30. Can you still get there?"

"Today?" Victoria wanted to rush to the hospital.

"Yes, today."

"I'll be there."

9

Victoria tried to pull herself together to drive to Macon. She wanted to be at the hospital, but she had to keep telling herself she was the only one who could get this piece of information. She drove while wiping the tears away. She rationalized that he would be in surgery so he wouldn't know she was there anyway. Sheriff Hawes said the shooter only trying to scare him, but what if the person was just a bad shot? Maybe someone wanted to kill Jeff too. She tried not to think about that. She could get back to Bennettsville as soon as possible. She only had three minutes once she got through security anyway.

Victoria declared this to be the summer Bennettsville went crazy. As the temperatures went up, it seemed that a portal to a weird alternative universe had opened wide with it. At times, she felt she had even lost her mind. She'd been threatened a few weeks before, and now while she was being threatened by some other unknown person or people, she was on her way to see the woman who'd stalked and shot her. Not only was she worried about Jeff, but she knew she was Jonathan's only hope. She didn't want to think about it that way. The newspaper had abandoned him, and now with Jeff in the hospital, what was she supposed to do? She arrived well before her time so she could go through the appropriate security checks before seeing Jennifer. There would be no time for pleasantries. She'd have to get straight to the point. She prayed silently.

Without makeup and in an orange jumpsuit, Jennifer Campbell was still a strikingly beautiful woman. She looked oddly at her visitor.

"How's your arm?" she asked.

The tone lacked all of the sarcasm Victoria thought it should have.

"It's fine," Victoria replied. "I have three minutes."

"I know why you are here," Jennifer cut her off. "You are in way over your head, Ms. James. There are secrets you will never know the answer to. You will solve this one just like they let you solve the last one, but you will never know the complete truth. The answer is in front of you. It's in front of everyone. A lot of innocent people will die. You should have never returned home and never gotten involved with that family. Do yourself a favor and get out of Bennettsville as quickly as you can. Take Jonathan Marlowe with you. He's a good man. Allison Blake and Martin Anderson are part of the cogs that turn the wheel that framed Jonathan. In a lot of ways, they are so clueless. Think about it carefully. Who were the most powerful people in Bennettsville? Dan Kennedy and Charles Blake. They are both dead in the span of two months. That leaves a huge power vacuum. Don't believe everything you see or hear, and don't even believe everything you write."

Victoria stared at Jennifer.

"You want to know why am I telling you this? I'm a dead woman already. I've got nothing to lose. And one more thing – you really should read. There are some great things at the Bennettsville Library. Is it 4:10 yet?"

"Time's up, Campbell," said the guard.

The blood drained from Jennifer Campbell's face. She slowly got up and began to walk away. Before she left the room, Jennifer looked back over her shoulder one last time. That was not the arrogant woman she had seen a few weeks before. She looked terrified. Victoria realized she was shaking as she stood up. She felt numb as she walked through the steel doors. She wondered about Jennifer's cryptic message. As soon as she got to her vehicle, she wrote down everything she could remember.

She checked her phone. There were no messages. She dreaded the drive back to Bennettsville. She called Margie and tried to keep her voice calm.

"How's Jeff?" she asked.

"He's out of surgery now. He's still groggy, but he's already asking when he can leave," she said.

"I'm glad to hear it."

Throughout the drive back to Bennettsville, she kept looking behind her to see if anyone had followed her. Once inside the city limits, she drove erratically to try to shake anyone off her tail. She'd turned her phone off. She didn't know who or what to trust anymore. She knew she wasn't heading to the hospital just yet.

She called Jeff. He sounded like she'd woken him.

"Hey, Vic," he said.

"Do we have matching scars?" she asked and laughed.

"I think mine might be a little bigger. Where are you? Please be careful out there," he said. "I'm still at the hospital. They won't let me leave. I may be able to leave in the morning,"

"I'll be there shortly," she said and hung up the phone.

"But I'm going to the Bennettsville Library first."

Jennifer had left something there, and she hoped that she was the first to find this mysterious package. Their appointment had been at 2:30 p.m., and they only had three minutes together. The time Jennifer mentioned wasn't even close to their appointment so it had to mean something related to the library and the location of whatever she wanted Victoria to find. She went to section 410. Linguistics. There were definitely lots of words being thrown around. She didn't know who to believe. No one had been telling her the truth lately. There wasn't much in 410. She pulled out each of the 410 listings and behind them was a paperback copy of Myra Evans' History of Bennettsville. The tiny village could date its founding to 1755, and the history was written in honor of its 250th anniversary in 2005. The book had no markings and didn't appear to have been part of the library's collection at all. She thumbed through it. There was an enveloped taped inside the cover. Victoria looked around to see if she was being watched. She was sure there were security cameras somewhere. She grabbed a few other books and headed to check them out.

"Hi, Ms. James," said a fresh-faced library assistant, who scanned her card and the books. "Is this your book, Ms. James? It's not ours; it doesn't scan."

"I'm sorry. Yes, that's mine. I didn't mean to put that in there with those. Thanks."

She smiled.

She needed a safety deposit box for all the clues she kept acquiring but not in Bennettsville, she surmised. Outside the library, she called Liz to let her know about her visit with Jennifer. She got Liz's voicemail.

"It went better than I thought. Give me a couple of days, and I'll let you know," she said.

She wanted to delve into the book and see what was in that envelope, but back in Bennettsville, she felt the walls closing in on her. She was on edge as it was, but her conversation with Jennifer confirmed some of her fears. The two wealthiest and influential men in the town were dead in the span of a couple of months. It wasn't a coincidence especially when Bennettsville was a peaceful town with few violent crimes. She wondered if Jonathan knew everything that was going on.

She opened the envelope as she sat in her car and read the note inside.

"I didn't kill Charles and Cassie Blake. No one would ever believe the truth. I had to confess. The secrets are in this book. If you want to know the truth, keep searching. J.C."

She couldn't read the history book in the car. She opened it and shook it to see if anything else fell out of it. No luck. She sighed. That was another mystery for another day.

At the hospital, she hesitated. She wanted to see Jeff, but at the same time, she didn't know how he'd react to her after the previous night, plus she really did not want to see his dad again. When she arrived at his room, she found two deputies standing at the door.

"You can't go in there, ma'am," one of them said.

"Could you ask him? I'm Victoria James."

The deputy nodded.

"You are allowed in. We have a short list of approved visitors."

Jeff was sitting up in his hospital bed and talking on his cell phone. He had an IV, and his right arm was in a sling. She waved and quietly sat down. She felt her heart race again.

"Do we have enough information yet? I want to close this case. Work all night if you have to."

He hung up the phone.

She smiled.

"How are you feeling?" she asked feeling slightly awkward.

"I need to get out of this hospital. I'm not taking any more pain meds. They are messing with my brain," he said and winced as he moved. "They are supposed to let me out in the morning if I behave. Vic, I'm sorry about last night. It was stupid of me to think we could pick up where we left off eight years ago without any warning to you."

She got up and moved closer to the side of the hospital bed. She reached for his left hand and held it for a minute.

"Why don't we talk about that when you are better? Okay?" she said, reaching out to touch his face. "How are you doing?"

"I got shot in the shoulder. They had to remove the bullet, and there was damage to the bone and tendon. I'm going to be fine. I'll probably be able to tell you when it's going to rain a day before it happens, but I'll be fine. I want to get out of here," he said. His words came out rapidly. She could tell he was agitated.

"What about the shooter?"

"Didn't get a good look at him."

"Where is your family?"

"I sent them away. I'm fine. My sister was like a mother hen.

Where have you been all day? Margie said you were onto something."

"I guess your anesthesia is finally wearing off. I went chasing down a few clues. Before you fuss too much, take a look at these."

She pulled the computer out of her oversized purse and placed it on his hospital tray. He motioned for her to sit on the edge of his bed.

"This is Jonathan's secret computer. It was hidden in a drawer at his house. It took me a while to crack the password. I spent some time in Jonathan's apartment to see if there were any hints. Fortunately, there were."

She pulled up the files for him and told him all about what Miss Myra told her.

"It doesn't tell us much, but does it tell us something?"

"I think so. I'm on them to get me the results of those DNA tests. Once I have them, I may have the answers, and we can get Marlowe out of jail soon," he said.

"You look tired. I'm going to leave so you can get some rest," she said. She touched his hand before leaving.

Victoria decided to return to her apartment for the night. It was closer than Margie's. If anyone was following her, it wouldn't matter where she was. They'd find her. She didn't like that Auggie was still with Margie. She'd rather have him with her, but she knew Margie would take care of him.

She slowly let herself in and turned on all the lights. Satisfied that there was no one hiding in the shadows, she locked her deadbolt and the chain. She also stuck a chair under the doorknob for good measure. She decided to take a closer look at Jonathan's emails. Most of the emails were only between Jonathan and Mr. Kennedy, but there were a couple that included a third party – Cliff Daniels. He was the president of a tech company near San Francisco. That made sense. She had an idea; she wasn't sure it would work, but she had to try. His personal cell number was listed in the email. Victoria looked at the clock – 10 p.m. On the west coast, it was only 7 p.m. She wasn't surprised when she reached his voicemail. She left a message even though it was a little awkward with him not knowing who she was.

She was surprised when she got a call back only a few minutes later.

"Victoria," he said. "I've heard so many good things about you from Dan and Jonathan. We were hoping to ask you on board when things got rolling. Sadly, it seems none of this is happening."

"Jonathan is innocent, and I'm out to prove it," she said. "And I think you can help me."

"I'm all ears. I was hopeful about this new business venture."

"How soon can you be on a flight to Atlanta? I'll pick you up and drive you to Bennettsville."

"Is there an airstrip near Bennettsville? I have my own plane, and I can be there tomorrow," he said.

Since Dan Kennedy wasn't around to make the announcement, Cliff Daniels would be. She knew she could get a lot of media attention for a news conference, and she knew just what to write.

10

The deputies allowed her to slip quietly into Jeff's hospital room the next morning. He was on his phone when she arrived. She was surprised he was alone.

"You've been busy from what I hear," he said.

"How so?"

"Cliff Daniels?"

"Yes, he's arriving this afternoon, and he's holding a news conference tomorrow outside the small business association office."

"What's he announcing?"

"Aw, Jeff, I don't want to spoil the surprise, but how did you know he was coming?" she asked and then laughed.

"A little birdie told me. This isn't television, you know," he said.

"No, it's even better than that. I get to see the reaction on the faces of some people. Who knows what will happen tomorrow? Besides I think this little publicity stunt is just what we need to draw out the real killer. Whoever it is thinks this deal isn't going through, but I've got news."

"I guess Marlowe isn't the only one at the paper with a dramatic flair," he said and laughed.

"Where is everyone?"

"I sent them away. Speaking of, I heard that you didn't go out back to Margie's house last night."

"No, I went to my apartment, and I survived. I'm not going

to live in fear. I'll just add more locks. I'll be going to get Auggie shortly."

"Good, you can take me with you, after we stop by the drug store," he said and winced. "They gave me my marching orders. I was just waiting for my ride."

Although he was supposed to be resting and recovering, Jeff spent most of the day on the phone, tracking down DNA results and other forensic tests. Victoria made plans for the big news conference. There were some hotels in Bennettsville, but they opted to take Mr. Daniels to a bed and breakfast on the outskirts of town. Victoria was relying on the blue hairs at Jake's and Miss Myra to spread some rumors over the next 24 hours. It wasn't every day that someone arrived in his own plane into Bennettsville.

Victoria knew whoever killed Dan Kennedy also knew about the business plan despite the heavily-guarded secret. The announcement should ferret them out. Victoria still had some of Mr. Kennedy's money left from the evening gown purchase and tried to find the most businesslike suit she could for the event. She thought about Jennifer Campbell's look - a sharp pencil skirt and blazer and perfectly pressed shirt.

The next morning, she tried them on in her apartment and stood in front of the full length oval mirror.

"What do you think, Auggie?" she asked.

He barked twice in approval.

She pulled her hair into a neat French twist and took a deep breath as she headed to the news conference.

She arrived well in advance of the event to ensure all the details were in place, and then she headed to the bed and breakfast to pick up Cliff Daniels. He was in his 30s with dark hair and brown eyes.

"Good to see you, Victoria," he said as she walked inside.

"Are you ready?" she asked.

"You do look like a CEO," he said. "I hope this plan of yours works."

"Oh, Cliff, you have no idea how much I hope it works."

News media began arriving about 15 minutes before the event. Victoria watched for familiar faces. Usually, she was on the other side of this type of event, but she was thrilled to see she could draw a crowd. She saw reporters from the television stations, as well as the Herald. She wasn't surprised to see Ed and Martin come in together. Allison Blake arrived just in time. Wearing a sling, Jeff was in the back of the room, and Victoria hoped he had some good news for her.

Victoria approached the podium.

"Good morning and thank you for attending," she said. "This event is a mix of sadness and joy. What we called you here for was supposed to have been announced by Dan Kennedy at the Bennettsville Masquerade Ball. As you know, Mr. Kennedy was killed at the ball. We know that he would have wanted his dream to live. I want to introduce Mr. Cliff Daniels, the president and CEO of the Daniels Group, based in San Francisco. Mr. Daniels heads several companies and was preparing to launch a new endeavor with Mr. Kennedy. Please welcome, Mr. Daniels."

Victoria applauded as she stepped back and allowed him to take the podium.

"Dan Kennedy and I met at a publishers' convention a few years ago. We had lunch and discussed the new world of digital media and publishing. There are a few giants in the land so to speak, but we thought we could take some of what newspapers do best and combine it with those giants who publish electronic books and sell clothing on the same website. We'd also have a news blogging desk, as well as traditional journalism combined at one website.

"That brainstorming session led to many meetings and conversations, and today, I'm pleased to do what Dan Kennedy was not able to do. I'm here to announced this start-up company has a launch date of Sept. 30, and Ms. Victoria James will be chief operating officer of Dynamix Media."

Victoria made her way back to the podium and saw Jeff approaching her with a piece of paper. She took it and looked down at the paper. She smiled. It was exactly what she wanted to see.

"Ladies and gentleman, actually, I'm not going to be the head of the company. You see, the real head of this company is Mr. Jonathan Marlowe."

There were several gasps, and people began to talk as Jonathan walked to the front of the room.

"You aren't supposed to be here. You are supposed to be in jail," shouted Martin Anderson.

"Allow me to explain," said Victoria. "You see Dan Kennedy had kept all of this under wraps to everyone within Kennedy Publishing. He wanted new blood, new vision, but someone intercepted a few of Jonathan's emails to Mr. Daniels. He was furious because he wasn't the one tapped for the new position, and then there was his retirement to worry about. What if something happened to the Herald? He'd never liked Jonathan before so why not make him the fall guy? No one knew about this venture except someone in California and a few people in Bennettsville. Why not make it all go away? Isn't that right, Ed? Why not dress up like Jonathan on the night of the ball and shoot Dan Kennedy yourself? You had an alibi. You were supposed to be at the newspaper - for most of the evening, that is. You lied to me about Martin Anderson and the story that ran the day after the ball, Ed. You said Martin came to the news building, hijacked my story, and forced you to print something else. That couldn't have been true because he was on lockdown at the crime scene. And I'm positive he couldn't come up with a story and dictate it to you over the phone like I did."

"You can't prove any of this," Ed said.

"Actually, we have the wig, and it had strands of your hair and DNA in it. Also, you lifted Marlowe's gloves. While those had the gunpowder residue, so did your shirt that we picked up at the dry cleaner," said Jeff, as he made his way to arrest Ed.

Immediately, the questions began flying.

Victoria backed out of Jonathan's way, and she let him answer the questions. Mr. Anderson's face was red with embarrassment as he marched out of the news conference. Victoria wiped a few tears from her eyes. She was relieved this nightmare was over. She stared at Jonathan as he took over. He was such a natural.

"How did it feel to be accused of murder and exonerated in the same week?" "How did you became CEO of the brand new venture?" "What did he think of his supervisor framing him for murder?" The questions seemed endless.

Jonathan smiled.

"I know you have a lot of questions, but there's only one thing I want to say as of now. I have to thank my dearest friend, Victoria James. She's an intelligent and determined woman, and if she hadn't been on my side, I'd still be in prison."

He glanced at her, and she felt the strangest sensation as he spoke those words.

Then, with a flourish, he dismissed the crowd.

"That's all we can tell you at the moment. We will have another press conference soon. Thank you for coming."

They left the main room and headed down a hallway for a smaller conference room, where they stay until the press left.

Victoria couldn't contain herself and gave Jonathan the biggest bear hug she could.

"I'm so glad to see you," she said with her arms tightly around his neck. "I know that orange is not your color. I was so worried."

She pulled out of the embrace to wipe the tears of joy from her eyes. She was beaming with a large smile and crying at the same time. He smiled.

"I'm forever in your debt, Victoria," he said.

He reached out and touched her cheek to wipe her tears away. There was something different about his touch. There was an electricity she hadn't felt before. Her heart began to race.

"So you deciphered my clues and fed my cat. You saved me. Are you sure I can't persuade you to marry me?" Jonathan asked with a smile. He leaned back against the table in the conference room and folded his arms against his chest.

A couple of weeks before, she would have laughed and completely brushed that comment off. But because of the emotional roller coaster she'd been on for the past few days, Victoria blushed and stammered as she tried to think of something to say.

"Angelica hates me. She'd come between us," she said stumbling over the words.

Jonathan raised an eyebrow at her and moved his right hand to his chin as if he was trying to figure out what was going on with her. She didn't give her usual excuse. She turned her glance to Cliff to avoid making eye contact with Jonathan, but she could feel Jonathan's eyes boring deeply into her. She felt as though her soul was exposed to him. Those same butterflies she'd felt a few days ago with Jeff had reappeared.

"We are serious about having you come on board with us," said Cliff.

"I'll have to think about that one," she said. "I might be up for a career change at that."

"You'd make a fantastic vice president of marketing and public relations," Jonathan added. "You did a wonderful job getting everyone here, and you were made for that suit."

She smiled.

Jeff knocked on the door and came in.

"Deputy Hawes, I owe you a debt of gratitude," Jonathan said as he reached out to shake Jeff's hand.

It was a brief interaction as Jeff shook his head.

"You owe Victoria, not me. She pulled all of this together. When Ed pushed her out of the newsroom, she began to get suspicious of him. She hacked into your computer and searched a crime scene. I think she did a few other things I don't know about. She might have a future on the force," he said and smiled. "We still have some loose ends hanging now."

His phone rang.

"I've got to take this," he said and walked out of the room.

Cliff Daniels' phone also rang leaving Jonathan and Victoria alone.

"I like this look on you, Victoria," he said.

"Thank you."

"What's happened to you in the four days I've been gone? You seem -," he paused as he studied her. "different."

His gaze penetrated her soul. She wanted to escape. A smile came across his face as he watched her.

He knows, she thought. She shook her head.

"Nothing. Everything is fine," she said nervously.

"Is it your deputy?"

She smiled and glanced at him.

"He's not -" she started.

"Your deputy. Yes, I know. You keep saying that," Jonathan said as he grinned.

Jeff walked back into the room. His face was ashen and serious.

"Vic, I need to talk to you," he said.

She walked into the hallway.

"Where did you go the day I got shot?" he asked.

"I visited Jennifer Campbell in prison. Why?"

"She'd dead. There was some kind of prison violence in the courtyard, and she was killed - stabbed by another inmate."

Victoria felt the blood drain from her face as she remembered Jennifer's last words to her. She was right. She predicted Jonathan would be freed, and that she was a dead woman. Victoria thought about the history book inside her purse and Jennifer's note. She thought about the leak in the police department. This was only one layer; there would be more secrets coming out in Bennettsville.

"Jeff, I think you have more than a leak in your department."

"Vic, that's what I'm afraid of."

MURDER RUNS DEEP

MURDER IN THREES

A Victoria James Mystery

DIAMOND KEY PRESS

1

Summer turning into fall in Bennettsville didn't mean much as far as the seasons went. The residents traded in church league softball for high school and college football and their sandals for boots. Other than that, there was little change. The south Georgia fall was still warm by the rest of the country's standards. The leaves didn't start to change color until about Thanksgiving. The shorter days meant quieter times; that was what Victoria James was hoping for - quiet.

The summer had been tumultuous.

Bennettsville had lost three of its most prominent citizens, and the Bennettsville Herald watched as its publisher, managing editor and business writer/editor had to be replaced for various reasons. Victoria had decided to stay at the Herald for a little longer. With the forced restructure of the newsroom, Victoria had one request. She asked to cover the education beat as Liz Camden, the former education reporter, moved to an editor position to cover for Matt Sanders, who moved from the metro desk to fill Ed Grady's position as managing editor. Ed was awaiting trial for the murder of Dan Kennedy, the Bennettsville Herald publisher. Dan Kennedy's wife, Michelle, had taken over as publisher.

As education reporter, Victoria knew she'd have less opportunity to run into Jefferson Hawes, Bennettsville's Sheriff Department spokesman, and Jonathan Marlowe, the Herald's former business editor turned CEO. Victoria had histories with them both, and she still had feelings for them both. She tried to avoid their phone calls and from running into them outside of work, but after about four weeks, she was running out of excuses. Work was the only place she could hide, and Bennettsville just wasn't that big of a town. Victoria found herself covering the smallest of stories that weren't even related to education, and she was wearing herself thin.

"So how was the school board meeting last night?" Liz asked when Victoria arrived at work.

"It was boring as usual. The big news was there are new science textbooks coming next year for the high school. The story was in the paper so why are you asking, Liz?" she asked as she sat down at her cubicle.

"Aren't you here a little early?"

"Why? It's 9 a.m."

"You worked until 10:30 last night."

"I have a lot to do," Victoria said.

That was her standard excuse.

Liz walked into Victoria's cubicle.

"Victoria, I have a favor I need to ask," she said.

"Sure, what is it?" she replied without looking up from some papers she had on her desk. Liz knew she wasn't busy, but Victoria tried to make herself look it anyway.

"I need you to interview Jonathan Marlowe."

Victoria swiveled her chair to face Liz.

"No, no, and no. Absolutely not. I cover education, and Jonathan Marlowe falls under business. Two beats I won't cover anymore - business and cops. You know that," she said bluntly.

"Victoria, Michelle wants a story on the company her husband was killed over."

Victoria turned away to face her computer screen and hide her face from Liz.

"You have a business reporter. The new guy - what's his name? That's his job, not mine," she said.

"His name is Todd, and he's left numerous messages. Jonathan's assistant finally called back late last night with a voice mail that said the only person from this newspaper he'd talk to would be you."

Victoria turned her chair back around to glare at Liz. That sounded like something Jonathan would do.

"I'm begging you. I really like my new job," said Liz. She clasped her hands together to dramatically emphasize her point.

"And I'm sure we will have to do a face-to-face interview not one over the phone," Victoria said and sighed. "You owe me. You owe me big time."

Liz smiled.

"Thank you. Here's his office number."

Liz handed her a piece of paper, and Victoria stared at it.

The idea that someone could have feelings for two people at the same time bothered her. She couldn't have a relationship with both of them, and she didn't know what to do about it. Victoria was not good at confrontations in her personal life. She felt it was better to close herself in and keep both men away. She didn't want to hurt anyone. She loved them both. This was a no-win for someone, and Victoria knew she would also be hurt in the process.

"We want to run it Sunday," Liz said as she walked away.

It was Wednesday so she needed to call him right away. She took a deep breath. Her fingers began to shake as she dialed the number.

"Good morning, Dynamix Media," answered a perky voice.

"Yes, this is Victoria James with the Bennettsville Herald. I'm calling to schedule an appointment with Mr. Marlowe," she said in the most professional voice she could muster.

"Hold please," she said.

She took several deep breaths as her heart began to pound. She hadn't heard his voice in a month.

"Victoria," Jonathan said in his velvety voice that always made her melt.

"Jonathan, I'm calling to set up an interview with you."

She was nervous, and her voiced cracked She tried to sound professional, but she was failing. It made her angry.

"Would you meet me at my office at 6 o'clock?" he asked.

After hours - why after hours?

Her head began to swim.

"Are you sure we couldn't meet earlier?" she asked.

"You were fortunate to catch me. I have meetings all day, and I know when your deadline is," he said.

She didn't like it when someone else controlled things.

"I don't know where your office is," she said.

"We're on the seventh floor of the bank building," he said.

"I'll see you at 6 p.m."

"I look forward to it," he said. "And don't forget your camera. You are the only one from the Herald allowed here."

Even though Liz was only two desks over, Victoria sent her a text.

"I'm going at 6 - alone. You owe me."

Victoria didn't have any work to do. She was still trying to decipher the cryptic message left by Jennifer Campbell. Myra Evans' book on Bennettsville history was supposed to contain a key. She wondered what the key was. She had read the history several times, but nothing out of the ordinary had appeared in it. The murders earlier in the summer were supposedly connected. She couldn't see it. She knew it was probably time for a visit to Miss Myra, but she hadn't made the trip over. Miss Myra was prone to turn the tables at any time and say things Victoria didn't want to hear.

Just before lunch, a flower delivery arrived. It was an arrangement of two dozen fuchsia roses mixed with stargazer lilies and white carnations. Those were her favorite flowers, down to the color of the roses, and she knew before reading the card that they were from Jonathan.

Her hands shook as she pulled out the card. The thought of being alone with him made her nervous.

"I'm looking forward to meeting with my dearest friend in the world this evening," it read.

She hated shutting everyone out, but she was so confused about how her feelings could turn from lifelong friendship into something else practically overnight when she still had feelings for her first love. After a month, she still hadn't sorted them out.

Around 5 p.m., she left the newspaper and walked to her apartment building. She'd contemplated moving after all of the break-ins she had experienced during the two murder investigations, but she liked living in downtown Bennettsville. She just added a couple more locks to her door.

Auggie was happy to see her. She hadn't spent much time with him over the past month either, but she had been scared to be home too much in the event that Jonathan or Jeff decided to come by. Despite her degree in English and her work in communications, she didn't have any idea what she would say to them.

She pulled out the suit she wore for the news conference announcing Jonathan as president of Dynamix. She remembered it made her feel powerful and confident that day, but she hadn't worn it since then. She put it on with her only pair of black stilettos. The suit was too big now. In addition to hiding from everyone, she wasn't eating much and had lost about 15 pounds. She piled her light brown curls on top of her head in loose bun. She stared at herself. At least she looked confident; she felt like jelly on the inside. After taking several deep breaths, she headed to the savings and loan building, one of the town's tallest landmarks with seven stories. Dynamix took the whole seventh floor. She walked the few blocks but wondered what she had been thinking by wearing those heels.

There was no one at the reception desk when she arrived. She stood and waited. Soon Jonathan appeared through the double doors. He was wearing a silk gray suit with a black tie and matching silk scarf in his pocket.

Her heart began to pound as she saw him.

"It's so good to see you," he said, grabbing her hand. "Please come this way."

"Thank you for the flowers. They were beautiful," she said.

"I remembered you loved pink roses and stargazer lilies," he said. He smiled.

She didn't say anything else as she followed him to the door and into his office. He had a wall of windows overlooking Bennettsville. She walked over to the windows and looked down. The sun was setting, and the view of the orange and pink hues settling over the city's historic buildings was stunning.

"It's not a big city, but it's still lovely to look at, isn't it?" she asked.

"Not as lovely as you," he replied as he stood next to her and took in the view.

She turned to look at him and smiled.

"Please have a seat," he said pointing to one across from his desk.

Victoria tried to begin the interview, but Jonathan interrupted.

"Oh no, Victoria, we are not doing this interview until you tell me why you've avoided me for the past month."

"I've been busy, and I know you have, too."

She looked at her notebook to avoid eye contact. She was a bad liar, and everyone knew it.

"Let's see, you turn 31 in a couple of weeks, and I've known you since you were 6. I know what job you have, and I know how long it takes you to write a story since I sat in the cubicle next to yours for seven years. School board meetings are once a month. You've been avoiding me, and you can't lie to me. I haven't seen you at Jake's. Your apartment lights are never on."

"I've just been working late is all," she said.

"Are you finally dating Jeff?" he asked.

She shook her head.

"And why? He's free. Isn't it what you always wanted?"

"I can't cover crime and date the sheriff's spokesman. It's a conflict of interest. He's a source," she said.

"But you aren't covering cops now, are you?"

She didn't know what to say. She looked down at her notebook. He moved from his chair and sat on his desk in front of her.

"On the night of the Bennettsville Masquerade Ball, I'd never seen a more beautiful woman."

He leaned down and gently lifted her chin so he could look into her eyes.

"When I came to pick you up, I saw something in your eyes. I'd seen it before. I see it now."

She closed her eyes.

He knows.

She fought the urge to get up and run out of the building. She could feel the tears forming. She opened her eyes.

"It was the way you looked at Jefferson Hawes when you thought I wasn't looking at you. It didn't register at first, but as I sat in prison, I had a lot of time to think. Knowing that you were in love with me helped me get through the most difficult days of my life. And when I saw you at the news conference, the look had intensified. Even though you wouldn't maintain eye contact with me, I could tell."

She tried to look away. She tried to fight back the tears. She tried not to melt at his voice. She turned her head, and he dropped his hand. She stood back up and walked over to the windows.

"Please stop," she pleaded with her back toward him. "I can't be in love with two people at the same time. They put women like me on those horrible, daytime talk shows as they fight over paternity tests. I don't want to hurt either of you. I'm so conflicted. Life was so much easier when Jeff was married to someone else, you were simply my best friend, and I was a miserable spinster with a Yorkie."

"I want you to come to work for me," he said.

"I can't," she said, looking at the floor and shaking her head.

"Why? My offer is still open from the first time we talked about this. I'd pay you twice what the newspaper is."

"I'm married to the Herald," she said trying desperately to change the subject.

He ignored that remark and ran his eyes over her.

"That suit is hanging off of you. Have you eaten in the past month?"

"Maybe," she said. "I don't know. Please just let me do my job and go home."

Jonathan nodded his head and went back to his chair. She tried to focus on the questions she wanted to ask. They spent the next hour talking about her story. Victoria kept her eyes on her notebook for most of the interview. Fortunately, she knew the answers to most of the questions she was asking. All she could hear was his silky voice in her ears. Her hands were still shaking. She was having difficulty concentrating. He knew how she felt about him. As she finished the interview, she stood to get her camera. She could take a photo and then leave.

"Where would you like to have your photo taken?" she asked.

"I'll put on my fedora, cross my legs at my ankles and have my hands in my pockets while I lean on the desk," he said. "How's that?"

"Somehow, I think you've given direction for that photo pose before," she said and tried to laugh.

"Sometimes, it's with the arms folded instead of hands in pockets - your preference," he said and shrugged his shoulders.

She struggled to put her lens on her 35-mm digital camera, but her hands were shaking too much.

"Let me help you," he said, taking the camera and lens from her. As it clicked into place, she reached out for the camera, and he grabbed her hand pulling her close. He rested the camera on his desk. He caressed her face and gently kissed her on the lips. She closed her eyes and felt her knees weaken. He moved his hands down her body until he stopped at her waist. His lips trailed down her neck. She felt intoxicated as he pulled back and looked into her eyes.

"Victoria, come home with me tonight," he said.

The sentence jarred her back to reality.

"I can't," she said breathing heavily.

"Why? I know you can't tell me that you don't want to."

Yes, she wanted to. She couldn't think of anything else she wanted at the moment but to be with him.

"I went through it earlier with you," she said. "I don't want anyone to get hurt. It's not right for me to feel the way I do."

"Victoria, I've been in love with you since I was 6 years-old, and you gave me one of the chocolate chip cookies from your lunch after the boys on the playground wouldn't let me play with them. You sat in the dirt with me that day in your red and white polka dotted dress. You had matching red ribbons in your twin pigtails, and you tried to cheer me up. All I could think was 'I'm going to marry her one day.'"

Victoria blushed and tried to look away.

"I went to New York and London because of you," he said as he gently touched her face, forcing her to restore her gaze at him. "And I came back because of you."

She was surprised at that statement and stared at him.

"When I heard that Jeff had gotten married, I was ecstatic," he continued. "I thought I had my chance. I came back, and you moved to South Carolina for a year. I waited for you. But you still weren't interested."

He kissed her again. He pulled the chignon from her hair, and it spilled onto her shoulders. He gently stroked her hair and whispered in her ear.

"Please give me the chance to make you forget about him."

2

Jonathan and Victoria took the elevator to the parking garage. There, they noticed several police cars with their blue lights flashing. As they got closer to the scene, Victoria pulled out her notebook and phone, but she almost dropped them as Jeff Hawes walked toward her.

"Ms. James with the Bennettsville Herald, why do I keep finding you at my crime scenes?" he asked.

"Just lucky, I guess," she said. "How's your shoulder?"

"Healing. I can predict the weather better than the guy on the news. What brings you here?" he said as he stared icily at Jonathan.

She glanced at Jonathan.

"I was interviewing Jonathan for the paper. We were going to get something to eat, and he was going to take me home," she said trying to maintain her composure, but she felt as though she'd been caught in a lie.

Her hands were shaking as she sent Liz a quick text to let her know she was on the scene.

"I thought you were covering education these days?" Jeff said.

"The paper wanted a story, and I requested Victoria. She's the best they have, and I didn't want an intern botching my story," Jonathan interjected.

"What can you tell me?" she asked Jeff.

"Off the record, we have a dead deputy. He wasn't on duty when it happened, and we still have family to notify."

"Dead deputy," she repeated slowly. Her eyes widened.

Could the Bennettsville mastermind be at it again? We really need better name than that, she thought. She felt the familiar adrenaline rush of being at a crime scene and knowing there was a big story about to unfold. She hated covering education, and she knew she obviously couldn't hide from Jeff and Jonathan anymore."What aren't you telling me, Jeff?"

"That would be for another time and place," he said.

She turned to Jonathan.

"I think I'm going to have to take a rain check on tonight," she said. "I'm sorry."

"Ah yes, I remember. A reporter's job is never done, and I will take you up on that rain check. I promise," he said. "Do you want me to stay and take you to the news building so you can write? You walked over."

"I can make sure she gets to the news building," Jeff interrupted. "I'm sure she's going to linger here until she gets enough information."

This was exactly the scenario she was trying to avoid - the testosterone battle between the two of them with her caught in the middle.

"I can take care of myself. It's only a few blocks," she said. "What else can you tell me?"

"We have to notify his next of kin."

Victoria's phone began to ring. It was Liz. Victoria indicated she needed to take the call and walked away.

"So, how did your interview with Jonathan go?" Liz asked.

"Very well."

"In the course of a couple of hours, you are doing the two things you told me you absolutely would never do again. You can't do it all."

"Yes, I can. You haven't filled my slot yet so put me back on this."

"Are you sure?"

"Just forget what I've said. Everything I was trying to avoid has come to the forefront again so yes, I'm sure. This is what I do best anyway. Covering the school board is so boring. If I hear another argument about textbooks or banned books, I think I'll scream."

"You know when deadlines are," said Liz.

As Victoria hung up, she surveyed the scene. The body was facedown and sprawled out in the middle of the deck. She couldn't see too much. Deputies took photos and looked for other evidence. Jeff was expressionless as though he couldn't believe what was happening. He shook his head several times. The parking deck was well-lit, and she could see the faces of the other deputies on the scene. One of them walked over to Jeff and started pointing at Victoria. He glanced in her direction a couple of times and shook his head. She wondered what that was about.

Jonathan observed the scene with Victoria. He seemed hesitant to leave her there. After about 15 minutes, Jeff headed back towards her.

"Deputy, I have one final question. Could the murders of Charles and Cassie Blake, Dan Kennedy and this deputy be related?"

She stared at him and waited. He didn't answer the question right away.

"I don't know," he answered.

"I'm going to the office to file a story. Jonathan, thank you for the interview."

"Deputy Jackson, are you heading back to the station?" Jeff asked one of the deputies standing nearby.

"Yes, sir. I was on my way."

"Please drop Ms. James off at the newspaper. She doesn't have a vehicle with her."

Victoria was aggravated because everyone seemed to want to control her actions, but she didn't feel like arguing. She needed to file her story.

"You don't have to do this," she said to the deputy when she was out of earshot of both Jonathan and Jeff.

"No mind at all, ma'am, Gotta follow orders," he said.

"Thanks. Did you know the victim?"

She looked at the young deputy's face. In his early 20s, he looked shaken by what he'd seen.

"Don't quite know the words, ma'am. Billy Ray Spears. He was like a daddy to me in a way. He made me want to get rid of all the bad guys. Him and Sheriff Hawes, well, I looked up to 'em. I owed 'em a lot," he said with his thick Southern drawl. "I can't believe he's dead. Shot in cold blood."

"I'm sorry for your loss," she said as they arrived at the newspaper. "I'll probably do a follow-up on him. Could I call you to get a couple of quotes?"

"I'll try, ma'am. Can't make a promise," he said.

"I understand," she said.

"You be careful, ma'am. People ain't right no more," he said.

She nodded.

"Thank you."

She was at the newspaper for only about an hour before she headed the few blocks to her apartment building. She couldn't put the name of the deputy in the story even though Jackson had unintentionally given it to her. She walked up the stairs and noticed Jeff sitting outside her door.

"How did you get in?"

"Your nice neighbor, Becky."

His presence unnerved her. She unlocked her door to see Auggie standing right inside. She picked up the pooch who wagged his tail excitedly upon seeing her.

"I guess you want to come inside," she said to Jeff who followed her inside.

"What's going on with you? You won't return my calls. You're never home. You don't go to Jake's anymore. You don't respond to texts. If I show up at the news building, they send some kid to talk to me. I think his name is Andy. Are you dating Marlowe?"

This conversation sounded familiar.

"Jeff, I'm not dating anyone. They wanted a story about Jonathan, and he flat out told them he wouldn't let anyone interview him but me. So I had no choice."

"You did more than interview him."

"Excuse me?" she narrowed her eyes at him.

"I saw how you looked when you came off the elevator, arm-in-arm. Your hair had a windblown look; and - "

He paused. He pulled her close to him and kissed her. He surprised her, taking her breath away, and then as suddenly as he'd kissed her, he let her go.

"And you were slightly out of breath and your cheeks flushed just like you are right now."

Victoria didn't know what to say.

"Are you dating him?"

"No, I'm not," she tried to regain her composure, what little of it was left after encountering both Jonathan and Jeff in one night. "Could we please talk about something else - like why you are here?"

"There are two reasons. I lost you once, and I don't want to lose you again. And I know there's something you aren't telling me."

"About what?" she asked, ignoring his first point.

"Knock it off, Victoria," he said. "About my case; about these murders; about the Bennettsville mastermind or whatever. And why are you still living here? I thought you were going to move."

"There's not a lot available for a single woman who gets paid what I do, and I don't want a roommate."

"Marlowe would pay you well to work for him, and if you aren't dating him, it shouldn't be a problem."

Victoria ignored that remark too and went to the bathroom where she changed into a pair of sweat pants and a tank top and pulled her hair into a ponytail. She got Myra Evans' book off her bedside table and pulled out Jennifer Campbell's note professing her innocence.

"Pull up a chair," she said.

She told him about her prison visit with Jennifer Campbell and how she hinted there was more going on in Bennettsville that met the eye. She showed him the book she found in the library that wasn't part of the library's collection, and its cryptic note.

"You told me there was a leak in the department, but we both know it's more than that. Jonathan was arraigned less than 12 hours after his arrest and quickly transferred to another facility."

Jeff looked over the information.

"Remember when I asked you to go the Labor Day picnic with me and take photos?" he asked.

"Yes."

"The deputy who was killed tonight was in the photos you took. He took the envelope from Martin Anderson. He's also the one who insisted on working the picnic which everyone begs off," he said.

"What about the young deputy who drove me to the newspaper?"

"Name's Freddie Jackson. He's worked at the department for a couple of years. He's not from here. He grew up in foster care. At 16, he had one run-in with the law - breaking and entering, but he was sent to a boot camp that gave him some purpose for his life. He came to Bennettsville as part of a program my dad was doing to help kids like him. The force teamed up with Teens With Purpose program. Kind of a do-gooder program. It lasted for a couple of years. Jackson was one of the success stories. He went through the program. The charge was expunged from his record, and he's been able to turn his life around. He was here for several months as a teen, moved away for a while and came back two years or so ago."

"Seems like a nice guy," she said.

"He spent a lot of time at our house when he was going through that program. My dad mentored him. I almost thought I had a younger brother for a while there."

"Yeah, he mentioned your dad, and he said that the dead deputy was another role model for him."

Jeff narrowed his eyes and started to say something, but he shook his head instead.

"And what about that one deputy who was on the scene? He didn't seem to like the fact that I was there," she said.

"His name is Lucious Smalls. He was a partner of Billy Ray's at one time."

"Isn't he a little old to be out on a beat?"

"I think Lucious sleeps in his uniform, Vic. He never married and lives alone. He wasn't working the scene, but he got a call and hurried over. He thought I called you, and he was giving me a piece of his mind about that."

"Why?" she said

"I'm not sure. Last I heard, he and Billy Ray weren't exactly on speaking terms."

"Really?"

"I've said too much," Jeff stopped talking and turning his attention back to the papers and book.

Victoria wondered what he was holding back. His face looked grim.

Maybe, Bennettsville's mastermind wasn't the only one who had secrets, she thought.

"How does this all connect?" she asked.

"I'm not sure, but I wish you'd told me about your visit with Jennifer Campbell earlier. Her death in prison wasn't random. It was calculated. There will probably be more dead bodies before all this is done."

"I don't understand this history book. There are some markings in here and numbers. I wonder if Miss Myra has any answers? What about Jennifer Campbell's personal effects?"

"If we'd gotten this sooner, we might have been able to find something. But now, it's probably too late," he said. "You know, I have an idea. What hours do you work tomorrow?"

"Whenever to whenever. I have Jonathan's story to write tomorrow, and I have a dead deputy to follow-up on."

Jeff smiled.

"I'm glad you're back on my beat, Ms. James with the Bennettsville Herald. And wear some sensible shoes tomorrow. The sexy ones you had on earlier might have caught Marlowe's eye, but they won't be good for where we're going."

"I'll talk to you tomorrow, Deputy," she said as she walked to the door to open it for him.

"Is that a promise?" he asked with a wink.

He paused at the open door and touched her cheek.

"I messed up, Vic," he said. "I almost messed up again."

He leaned forward as though he was going to kiss her, but his phone began to ring. He cursed under his breath and turned to answer it.

"Hawes," he said.

She watched his body language and could see his profile. It wasn't a long call, but it wasn't good. Jeff's brow was furrowed, and he slowly ran his fingers through his hair as if he was trying to make sense of the call he'd just taken.

"Another deputy has been killed. He was off-duty, too. He was shot. I have to go down there," he said.

"Who was it?"

"Jack Ford. We don't know what happened."

"Were you suspicious of him?"

Jeff nodded.

"And your question about if these murders were related makes me think you could be a target - again."

"I'm going with you."

"Why doesn't that surprise me?"

"I'll take my own car," she said.

3

Jack Ford was another deputy who'd been on the force for more than a decade. A 12 year veteran and lifelong Bennettsville resident, he was married with two small children and was found, lying face down in a puddle of mud, at a spot, known as a fishing hole and lovers' lane. It had been a fisherman who found him. He'd been shot once in the back of the head. It looked like an execution, Jeff said, but that was off-the-record. She stood and watched the deputies do their job. She knew this was hard for them. He was one of their own. She gathered more information that was off-the-record. In fact, most of what Jeff told her had to be off-the-record. After she showed him the history book, he told her even more things she couldn't use.

Jackson had let it slip that the other deputy killed that night was Billy Ray Spears. He'd been with the department for 15 years. With two ex-wives, an ongoing custody battle and a drinking problem, Spears had been on administrative leave a couple of times, but somehow he managed to stay in the department. She didn't say anything to Jeff; she stayed out of the way and listened. Billy Ray was shot execution-style, as well. Billy Ray had less than an exemplary record.

Why did Jackson consider him a role model? Did he not know this? she wondered.

Jennifer Campbell's words and her face haunted Victoria. And Margie, Jeff's sister, had hinted that Bennettsville's crime problems were part of something else. All of a sudden, Bennettsville started to feel like a scary place. It was just something about the deputies being the targets.

She stayed on the scene for about an hour. She texted the newspaper for most of the time there. They updated her stories, which didn't give the IDs or the fact that they were both deputies. She was more than a reporter covering the events. She felt connected to this case as she was connected to the others. She didn't know how they were linked, but she'd find out.

Jeff didn't notice as she walked back to her car and drove away. It was close to 1 a.m.

When she got home, she carefully checked her apartment. No killers leaving notes outside her door; no break-ins; no one waiting. Maybe it was safe to go inside. Auggie was happy to see her. Her Yorkie's entire body shook in excitement as he greeted her. She picked him up and held him close. She thought about Jeff and Jonathan. She wasn't a religious person, but she believed an intimate relationship was just that - intimate and not casual. It was something shared by two people in love. She thought she'd found that person in Jeff. They dated for about six years. He was the first and only man she'd been with. She knew she loved Jonathan, but it was different than what she felt for Jeff. Her love for Jonathan had grown out of years of friendship. She never thought there was any chemistry with Jonathan, but it was strong and getting stronger. She wondered if her only connection to Jeff now was their chemistry. She knew she didn't have the deep friendship she had with Jonathan - not after his marriage and recent divorce. She guessed what they said about men and women not being able to be friends was true, at least in this case. But she also knew what they said in Bennettsville about women who were involved with more than one man. They had words for women who felt the way she did, and they weren't nice.

She tried to keep the labels from sticking to her as she looked out the window to see the light of the full moon streaming in. The night started out so much differently. She had about a month of nights where she actually slept, but now it was time for another sleepless and restless night.

She was awake before daylight and decided to get up. At 6 a.m., Jake's would be open for breakfast. Somehow, she knew that she was on the blue hairs' gossip menu for the morning, but she didn't care. She couldn't remember the last meal she'd eaten. Jonathan was right. She'd lost about 15 pounds in a month. He had said she was pining away before. Now, she knew what that meant.

When Victoria walked into Jake's, there were a lot of surprised faces. Even a couple of the blue hairs greeted her. Usually, they talked about her amongst themselves as she walked by. Tommy at the grill also said hello.

"The usual?," he asked.

"Cheese grits and bacon will be fine."

"And the sweetest tea I've got or is it coffee today?" he asked.

"Tea definitely."

It was crowded for a Thursday morning. She could hear the blue hairs' gossip about another set of murders in Bennettsville, and she didn't pay attention to any of the other restaurant patrons. She'd sat at Jake's many times and stared into space. Despite the clanging of silverware, the low roar of the blue hairs and the sizzle of the grill, it was a place where she could clear her head.

She wasn't sure how long it was before her plate arrived in front of her. She wasn't paying attention to her waitress, but looked up when two plates were placed on the table.

"Oh I only ordered - " she started.

She looked up to see Jonathan.

"Welcome back to Jake's, my love," he said as he sat in front of her.

"Hi." she said. Memories of the previous night rushed like a freight train through her mind. She felt herself blushing.

I'm 30. I'm too old to blush, she thought. She looked at her plate.

"There's nothing to be embarrassed about. In fact, I should be the one who is embarrassed. I behaved poorly last night, springing all of that on you without warning. After your month in hiding, I wasn't sure if I'd ever see you again," he said as though he could read her mind. "And stop looking at me like you are afraid of me. I'm not a vampire, although that's been in the long list of things people have said about me."

She smiled.

"That's better. You know the blue hairs are talking about you today."

"I'm not surprised. I think I gave them a lot of material last night."

"Yes, I heard the deputy didn't stay all night and that you and he went somewhere together."

Again, she felt as though she'd been caught doing something she shouldn't.

"How do you know all that and not know that two deputies were killed in one night? I followed Jeff to another crime scene. I'm getting used to seeing dead bodies without throwing up. I never thought that would happen."

"There was nothing about dead deputies in the paper - just two dead bodies."

"Official line."

"Since I didn't get to buy you dinner last night, I'm glad we could have breakfast together. I do hope the next breakfast I have with you won't be here. I can think of some much more intimate places to have it," he said with a wicked smile. "I didn't know this until today, but the blue hairs like to gamble. They've started a pool to see who you will end up with. They've divided into two factions - one with me and one with the deputy. He's currently favored to win, but I will try to bring the odds in my favor."

She looked down and tried to eat.

"You are beautiful when you blush."

"You just like to torture me," she said hoping her comments would turn his attention elsewhere.

She looked up to see his smile.

"I've always wondered why you sit in the booth with your back to the door," he said.

"Why?" she asked as she turned to see Jeff walking in the door. She should have known going to Jake's would be a bad idea.

"Good morning, Vic," he said. He glared at Jonathan.

"Good morning to you, too, Deputy Hawes," said Jonathan.

Jeff ignored Jonathan.

"Why don't you join us? The more the merrier," she said.

"Vic, what's your plan for today?" he said as he slid into the booth next to her.

"I've got my Sunday centerpiece to write, and then I think that's it. I need to talk with Liz for a little while."

"There was a third murder last night."

"What?"

"I've got a news conference planned for 10:30," he said. "Then we'll follow up on Jennifer Campbell."

"I'll be there. You don't want breakfast?" she asked.

"Not today. I don't have much of an appetite," he said. His eyes burned into Jonathan as he turned and marched out of Jake's.

Jonathan smiled and shook his head. He started to stand up.

"I have to get to my office, but what's this about Jennifer Campbell? This is the same double murderer who shot you and is now dead Jennifer Campbell?" he asked.

"Sit back down, and I'll tell you."

4

Liz was one of the few people in the newsroom when Victoria arrived. She didn't see Victoria at first; she was nervously tapping an ink pen on the desk as she read through emails.

Victoria gave Liz the rundown of the night's events and what she was working on for the day.

"That's not what I want to know about," said Liz. "There were some people who said Jonathan was gay. I didn't believe them. I always thought he was amazingly sexy. And he wanted only you to interview him."

"Jonathan's been a friend of mine for a long time."

"But he's more than a friend to you. He risked going to jail for you during the Blake investigation, and you stuck your neck out for him by bringing finding the real killer when he was wrongly accused. Thanks for doing that, by the way. I got a promotion because of you," she said. "And what about you? Why have you been avoiding him?"

"It's complicated."

"Uncomplicate it, then. I know that's not a real word, but you know what I mean," she said. "I love the flowers he sent. They're gorgeous."

"Thanks."

If she only knew. Victoria wondered if she was making things too difficult.

Writing the story on Jonathan was easier than she thought. She wanted it to be perfect, and even after she turned in it, she was skeptical. It could have been better.

"Liz, I'm heading to the news conference."

"Loved your story on Jonathan, and that photo - every woman in Bennettsville will be after him if they aren't already."

"I guess I should go 'uncomplicate' my life then," Victoria said and tried to laugh.

"What time should I expect your news conference story?"

"I'll pop back in after the conference. It shouldn't take too long. I've got it partially written already. You might not see me the rest of the day," she said.

There was so much she needed to do - like take another look at Miss Myra's history and give Miss Myra a visit. She wondered where Jeff was going to take her to look for clues on Jennifer Campbell. She should have said something to him earlier. She could kick herself, but she knew she was getting in way over her head. She wanted some things to be quiet. What if there was something else really was going on? Since summer, she'd been threatened with jail, stalked, and shot. Then, she watched her closest friend go to jail and had seen three dead bodies as well as come in close contact with a severed finger. By helping Jeff with his investigation, she could be in danger again.

Bennettsville didn't have a huge news force of its own, but sometimes, reporters from Savannah showed up for press events. They were on hand for the last two murders to rock Bennettsville. She suspected with three deputy deaths in less than 12 hours there might be more interest than usual. Her plan was to keep her mouth shut. She'd let the other reporters ask the questions on this one.

The third deputy to die had been with the department for 10 years. Kyle Foster was found outside his house around 3 a.m. with a bullet in the back of his head. Jeff didn't give much information out on Foster except that he was a divorced father of two.

The reporters asked about the connections. Jeff was tightlipped.

She knew he wasn't going to say anything to jeopardize his investigation. He only allowed a few questions before he dismissed everyone. Although he'd been the department's spokesman for only a few months, he acted like he'd been at it for years. He was a natural at dealing with the public, even if he did have a few moments when he mirrored the gruffness of his father.

After the news conference, she dashed back to the news building to insert the snippets of info. She walked to her cubicle. It was starting to look like a florist shop. Not only was there the large arrangement from the previous day, now there were two dozen red roses on her desk.

"Red suits you," read the card.

She turned in the updated story and passed Liz on her way out. She was to meet Jeff in front of Jake's.

"'Just friends' don't send 'just friends' two dozen red roses," Liz shot back as Victoria walked out.

Victoria ignored the remark.

"I'll see you later, Liz," she said.

Jeff had said sensible shoes. She wondered where they were going. She saw his white pickup truck before she made it to Jake's. He slowed down.

"Need a lift, ma'am ?" he asked through the open window.

"Where are we headed?" she asked as she opened the door and climbed in.

"To the mill where she lured you. At the time, we didn't need to take a closer look. She had the computer, which we took with us. I checked evidence today, and the computer is missing."

He rubbed his forehead with his left hand, keeping his right hand on the steering wheel.

" I just have a hunch. I hope it pays off," he said.

"Jeff, what did those three deputies have in common?"

"Besides the fact that they all worked for the department, I'm not sure. That's another one of the mysteries I'm working on right now. Spears was working a desk; Ford did a lot of traffic duty; and Foster was the first deputy I had assigned to watch your apartment before Jennifer Campbell was arrested. I thought he'd been fired; turns out he was just on administrative leave."

Jeff paused. She could tell he was thinking about something.

"Vic, I don't know that you are safe given the facts," he said. "How long before you move out of that apartment?"

"I'm not going anywhere, Jeff."

"Do you have the book with you?"

"Yeah, I stuck it in my purse. I thought we might need it."

"See if it says anything," he said.

There were several mentions of the mill in the history, but only one of them had anything on it. Marked in red ink on the day the mill closed, Oct. 2, 1994, were the numbers 8509. She mentioned it to Jeff. She scoured the index for other references to the mill and its owners.

Jeff had keys to the mill.

"How is it you have the keys to this place?" she asked.

"You know who owns this place right?" he replied with a question. "The property belongs to the Blakes. I'm still on Allison's good side. She gave them to me."

Victoria nodded.

The mill had a couple of large buildings on the site with multiple warehouses. There was an office building as well.

"This could take a while," he said as he looked at the buildings.

"Is this an office number or something?"

"I'm not sure. Let's check the building where she brought you first. We'll worry about the numbers after that. Glad to see the sensible shoes," he said.

She followed him into the loom building. It was a cavernous room with large industrial looms inside.

"What are we looking for exactly?" asked Victoria.

"You've helped me solve two murders and now you ask? Welcome to detective class 101, Ms. James," he replied. "Try to find anything out the ordinary."

There wasn't anything that fit that description. Besides the pigeon droppings, cobwebs and machinery, there wasn't much left in the room at all. As she walked around the spacious room, she noticed the package from the dressing the paramedics used on her arm after Jennifer Campbell shot her. There were a few brownish spots on the floor. She wondered if that was her blood. She shivered to think that Jennifer might have missed. Or maybe she missed on purpose.

What really happened to Jennifer Campbell? she thought.

"Did you find anything?" Jeff asked.

"Not really," she said. "Just the evidence that I'd been here before."

She handed him the bandage wrapper than had been tossed on the floor.

"How's the arm doing?" he asked.

"It's healed. I try not to think about it much," she said. "How long are we staying in this building anyway? There are so many others to check out."

"What exactly does Miss Myra say in her book about this place? Maybe there's a clue as to where we should head next?"

"It's a boring book. It's almost like she went to the Herald and rewrote the headlines for the day. I can't tell you how many times I've fallen asleep trying to read this thing," she said. "She tells much better stores in person."

Jeff smiled.

"That's true."

There were no numbers on the outside of any of the buildings. During their walk through the complex, Jeff received a phone call.

"Ballistics confirm that the same weapon was used in all three of the homicides. Vic, I don't know how much longer I'm going to be able to stay here, but I can't leave you alone."

"You're my ride so I'd appreciate you not abandoning me," she said with a laugh. "Why don't we check the admin building? Of all the buildings, that one would make the most sense of having numbers on doors, don't you think?"

The administrative building was a small two-story building at the opposite end of the campus. Victoria was right; many of the offices had numbers on them instead of nameplates. There were metal desks and wooden chairs scattered around. Some of the offices had metal file cabinets. It was definitely stuck in a different era with its painted cinderblock walls. Most of the offices were devoid of light fixtures and stripped of any machinery. There were no papers anywhere to be seen.

"Jeff, here's an 85," she said.

Unlike the other offices in the building, this door was closed.

"Don't touch it," he said and pointed to a piece of wire wrapped around the knob. It appeared to lead inside the office. "That could be dangerous."

"Does Bennettsville even have a bomb squad?"

"Not really. We usually have to call in another department. I have a buddy who served in Iraq I can call to at least look at this," he said.

"You aren't going regular channels, Jeff?"

"Vic, you are the only person I trust right now. I don't even know what to tell my father," he said. "I usually talk to him about a lot of stuff. He seemed to miss the job. I mean, after 40 years in the department and more than 20 as sheriff, it was tough for him being retired. Fishing bores him, but he keeps going to the shooting range."

Victoria nodded.

"Well whatever is in that office must be huge," she said.

"I need to get you out of here. It's not safe," he said.

"Are there any other sets of keys?"

"Possibly, but these are the masters."

"Do you want to see if there's an 09 in here somewhere? I mean, it's only going to blow if you and I trip it."

"For a few more minutes and then we are leaving."

The continued search proved fruitless. Once outside the building, Jeff asked for Victoria's phone. She raised an eyebrow at him.

"I'm paranoid, Vic. I'm sorry," he said. "Is there any place else you can stay? Any time I find you in the middle of one of my investigations it gets dangerous."

"Maybe I should buy a Rottweiler?"

"Might not be a bad idea. Auggie isn't much of a guard dog," he said. "I've got a better idea."

He took her phone and called his buddy, Stan, who'd served in the Army. Stan was shot by a sniper and lost part of his right leg. He ended up going to technical school and started his own business working on computers after he returned home. Victoria didn't hear much of their conversation except that they were meeting later.

"Do you need to go back to the paper?" he asked when he'd finished the call.

She shook her head.

"Liz hasn't called all day. I told her I was working on something. Besides, I have more comp time than I can ever use."

On the drive back into town, Jeff didn't say much; she could tell from his furrowed brow and the grimaces he made every few minutes that he was thinking. As they waited for a light to change from red to green, he slammed both of his hands on the steering wheel, startling her.

"This just doesn't add up," he said.

"Where are we going?" she asked.

He didn't answer. He turned onto a cozy street in a neighborhood. She knew he lived in a quaint craftsman cottage like Miss Myra Evans did. There were lots of those in Bennetsville. He turned in the driveway.

"Is this your house?"

"Yes, but it's not what you think. As much as I'd like to seduce you right now, I don't have time for it," he said.

He smiled and winked at her. She followed him inside the cottage. It seemed when his wife left she took most everything with her. There were few furnishings in the house.

"To prove I'm a man of my word - you stay out here for a second," he said, tipping his cowboy hat as he went into the back of the house. After a few minutes, he came back with a small box and handed it to her.

She looked at him. She was confused.

"Open it," he said.

She opened it. Inside was a small handgun. Horrified, she immediately handed it back to him and shook her head.

"Didn't I teach you to shoot when we dated?"

"Well, yes, but I never liked guns," she said.

"I don't care if you like it or not. Besides, you need this. My hunches aren't always right, and I'm hoping this one is completely off base. But I'd rather be safe than sorry."

He abruptly turned and headed for his truck with her meekly following.

"And just so you know, yes, that gun belonged to Lacy, but when she took everything else out of the house, she left that. I'll buy you one, but for now, keep this."

"Don't I need a license for one of these?"

"Yes, you do. I'll help you get one, but in the meantime, I'd rather you be alive and facing charges than dead."

His statement sent a chill down her spine. She was quiet at they started to drive again. About 10 minutes later, they pulled up at the local indoor shooting range.

He handed her ear protection.

"Do you remember any of this?"

She nodded at him and covered her ears. Some of their dates had consisted of going to the shooting range. There wasn't much else to do in Bennettsville - two movie theaters, one roller skating rink. In the spring, summer and fall, there were plenty of outdoor activities, but in the winter, Bennettsville was dead. And of course, hunting was a major pastime, but not for Victoria.

She had been a pretty good shot at one time. He'd even given her a gun once, but after they broke up, she got rid of every reminder of him she had.

"Just back up, Deputy," she said.

She didn't want one of those movie scenes where the valiant boyfriend taught the weak woman how to shoot and stood behind her to steady her hands and show her how it was done. According to the movies, the scenario would end up with sparks flying between the lead characters as they got in such tight quarters together. If she got in that situation, she knew she'd melt in his arms.

With her weight evenly distributed on her feet and her hands in the proper position, she took aim. She fired 10 rounds from the 9 mm handgun into the paper target ahead of her. She actually felt the tension leave her body as she fired.

"A little rusty but not bad. You do remember what I taught you," he said as he looked over the target. She didn't hit the center, but she did get all the rounds into the target itself. "Do it again."

The more she practiced the closer her shots got to the bull's eye. Jeff seemed impressed.

"You've helped me solved two crimes, been shot, aren't afraid of a dead body. Now, you proved you can still shoot. Maybe you should be working for me, Ms. James."

She laughed.

"I love what I do. Why does everyone want me to change my career?"

"I'm going back to the mill tonight. There is power to the offices, and Stan is going to meet me there."

"I want to go," she said. "I gave you the clue. I want to be there."

"If it doesn't go well, I don't want you there."

"Then I'll stand outside. I have a gun. I can protect myself," she said and grinned.

"There's no telling you 'no,' is there?"

"No, there's not," she said.

5

What was so important in that room that it was booby trapped? Victoria thought as she stood outside the abandoned office.

Jeff had tried to make her stay in a tiny office in one of the warehouses, but it was too creepy for her. She decided she'd stand outside the building. Maybe it wasn't the wisest choice, but she had confidence that no one was going to be hurt. Despite its remote location, there were some lights outside - an attempt to keep trespassers at bay. She paced back and forth like a sentry in front of the building. There wasn't much else she could do. She clutched the gun because Jeff had instilled enough of his paranoia into her. She wished she could pull out the history book to find another clue, but it wasn't light enough for that. She rejected the urge to text Jonathan extensively. She did send him a "thank you for the roses" text, but there wasn't much after that.

She was sure she'd paced about two miles before Jeff emerged from the building.

"I should have known," he said. "Come on."

He didn't wait on her. He turned and headed back down the dark hallway. At the doorway of office 85, he paused.

"It wasn't real; it was meant to frighten people away," Stan said.

She walked in the room and looked around. There wasn't a desk in this office. There was only a chair with several files in it and masses of intertwined wires. There was even a digital clock to give the impression of a timer.

"If someone had tripped the initial wire, it would have caused the timer to go off. I'm thinking the timer would have been set for a short period of time so it would have spooked whoever tripped it, and they would have run for their lives. There is a fuse, but it was rigged to these firecrackers which would have gone off to give the sound of some type of explosion."

As she listened to Stan's explanation, Jeff flipped through the files.

"Jeff, thanks for the memories. I'm going on now," said Stan.

"Thanks, Stan," he said. "We could use you in the department."

"If I ever get desperate, I'll call you," he said.

"Jeff, what's in there?" asked Victoria.

"It will take me a little while to go through them, but there appear to be some financial records of all three of the deputies who were killed. There are also confidential personnel records in here with information from internal affairs. There's a fourth deputy in here - Trevor Miller. He left the department right after Jennifer's arrest. I think he moved to Atlanta. There's info on other deputies too."

Jeff shook his head.

"I don't have time for a trip to Atlanta."

"We found the 85 but what was the 09 part of it?"

"I know what it stands for."

"I need a story. I have to be able to justify my little side excursion today. I told Liz I was researching."

"Always the reporter, aren't you? The same weapon killed all three deputies, and we are looking at possible connections. I can't give you much more than that right now. Just trust me, Vic, please," he said.

"Something else. Anything?"

He put his hands on his hips and stared at the ground for a few minutes. He walked over to her and put his hands on her shoulders. He wasn't smiling as he spoke.

"I'm afraid this is going to be very ugly, and what you print could jeopardize your life," he said. The tender look in his eyes pleaded with her not to press the issue.

"I'm armed and dangerous, Deputy Hawes," she said and winked.

"Don't make jokes. I'm serious," he said.

"I know you are, Jeff, and I appreciate your concern."

"Vic, I can't tell you anything else now."

Jeff drove her back to her storefront/apartment building and walked her to the door.

"I won't follow you upstairs. I was wondering if you had plans for this weekend. Maybe we could go to dinner?"

She smiled and nodded.

She rushed upstairs to greet her Yorkie, Auggie. He was always a welcome sight. She picked him up and sat down on her bed next to the window overlooking the main thoroughfare. Through the gauzy sheer curtain, she could see that Jeff hadn't left yet. She wondered what he was doing.

Her journalistic sensibilities began to get the better of her. Three dead deputies and cryptic numbers. She decided it was time to do a little research of her own. It was in moments like those that she was thankful for technology as she typed the three names into a web search.

All four of them had been placed on administrative leave for a variety of charges including assault and bribery in 2009.

"How were these men still on the force?"

There was only one story on the web search. She tried a variety of combinations of key words with no additional success. She accessed the newspaper's database using her employee account, but she still only found the one newspaper article. It was written by a reporter named Cory Streeter. She vaguely remembered Cory. He only worked at the newspaper for a few months. He was killed in a car accident three days after the story came out. He lost control of his vehicle on the rain-soaked Jefferson Davis bridge and plunged into the river. The investigation concluded Cory's brakes had failed.

That does look fishy now, doesn't it, she thought.

She looked up the story on Cory Streeter's accident and follow-up. Jonathan had written them. She wondered if Jonathan would be at the diner for breakfast and if he would even remember anything about them. She looked at her phone. It was close to 1 a.m. She smiled and shook her head. She never seemed to get to bed before midnight.

6

Victoria wasn't a huge shopper, and she didn't have much closet space in her loft apartment. There wasn't much color in her wardrobe at all. She mainly had a couple of pairs of black pants and different tops to go with them. There was the one business suit and a formal she'd probably never wear again. Plus, a couple of dresses. No red except for the red and white polka dot dress that she had bought to attend a party. It had a retro theme. She remembered Jonathan commenting about the dress then, and she knew why now. She could recall the day they met, but she didn't remember what she wore.

She quickly pushed the red dress aside and decided on a black pair of pants and black shirt. She was going to be writing follow-ups on the murdered deputies. It seemed appropriate.

She found her usual spot at Jake's and hoped Jonathan showed up. She had written down a few of the facts into a notebook and started to make a small graph. She got lost in thought as usual, only snapping out of it when a single red rose was placed across her notebook.

"Good morning, Victoria," Jonathan said smiling.

He was wearing an immaculately tailored suit and his fedora.

"My cubicle is starting to look like a flower shop. Thank you," she said.

"I know what your cubicle looks like. It needed some dressing up."

"You are just the person I wanted to see this morning."

"That's music to my ears."

"Do you remember Cory Streeter? Cop reporter five years ago. He was killed in a car accident. You wrote the stories about him and the investigation into his death."

"Ah, I knew it was too good to be true. You only want me for work-related things," he said and sighed. "Yes, I remember it well. Why?"

"Three days before he died, he wrote a story about four deputies who were placed on administrative leave because of various charges including assault and bribery," she said. "There were no other stories. No follow-ups done."

She looked at him.

"And let me guess, three of them were killed the other night?" he asked.

She nodded.

"What about the fourth?" he asked.

"Jeff said he moved to Atlanta right after Jennifer Campbell was arrested."

Jonathan nodded.

"With Cory gone, they had me doing double duty. What were you working on then?"

"Courts and government," she said. "Charles Blake was still mayor."

"Jeff wasn't the spokesman for the department at the time. He was still pulling traffic duty. The elder Sheriff Hawes told me in no uncertain terms to 'back off,' and I do believe he used a few expletives. I went to Ed, and Ed told me he would get the paper's lawyers involved."

Victoria took notes and shook her head.

"Jennifer told me there was more going on than anyone knew, Jeff's sister, Margie, hinted at corruption. Jeff told me there was a leak in the department."

"There's always been a good-ol' boy system here in Bennettsville and Daniel County, you know that."

"I know, but I didn't know they were dangerous," she said.

"Any time there's money and power to be had, there's danger."

"Jeff gave me his ex-wife's gun yesterday, and then he took me to the shooting range."

"You could always move in with me," he said and grinned.

"I'll keep that under advisement."

"He's right though. If you start digging for more details, you are liable to wind up like Cory Streeter. Your life has been threatened before, and if Jennifer Campbell didn't kill the Blakes, then who did? And why? You can't keep your head in the sand. I understand your journalistic brain, but you can't discount that things could go wrong for you very quickly. What's important to you?"

She took a deep breath as he reached across the table and grabbed her hand.

"Do you really want to chase police cars all your life? Do you want to risk being shot and threatened and live in so much fear that you have a gun?"

She looked at him.

"Life is short. How long until you decide to be happy for you?" he continued. "Speaking of happiness, what are your plans for a week from today?"

"Nothing that I know of. I can check my schedule. Why?"

"As I recall, someone turns 31 next Friday. Would you allow me to take you to dinner?"

Birthday, she thought.

Her mother would be calling that day to ask about her biological clock and the possibility of grandchildren. She didn't want to think about 31. It sounded old.

She smiled.

"I'd like that, provided the cop killers don't kill me by then," she said.

"This isn't a joking matter."

"I'm sorry. Who could be behind all of this?"

"I don't know, but I can bet one person in this town who does.

She won't hesitate if you ask the right questions."

"She was on my list."

"Victoria, please be careful. Whoever has done this has left a trail of bodies. They've taken people like Jennifer Campbell and me and had us put in jail and falsely accused. They don't care about people. You are expendable to them, but you aren't expendable to me."

"Thank you, Jonathan," she said. "What about you, Jonathan, are you happy?

"That's an odd question, Victoria. I do know what would make me very happy, and I'm working on that," he said and winked at her.

"I just never saw you as a CEO. You have always been such a free spirit."

"A means to an end, my love. It's a means to an end," he said. "I have meetings all morning so I must go."

She smiled.

"I'd forgotten how much I missed our breakfasts here," she said.

"Some things don't have to change," he said as he left her seated there with her back to the door.

She couldn't head to Myra Evans' home yet; she'd have to wait. It was too early to go to the office. She mulled everything Jonathan had said about Cory Streeter and the danger. Maybe she was dismissing all of it too quickly. After all, Jeff gave her a gun.

"Marlowe isn't here this morning?"

"He just left," she said without looking up at Jeff who took a seat across from her. She knew he was keeping all of this information from her. She knew he was part of the department in 2009. He would have known about all of this. What did he have to hide?

"What's on your agenda today?"

"You know, Jeff. I have three dead deputies and a follow up or two," she said without looking up.

"What's wrong?" he asked.

"Jeff, what happened in 2009 with those four deputies?"

She looked at him. His jaw had tensed and his eyes had turned to that familiar steely gray she only saw when he became angry.

"I found one newspaper article from 2009 implicating the four of them, and three days later, the reporter covering it was dead. Jonathan covered it and was told by your father to keep his nose out of police business. Why were they still on the force? They were facing serious charges."

"Back out of this now, Victoria. Don't -"

"You sound just like your father, Jeff. Don't stick your nose in. Keep out of police business," she said. "He used to like me when I dated you, but when I started in this business, he did a 180. I was afraid of him."

"Vic, I can't - "

"Why not, Jeff?"

"You need to lower your voice," he said by giving the example with a soft, slow Southern drawl. "No one needs to hear this conversation. I should never have allowed you into this investigation. Go apply for your gun permit today."

He got up from the table and walked out of Jake's.

Maybe she was taking too cavalier of an attitude with all of it. She wasn't sure, but there was something about being told to butt-out of the situation that riled Victoria especially when Jeff wavered between wanting her help and pushing her away. She headed into the news building bearing that anger.

Liz met Victoria as soon as she walked in the door.

"Rough night?" Liz asked.

"You could say that. I'm running up against a wall with a certain deputy."

"Ah well, there's someone else who's interested in talking to you. The mayor called and wants you to come to his office," she said.

"Why? I don't cover government any more. I have my hands full with three dead deputies."

"I know, but just find out what he has to say."

"Fine."

"And what do you have on the deputies?"

"Nothing but something suspicious happened in 2009 that

Detective Hawes will not comment on."

"Sounds interesting."

"It is, but I've been warned it's dangerous ground. I'm going to do a little more research before I write anything," Victoria said.

She explained to Liz about the single article and Cory Streeter's suspicious death. She omitted Jonathan's comments and the fact that she now had a gun. Going to see the mayor would be good since she had to go apply for a gun license in the government building anyway.

Frank Barton succeeded Charles Blake as mayor of Bennettsville after the last election. Mr. Blake had maxed his terms and couldn't run again. She didn't know what anyone saw in Mayor Barton. He had little personality and wasn't very likeable. She'd covered the election. It was a close one, and neither candidate was strong. The voters were divided. After four years in office, he'd hadn't done much to win over his detractors.

"Ms. James, so good to see you," he said. His handshake was limp, and his palm was sweaty.

She thought he was trying to conjure up a little bit of a personality, but he was failing.

"Now Ms. James, you know the election is right around the corner," he said.

She nodded.

"And Bennettsville, it used to be such a sweet little town, quiet with little going on. But what has happened over the summer? First, the Blakes; then your publisher; now three sheriff's deputies."

She continued to nod. She wondered where was he going with this.

"The constituents are unhappy. They don't feel safe with murderers running around."

"That's not my job, Mr. Barton."

"Oh I know, but you have to stop writing these horrible stories. People are afraid. My numbers are going down in the polls, and I can't have that."

"I'm sorry, Mr. Barton, but I'm not going to stop printing the news. If you have problems, take them up with the Bennettsville Sheriff's Department not me."

"How about a good news' piece on me? I need to raise these numbers."

She raised her eyebrow.

"I cover crime not government."

"Oh dear. This is not how you are supposed to act."

"Why don't you call Deputy Hawes? He's the spokesman for the department. Come up with some kind of anti-crime bill or something, and then call me."

She got up and walked out of the mayor's office.

7

She headed to the Bennettsville Sheriff's Department headquarters. Jeff had arranged for a couple of deputies to speak with her on her deputy follow-up story. The Bennettsville adage of "Never speak ill of the dead. God rest their souls" was in full gear as she received glowing comments about the three deputies who'd obviously spent part of their careers in shady territory.

Deputy Jackson was almost teary-eyed as he talked about how Spears helped him and acted like a "daddy" to him when he first joined the department.

"Do you want to comment, Deputy Hawes?" she asked. "I feel like I'm rewriting the Blake story all over again."

He paused.

"I think you have enough without me saying anything."

That surprised her a little.

"Sorry, you are the department spokesman, and you are a required quote for my story."

He thought for a moment.

"Fine. Here's my official quote. The Bennettsville Sheriff's Department grieves the loss of three of its own. We are currently searching all avenues to bring their killer or killers to justice."

He gave her a fake smile.

"Happy now?" he asked.

"Sure."

"I'll walk you out," he said.

She noticed Lucious Smalls standing outside the conference room as Jeff escorted her out of the headquarters. She wasn't sure if he had been waiting for her or not. She thought it was odd.

She paused.

"Deputy Smalls, do you have anything you'd like to say?" she asked.

Jeff seemed surprised that Victoria would stop and talk to him.

The two men looked at each other. She wasn't sure what their glances signified, or if she was reading something into it or not. He clenched his jaw, and she noticed as his eyes narrowed at her. He mumbled something and turned away.

"Jeff, what's going on?"

"I can't answer that right now," he said.

She spent a few hours in the news room putting together the follow-up piece on the deputies. She didn't put any mention of their administrative leave from 2009 in the story, although the detail nagged at her. Innocent until proven guilty, but so many charges just swept away and by whom? She wanted to research it a little more.

She always liked visiting Myra Evans, and Miss Myra seemed to like having her over.

"So good to see you, my dear," she said as she greeted Victoria with a hug and a peck on the cheek. "Would you like some sweet tea and pumpkin bread? I made some this morning."

The aroma of nutmeg and cinnamon hung heavy in the air. Yes, she'd made pumpkin bread, and probably lots of it. Miss Myra couldn't have weighed 90 pounds soaking wet, but she always had freshly made cookies or sweets of some kind. Victoria wondered what she did with them all.

"I'm fine, thanks," she said.

"Shame to hear about those deputies being murdered. Bless their hearts," she said, leading Victoria into the parlor.

Miss Myra smiled at Victoria and looked at her like she was awaiting her questions. Victoria pulled the history book out of her purse.

"Oh you want to know about my book. I'm so happy; so few people have read it."

She explained to her about Jennifer Campbell and the cryptic numbers written inside the pages. She omitted quite a few details, but she gave Miss Myra enough to start with.

"You think these deaths are related?" Miss Myra asked.

Victoria nodded. Miss Myra's expression changed. Instead of her usually cheerful self, she grew serious and the smile vanished. She dropped her voice to a whisper as she moved to a chair closer to Victoria.

"There are things you just don't talk about in Bennettsville. There's a system that's been in place since the town's founding. It's not one family or one person, but there are things you don't want to start meddling in. History is being repeated. History will always been repeated. When one person gets too close to the truth, people start to die in unexplained ways. The truth will never completely come to the surface. Tread lightly, Victoria; tread very lightly."

Miss Myra got up and walked toward the kitchen.

"Wait. That's all you are going to tell me?"

"I'm 84, dearie. You don't live to this age without being very careful. Of course, I know secrets. Some are hidden in plain sight. Your detective knows more than he's telling you, but even he doesn't know how deep this goes. The old-timers know, and we play the game. It's all about the game. If you want to live to be one of the old-timers, you need to toe the line. Drop this. It's for your own safety."

She cut several slices of her pumpkin bread and placed them in plastic bags, then she put them into a brown lunch bag and folded the top.

"Come and visit me anytime," she said handing her the bag. "And don't forget to visit the library. So many good things to read there. Take Jonathan there, too. We always had such wonderful times at the library - he and I."

She hugged Miss Myra and walked to the door.

Once outside Miss Myra's house, Victoria sat in her car. She wasn't sure what she was doing anymore. She decided to take a drive to clear her head and process everything. She slipped into automaton mode and wound up at the Bennettsville Library. She pulled into a parking place not recalling any of the five-mile drive. Outside the library was a small park with picnic tables. On a Friday afternoon in October, the park wasn't too busy. Just what she needed - quiet and sunshine.

She spread everything out on the picnic table - her notebooks, the Bennettsville history book, Jennifer Campbell's notes. She thought about everyone telling her to stop looking into things. Jeff gave her a gun.

She had a war going on in her mind. As she listed all the ideals she held toward her profession, she thought she needed a superhero cape. They sounded so impossible - present the truth, uncover lies and corruption, inform the public. She thought she needed to add defend the weak and helpless to the list. A good journalist would keep pressing and fighting. There were lies and corruption that obviously went deep, but with all the warnings and all the dead bodies, she wondered if it was worth it. And in Bennettsville of all places. Little, insignificant Bennettsville. She wasn't ready to die. What was she going to do? And was she going to have any choice of whether she stayed at the Herald or not? Jonathan had even said that it wouldn't be long before Dynamix Media absorbed the Bennettsville Herald. Maybe she should take Jonathan up on his offer to work with him. She was probably going to work for him eventually anyway. In public relations for his company, she wouldn't have to worry about these lofty ideals, but she also felt like she would be doing everyone else a disservice or maybe even hurting them if she just walked away.

She wondered what Miss Myra had hidden in the library. At least with Jennifer Campbell she had a hint, "so many good things to read there" wasn't specific enough. She needed to focus on her task at hand, and by this point, she didn't even know what that task was. She realized she hadn't looked at her phone since before she left the newspaper to meet with the mayor. Liz, Jonathan, Jeff. Missed calls and texts from all three - not surprising at all.

Liz wanted a story, but Victoria had nothing. So her first call would be Jeff. Maybe she could get enough from him to stall Liz.

"Vic, I wanted to apologize for this morning," he said after he answered.

"No, you're right. I think I'm going to ask Jonathan for a job at his company. He'll pay me more, and I can have a life."

"Where are you?"

"Bennettsville Library Park," she said.

"I'll be there in 15 minutes - give or take."

He arrived with a couple of hamburgers and orders of fries.

"This isn't what I had in mind when I suggested having dinner," he said and smiled.

"Thanks though. I hadn't thought about eating," she said.

"What's going on with you?"

"I met with the mayor, who wants me to stop writing about crime but for totally selfish reasons. Then I met with Miss Myra, who is as scared as everyone else in this town is. There's something about Lucious Smalls. I don't understand anything," she said.

She paused and took a deep breath.

"Besides, The Bennettsville Herald won't exist much longer anyway. Jonathan told me that when I was trying to find who framed him," she sounded dejected.

"I don't ever remember you getting discouraged. Being a journalist is all you ever wanted to do. You were always passionate about it," Jeff said.

"Maybe, I need to shift my passions elsewhere," she said. "There are other things I could do with my life besides work all the time and fight with you."

"I'd miss having you to fight with, Vic," he said. He smiled. Maybe it was just the sunlight, but she thought she saw a twinkle in his crystal blue eyes.

"Why are you here? Do you have any information for me? Are

you going to tell me what's up with Lucious Smalls?"

"And there is the Victoria James I know and -" he looked down as he started to say the word "love."

There was an awkward pause.

"The thing is, Vic - the ballistics show the murder weapon was a standard-issued weapon of the Bennettsville Sheriff's Department. It was the same weapon in all three of the shootings, and it didn't belong to any of the victims."

She stared at him.

"It was a deputy?" she said as her forehead wrinkled. "Why would a deputy do this? Do you think it might be Lucious?"

"You tell me. You're getting good at this. I'm not sure about Lucious. I heard he was placed on leave a few years ago. Seems like everyone on this force has been suspended at some point. He was drinking on the job, and his partner, Billy Ray, turned him in."

"Is that all Billy Ray did? Sounds like a possible motive in the one shooting . Did the incident affect Lucious' career?" she asked.

"It could have, but I can't say for sure. I'm trying to find connections between him and the other shootings," he replied.

"Why are you telling me all this? You gave me a gun and told me to stay out of things."

"Because I know you, and you won't back down. Besides, I'd rather the information come from me than to have you snooping around dangerous places to get it," he said.

"So who does the murder weapon belong to?"

"'Who did?' is the correct question. A young deputy by the name of Mick Evans. He was killed in the line of duty about 20 years ago by a dirty cop."

"Mick Evans?"

"Miss Myra's nephew from what I've been told. What did she tell you?" he asked.

"Like I said - 'stay alive; stop looking; read at the library.' I'm tired of cryptic messages. I didn't know Miss Myra had any relatives who were deputies."

"Vic, did she give you anything?"

"Some pumpkin bread, why?"

She pulled the brown bag containing the pumpkin bread and opened it. The pumpkin bread was in there, and so was a note.

"Get into the historic books' room. Find the volume on the original founders of Bennettsville and look behind the book. Miss Myra."

They quickly picked up the remainder of their lunch and threw it away. Jeff had a piece of the pumpkin bread. Together they approached the librarian at the reference desk and introduced themselves; each one of them flashed their credentials. The librarian smiled as though she'd been expecting them. The request to go to the rare books' room didn't seem strange to her at all. The room was locked and smelled musty.

"You can't take anything out of this room," she said. "When you are finished, find me so I can lock the room."

She gave Victoria a pair of gloves.

"The book is delicate so please be careful when turning the pages," she said as she placed it on a table.

Victoria sat down and put on the gloves. As soon as the librarian left, the two of them abandoned the book and went to the site she had pulled it from. They looked behind the other books and felt underneath the bookcase.

Jeff grinned as he pulled out a key to a safety deposit box, and there was an envelope taped next to it under the shelf.

"Look inside the book to see if there's anything," he said.

The book was about Frederick Bennett, one of the founding fathers. His daughter married into the Blake family. There were no pieces of paper stuck in the volume, and no markings on the covers. It seemed the book was a place holder.

"I guess we are off to Bennettsville Savings and Loan," he said.

"But how? They aren't going to just let us open a box without the right ID. Does this belong to Miss Myra? Why don't we call her?"

"If she had wanted to tell you about this in person, then she'd be here with you right now. What's in the envelope?"

"A note. It says 'Ask for box 8509. You will be asked for a password. Tell them - Mick Evans.'"

"There's that number again from the book and the mill," said Victoria.

"Yeah. Let's go."

With the key and the password, there were no additional questions asked. Victoria and Jeff were escorted into the vault and left with the large box. Inside the box were various newspaper clippings about Mick Evans. He had a promising start when he started in the department in the late 1970s. He received numerous citations and awards in the community and in his work. There were photographs of him and Jeff's father, shaking hands and smiling for the camera.

Then, there were the clips of his obituary. He was executed just like three deputies, and he was found near the mill face down in the mud on Oct. 10, 1994, at the age of 39. There was one final article. It had to do with the arrest of Mick's killer, but there was nothing else on the case. Inside the box were medals and mementos of a life well-served.

"He died when we were kids," said Victoria. "But one thing I don't understand is why there's nothing in Miss Myra's house. I never heard of this guy, and I go over there a lot. Miss Myra was one of my grandmother's friends. My grandmother never said anything about him. If he was such a hero, why the silence? No photographs, no trophy case, no clippings. Why here?"

Jeff shook his head.

"I don't know. I don't remember this either. I'm going to ask my dad," he said.

"And he never tells you to butt out?"

"All the time, Vic, all the time," he said and smiled. "Listen, I know I asked about dinner this weekend, but we have three visitations at the funeral home and three deputy funerals in the next 48 hours."

She nodded.

"I'll be stalking them," she said. "I'm sure I'll see you. I've got to go back to the news building. I'm sure there's something I have to write."

Back at the news building, she stared at a blank page on her computer. So much information that she could do nothing with. She eventually came up with something, but it was really short.

"Liz, I'm out of here. Three wakes and three funerals in two days," she said. "I'm taking part of my florist shop with me."

"Wow, calling it quits an hour before everyone else. You are being such a rebel. You are really taking time off," Liz replied and laughed. "You sure you don't want me to assign the funerals to the weekend person?"

"Even if you did, I'd still probably show up out of curiosity."

Victoria realized quickly that she wasn't going to be able to carry both vases at one time so she opted for pink roses, which were still beautiful.

Auggie was happy that she'd returned home for a few hours. He greeted her with his unabashed enthusiasm, wagging tail and puppy kisses.

"I'm so happy to see you too," she said. "I'll be here for a couple of hours, then it's back to work.

He placed his head on his paws and looked forlorn at her comment.

"I feel the same way," she said.

8

Billy Ray Spears' funeral visitation was that night. It was the first of the triple murder victim's final arrangements.

Victoria had fallen asleep after coming home. She awoke to discover she still had time to make it to the funeral home. Hodges and Sons was around the corner from her. She decided to walk. It wasn't the scene she had witnessed during the last Bennettsville murders. Most of those attending were Bennettsville deputies or people who worked at the department. His kids weren't even there. His mother and a sister seemed to be the only family he had left.

It was sad.

She saw Jeff. He was talking to his father, and from Jeff's facial expressions and body language, it didn't seem to be going well. He was angry. Sheriff Hawes looked her way several times during the conversation. She wondered if her presence was the cause for all the commotion. She also saw the mayor who ignored her.

Lucious Smalls was even at the funeral home for a minute Victoria saw him come in, but she also noticed several heads turn and people whispering. He signed the guest book and left without speaking to Billy Ray's mother or sister, but he did manage to throw an icy, penetrating glance her way.

After Lucious left, Victoria was greeted by an older man. She didn't recognize him.

"Howard Granger, Ms. James," he said as he held out his hand to shake hers. Howard Granger was sheriff prior to Jeff's father. She'd only heard of him. In his 80s, he had retired long before she joined the newspaper.

"Sheriff Granger, so good to meet you. You are a legend. I've heard so much about you from Deputy Hawes and others over the years."

"Ms. James, I know you are only doing your job, but remember what Sheriff Hawes always told you. Sometimes, it's best to stay out of police business."

"I've been hearing that a lot lately."

"Then you have some wise friends. Listen to them for your sake."

"What's going on that people are so afraid of?"

"The dead should stay buried. Don't dig up corpses. There are secrets in Bennettsville, Ms. James. Long dead; long buried. Bringing them up only wounds the living. Have a good day," he said and turned away.

Victoria stared as he walked away. She'd had enough. No one was going to dictate to her how to do her job any longer. There was information out there, and she was determined to find it. It was just a question of where the information was. She was focused as she left the funeral home. It would be back to the news building for her and searching the archives. She wasn't paying attention to her surroundings.

"Need a ride somewhere?" Jonathan asked as she passed him without a glance.

She turned to see him looking amused.

"You look like you've been booted out of the good ol' boys' club," he said.

"I'm going back to the newspaper to research," she said as she walked closer to him. "Wanna join me?"

"That was never the way I wanted to spend a perfect Friday evening. Would you have dinner with me?"

"Well, I -"

"There's no excuse; I'll buy. Besides, I want to thank you for the lovely story you wrote about me. I still have contacts at the paper. Liz brought me a copy," he said.

"Liz?" she said and raised an eyebrow. "Really?"

Jonathan smiled and opened the car door for her.

"I only have eyes for you," he said ."Besides, Liz never gave me the time of day when I worked at the Herald, but now that she perceives I have money and power, she's interested. Not a game I'm interested in playing."

"So, what brought you to the funeral home?" she asked as they drove away.

"Just a hunch."

"You have those, too?"

"More of a well-educated guess, I suppose. I know you, and there's a triple murder. Investigative reporting and solving crimes has gotten into your blood."

"My head is swimming. I'm so angry. Everyone tells me to back away, but they are all hiding something. It's like they are warning me but daring me at the same time."

"Only you would think they're daring you."

She laughed.

"You used to feel the same way."

"I do admit this juicy mystery piques my interest, and as boring as research might sound to some, I share your enthusiasm. Plus, there is a way to bypass Jefferson Hawes to get the info you really need to connect your dots and find your killer," he said. "But first, we are eating, and not at Jake's."

"That actually sounds really good. I hate to think what my arteries look like from all the meals at Jake's."

At dinner, Victoria had a difficult time concentrating.

"You seem miles away," Jonathan said trying to break into her reverie.

"I'm sorry. I'm not a sociable person tonight," she said and attempted to smile.

"Victoria, I know that look. I've seen the wheels churn many times, and I've enjoyed being privy to your inner thoughts."

"This case. All the other cases. This crazy conspiracy theory. Maybe there is something going on. I need to make a trip to the library. Miss Myra told me to go there, and she told me to take you, but she didn't say why. Don't they stay open until about 9 o'clock on Fridays?"

"The library it is," he said.

It was a good thing that Bennettsville was a small town. It never took long to get anywhere. They had plenty of time before the library closed.

"All right, Jonathan, if you were going to leave something cryptic in the library, where would you put it?"

"I used to spend a lot of time in the library as a small boy. My mother worked into the early evening, and she couldn't afford a sitter so I came to the library. Despite her age and being past retirement, Miss Myra continued to work. She and I had long talks about literature. She loved mysteries - codes and ciphers. I have an idea."

Victoria smiled as Jonathan continued.

"Not only she did like to talk to me about literature, but she also put me to work," he said. "She taught me how to shelve books and file. She used to tell me that her favorite part of the library was the reference desk, and she had secret hiding places in the library. She was fascinated with military intelligence. Believe it or not, she liked to read books about World War II. The thought of being a spy always appealed to her. She told the most interesting stories."

Victoria laughed.

"She still tells the most interesting stories," she said,

She followed Jonathan into the library. He smiled at the librarians.

"Good evening, Mr. Marlowe," one said as he passed the desk. He smiled and waved in response, but he didn't stop. He seemed to know exactly where he was going.

"World War II history is in section 940," he said. "I'm going to check a couple of places."

He looked through the stacks in section 940 and pulled out a couple of titles. Then, he felt underneath the shelf. He pulled out an envelope. Inside it was the title of a book, Ciphers and Spies. He smiled.

"She always told me she'd write a book one day with this title."

"So it doesn't exist?"

"It doesn't, but it's a good thing you brought me here. I know exactly what she's referring to. This corresponds to a hiding place in the library. It's where we will find the book to unlock the code. The next visit you have with Miss Myra please take me with you."

"I will. So where's this hiding place?"

He looked around to make sure no one was watching them and motioned for her to follow. They went into the reference section and headed to the back wall. The view was partially obstructed from the view at the front desk. Jonathan took several books off the shelf.

"Hold these."

They were obscure reference books and had fresh smudge prints among the layers of dust. Someone had recently moved them.

"Miss Myra and I would sometimes leave each other clues through her elaborate coded system. This was the place we started," he said.

Behind the books was a false panel. After removing it, he reached in and pulled out a notebook.

"This, my love, is what you are looking for. Whatever is in Jennifer's book - numbers or letters - will correspond to this, or at least they should, provided Jennifer's book is the real thing," he said.

She stared at him flabbergasted.

"You're my hero, Jonathan," she said.

"Don't promote me to hero yet. This key is no good if Jennifer's book isn't the right puzzle."

"You mean there might be another book? But there was a puzzle in Jennifer's book that we already solved or sort of solved. I don't know. It just posed more questions."

Jonathan smiled.

"I'll help you figure it out," he said and winked.

As they walked out of the library, Victoria admitted being confused. Jonathan was right. He was going with her on her next visit to Miss Myra. Obviously he knew Miss Myra better than Victoria did.

Their next stop was Jonathan's office.

"Stop giving me the vampire look. I promise to be a gentleman," he said as he led her to the conference room on the seventh floor.

"There's plenty of space, so you can put all your evidence on the table and organize your thoughts without fear of someone breaking into your apartment."

"Thanks. It helps to talk it through sometimes. Auggie really helped me when I was trying to figure out who was behind Dan Kennedy's murder."

"So let's lay out what you have," he said.

She pulled out her history book and numerous newspaper articles. She'd even kept important clues Jennifer Campbell had left her during the Blake murder investigation about the two women who had filed sexual assault charges against Charles Blake, then died just a short time later. She'd written down the dates on the articles in the safety deposit box as Jeff wasn't about to let her leave with anything in that box. She also wrote out other pieces to the puzzle - the names of the dead deputies, the people telling her to back off, the information left at the mill behind the fake bomb. They also created a timeline.

After about an hour, she'd laid out all of the pieces on the table and stood back.

She and Jonathan surveyed the table together. At the Herald, the two of them - business reporter and cop reporter - had collaborated on more than one project as unlikely as the pairing seemed. It was a small town, and the Herald didn't have a huge staff.

"Jonathan, do you remember Miss Myra talking about her nephew?"

"Vaguely. I do remember she took off about a month around his death, but she never talked about him when she came back. She was different after that happened. She put on a mask for most people, but I could see the sadness in her eyes. She'd sometimes trail off in the middle of stories as though she was lost in her own thoughts."

"I don't remember any of this," said Victoria.

"I thought it was curious that she never mentioned him again," he said.

Victoria thought for a few more minutes before trying to piece together the information.

"In 1994, Mick Evans, a stellar and decorated cop is gunned down near the mill for unknown reasons. An article says Bruce Cannon, another deputy, is charged in the murder. Charges are mysteriously dropped. Now, on the 20th anniversary of Evans' death, there are three police officers who are gunned down using Evans' service revolver. All of them have shady records including being arrested, but they had the charges dropped against them for multiple offenses in 2009," she said.

"If we were going to write an article, Victoria, who would we interview and what would we ask them?"

"I don't know, Jonathan. My first choice would be Jeff's dad, but he wouldn't answer my questions. Sheriff Granger would be another option," she said and then paused. "I wonder why those three deputies? They weren't even on the force when Mick Evans died. The only two who were there were Jeff's dad and maybe Howard Granger."

"Was Hawes the sheriff 20 years ago? I've always heard that the was on the level."

"Yes, he was sheriff then. Granger lost the election, but he still stayed with the department several more years working behind some desk," she said.

"As sheriff, he would have the power to file any type of charge he liked. He could plant evidence on the killer, and then have the power to mysteriously drop the charges. Seems like deputies have had things pinned on them then dropped for a long time now."

"True, but what if they really were tied to something shady. We know there's someone in the department or even higher up the food chain who is corrupted. You were out of Bennettsville too quickly after that sham of an arrest," she said.

"If Sheriff Hawes were here, what would you ask him? Maybe there's something in that history book you're missing, Victoria. I wonder what secret Mick Evans had uncovered. I think that's the whole point. Mick Evans was murdered at the mill. That's probably no coincidence. While you are looking for what he might have been investigating at the mill, I'm going to cross-check the three deputies. What about the fourth deputy? Did you consider him? How did he manage to get out of Bennettsville, and why is he still alive?'

"I wonder if Miss Myra knew what her nephew had uncovered."

"No more talking, Victoria. Look in your book," he said.

Victoria hadn't thought to check Miss Myra's history of Bennettsville for information on Mick Evans. There were two mentions. One was about his death, and the other was about his role in bringing three deputies to justice in a cover-up in the late 1980s. Billy Ray Spears Sr. was one of several people busted in a prostitution and drug ring. Spears used his position to protect the owner of a club on the outskirts of town and reaped the benefits. As she read it, she wondered if Charles Blake owned the club. Mick Evans learned about it and had them all arrested. Billy Ray wasn't in jail long though; they got out on a technicality. Nothing on what happened to them after it.

"Jonathan, you have got to read this," she said showing him the passage in the book.

"It could be a coincidence," he said.

"I went to the funeral home for Billy Ray Spears tonight. He didn't have a father according to the obituary. They usually list the parents in an obituary even if they are deceased. There were no photos of Spears with a man. Even the pictures they had of him on display as a child didn't show a father," she said. "Jeff's dad would have known this. There are lots of people in town that would have known this. Why hasn't anything been said?"

"Whose funeral is first?"

"Billy Ray's is tomorrow. Is this another part of Bennettsville's 'do not speak evil of the dead' code?"

"Possibly," he said. "It is very strange indeed. What about the other two? They would have been kids too."

"I feel like I'm missing something," she said.

"Do you know what time it is? It's nearly midnight. Let's try this with fresh brain cells."

She smiled and realized how tired she was.

"You know, I haven't gotten any phone calls," she said looking around for her phone. "I must have left it in your car."

"It's late. Why don't you let me take you home? And I'll see you at Jake's in the morning so we can go to two funerals. There's more to this. Whatever that code is and wherever it fits will unlock more than this investigation."

She smiled.

"You miss the chase, Jonathan?" she asked as she sat on the edge of the conference table.

He moved closer to her.

"I've got newsprint in my blood, and yes, I do miss it," he said. "Mainly, I miss working with you. You and I have made a good team over the years."

"Yes, we have," she said. "Jonathan, how long before Dynamix absorbs the Herald?"

"Now, that is quite a topic change, isn't it? You've always been known to speak what's on your mind."

"Well, I need to know. I have to figure some things out," she said.

"Such as?" he said with a twinkle in his eye. He touched her cheek and gently lifted her head as he leaned down to kiss her. His lips lingered on hers and then he pulled away to stack her newspaper articles into a neat pile as though nothing had happened, leaving her confused.

"One funeral inside and another simple graveside service tomorrow, then a visitation and funeral Sunday," he said. "And to answer your question as to why I stopped, my love, when we are together for the first time and I do mean 'when' not 'if' - it won't be for a brief few hours. I don't want a night or even a weekend. I want a lifetime with you. I've waited for a long time, and I'll not rush it."

"You sound sure of yourself," she said trying to be nonchalant.

Without saying anything, he put the papers down and pulled her close to him. He looked into her eyes before kissing her again, softly and tenderly, but still with enough passion to take her breath away.

"Not sure of myself, I'm sure of you," he said releasing her from his embrace.

With his right hand, he touched her cheek. He gazed into her eyes. Her heart was pounding.

"I love you, Victoria James. I always have."

9

Victoria had left her phone in Jonathan's car, and there were several missed calls from Jeff. She wasn't surprised. It was too late to call him back. She didn't think it could have been too important because he didn't leave a message. Once at her apartment, Jonathan insisted on walking her inside, and they found Jeff waiting on them.

"When you didn't answer, I got a little worried," he said. "I'm sorry. I'll go."

"No, Jeff, actually, I'm glad you're here," she said. "Come on in."

Victoria brushed past him and went into her apartment. She rummaged through her purse to find Miss Myra's book.

"Jeff, we've spent the past several hours researching and putting together my clues. Read this," she said as she shoved the book into his hands. She'd highlighted the information about Mick Evans and the arrest. "Did your father tell you that Billy Ray Spears' dad was a member of the department? Did anyone tell you that?"

Jeff's jaw dropped in amazement. He shook his head as he read the paragraphs.

"I can't believe Dad or Sherriff Granger didn't say anything. I never really talked to Billy Ray about his family. I thought he was raised by a single mom. That's all he ever said."

"The fact that both of you are in my apartment after midnight will be the topic of conversation tomorrow, but stuff like this goes unsaid. I just don't get this community at all," she said. "Why is it that Billy Ray Sr. and Mick Evans' memories don't even exist in this town?"

"I don't know, but I'm going to find out," said Jeff, who had his hands on his hips and looked as though he could spit fire from the anger welling inside him.

Jeff took several deep breaths.

"I feel like such an idiot."

"Jeff, what did you find in those papers at the mill?"

"All three of the deputies had records that should have ended their careers. That article Cory Streeter wrote was all true. They took bribes to turn the other cheek so drug dealers could sell their junk. It looks like Charles Blake even paid them to cover up some illegal gambling and prostitution operations. It's almost like Billy Ray Spears was his father all over again. He got three other deputies to help him."

"What about the fourth deputy in Atlanta?"

"He's dead, too. The next night; same gun."

"Jeff, it sounds like someone did some house cleaning," said Jonathan.

Jeff looked at the floor.

"Do the two of you know what you're saying?" he asked and shook his head. His face turned an ash gray, and his eyes welled with tears. "You're implicating one of the two men who I've practically idolized my whole life. They're the whole reason I went into law enforcement."

"Well, we don't know for sure, but it sounds like they tried to do things according to the rules. They had them arrested. The problem goes higher, much higher," said Jonathan. "Do you have the gun?"

He shook his head.

"What happened to Mick's gun after he died? Was he working on the night of his murder?" Victoria asked.

"No one knows what happened that night. Ballistics matched the slug that killed Evans to a gun registered to Bruce Cannon. He never went to trial, and he died in a motorcycle accident about five years ago."

"Five years ago as in Aug. 5, 2009?"

Jeff nodded.

"Who arrested them?

"My dad," he said choking back tears. He ran his hands through his hair. "I can't - "

Jeff quickly turned. He slammed the door as he left her apartment.

"It would be quite convenient to pin all of this on the ailing retired sheriff, don't you think?" Jonathan asked.

"Yeah, I don't really see him as a vigilante," she said. "What are we missing?"

"A huge puzzle piece, but I'm too tired to figure out what it is," he said. "I'm going home."

"I don't think I can sleep."

"Did you, by chance, read Mick Evans' obituary?"

"I skimmed it, but I don't have a copy."

"See if you find anything interesting there, and tell me at Jake's in the morning," he said.

10

In all the time she'd known Jeff, Victoria had never seen such an expression on his face. It was a mix - horror, rage, fear, disbelief, sadness - all at once. She couldn't sleep as that tormented look came up in her dreams repeatedly. After a couple of hours, she dragged herself out of bed and looked around for something appropriate to wear to two funerals and another wake. Her other pair of black pants and a simple dark blouse would work. It was still too warm to wear a sweater.

She wasn't sure who would be at Jake's this early on a Saturday. It was crowded as usual. She looked in the back of the diner and thought she saw Jeff. His head was bent over and his hand placed on top of it. She walked to the back of the diner.

"Jeff?" she asked.

"Vic, just leave me alone," he slurred his words.

She sat down at the table as the stench of alcohol filled her nostrils. Jeff reeked of a night drowning his sorrows.

"Sorry, not going anywhere," she said. "Want some coffee?"

"I had a lot besides coffee last night. I've had a pot of coffee since last night, and I don't want anything."

"I can tell. Where did you go after you left my place?"

"I don't remember, but I didn't drive. When the bar closed, I came here. I closed one place and opened another."

He placed his head on the table as Jonathan walked up.

"Good morning, Victoria," he said.

He stared at Jeff.

"Good morning, Deputy Hawes," he said.

Jeff simply grunted.

"Did you find anything interesting in Mick's obituary?" Jonathan asked as he sat down.

"Only that he had a wife named Angela and a 3 year-old son named Jackson. Miss Myra was mentioned. It was a glowing story about a fallen sheriff's deputy. Nothing unusual about it."

"When our good deputy wakes up, we should pay a visit to Miss Myra," he said.

Jeff sat up.

"What's Miss Myra have to do with this?" he slurred.

"Everything, Deputy Hawes. Every single thing," said Jonathan.

"Yes, but you aren't going to Miss Myra's like that. We're taking you home first to shower and change," said Victoria.

Jonathan helped Jeff to his car, and the three of them drove Jeff home. None of them said anything on the drive. After a long cold shower, Jeff emerged ready to head to Miss Myra's. He still looked awful, but at least he didn't smell like a bar anymore.

When they arrived at Miss Myra's, she greeted them with her usual cheerful smile. She hugged each of them as they came in, and then she led them to the parlor, where they found Howard Granger seated on one of the Victorian loveseats.

Jeff couldn't control his pent-up anger.

"Why won't someone tell me the truth?" he said with his voice raised. Jonathan stood in front of Jeff to keep him from lunging at Sheriff Granger.

"Jeff, I'm sorry," Sheriff Granger said in a low voice, attempting to diffuse Jeff's rage.

Miss Myra came into the room with a pitcher of sweet tea on a platter.

"Now, now, I won't be having any fighting in my parlor," she said. "I've seen enough death and destruction. Victoria, dear, did you figure out my riddle?"

She shook her head slowly, still confused, as Miss Myra placed the platter on the coffee table and sat next to Sheriff Granger.

"But you did, didn't you, my sweet Jonathan," Miss Myra smiled.

"Miss Myra," started Jonathan. "Mick wasn't your nephew, was he?"

She smiled and looked at Sheriff Granger.

"No, Mick was our son," she said matter-of-factly and patted Sheriff Granger's hand.

Jeff sat down. His rage diffused as he stared incredulously at them both.

"Sixty years ago, it wasn't proper what we did. Actually, what we did still isn't proper today," she said.

"I was married at the time," said Sheriff Granger.

Now it was Victoria's turn to sit down. She needed something to drink, and she wasn't sure sweet tea would do the trick.

"I went away until the baby was born, and he lived in Atlanta with my sister who was married and had children of her own. He visited a lot, and when he was a teenager, he moved in with me. He grew up to be a fine man," said Miss Myra.

"When he became a deputy, I was so proud. None of my sons wanted to follow after me," said Sheriff Granger. "I knew that Billy Ray Spears was dirty. I just couldn't prove it. Mick put his life on the line and was dead because of me. He finished what I couldn't."

"So what does Mick's death have to do with all of this?" Victoria asked.

"I think you have a funeral to attend," said Miss Myra cutting them off.

Jeff looked at his watch. The funeral was set for 11 a.m. graveside. Jeff bolted for the door.

"C'mon Marlowe and drive," he said.

"What's going on?"

"I confronted Dad last night before I went on my binge. He insisted he didn't have anything to do with the deaths of the three deputies, but he did tell me one thing. He was Mick Evans' partner at one time, and then was sheriff when Evans died. Whoever was cleaning up the department sees my dad as someone who allowed this to take place. It's the anniversary of Mick's death. I just hope we get there in time," he said.

Miss Myra stopped Victoria before she made it to the door.

"Dear, go back to the library. Tell Jonathan to remember the time I taught him about Bennettsville's history."

She nodded and hurried out the door to the car.

They arrived at the cemetery as the funeral began. It was a short ceremony with only a handful of mourners including Deputy Smalls, Deputy Jackson and Sheriff Hawes. As they began to disperse, Jeff watched his father's moves. Oakview Cemetery was the final resting place for Bennettsville residents for more than 200 years. It was a blend of history monuments and modern ones. Sheriff Hawes began walking toward another part of the cemetery. Jeff followed him, keeping his distance, ducking behind monuments when necessary. Sheriff Hawes stopped and bent down at one of the grave markers. As he did, someone else stepped up behind him and appeared in Victoria's obstructed view.

"Jackson, put the gun down," Jeff yelled.

Victoria and Jonathan tried to move closer. They could see Deputy Freddie Jackson with a gun in the back of Sheriff Hawes' head.

She could hear them talking, but she couldn't understand what they were saying, Jonathan and Victoria both fell to the ground and crawled to hear what they were saying.

"I'm not telling you again, Jackson. Put the gun down," Jeff said in a loud tone as he enunciated each word.

"He killed my daddy," Jackson yelled. "He's gotta to die to pay for it. They all gotta die."

Victoria got on her knees and peered over one of the more modern markers in the cemetery.

"I didn't kill him, son," said Sheriff Hawes. "He got to the mill before I did. We were supposed to meet an informant. I was his backup. I don't know what happened. They were early. When I got there, Mick was dead."

"No, you did it. Was your fault. Him and Mama were gonna move out of Bennettsville and start a life somewheres else. Mama said he stayed cause of you. Mama said he was afraid. Mama told me I had to do something about my daddy's death. It wasn't right. So, I found you. Made you think I cared. Mama told me to do that. Then, you let Billy Ray Spears do the same things his daddy did, and those other dirty cops who cheated and lied and took money from people. I knew I needed to kill all y'all."

"Don't do it, Jackson. You've been a good deputy," said Jeff.

"Why, Jeff? I'm already dead," he said.

Victoria heard a gunshot. She looked at Jonathan and leapt up from behind the marker. She saw Jeff standing there, and his father still kneeling. Deputy Freddie Jackson lay on his back.

Jeff bent down to see about his father.

"Are you all right, Dad?" he asked as he reached out his hand and help him stand.

"I'm fine," he said.

Jeff grabbed his father and hugged him for several minutes; Jeff's body jerked and shook as he cried tears of relief. Several deputies, who had watched the scene play out after the funeral, rushed to attend to Jackson. Sheriff Hawes stood motionless for a while before he wrapped his arms around his son. Victoria turned away. She felt like she was intruding on an intimate moment. As she averted her eyes, she noticed the gravestone where Sheriff Hawes had kneeled. The name on the marker was Michael Stephen "Mick" Evans.

After letting his father go, Jeff walked over to Victoria and Jonathan. He wiped his eyes and acted embarrassed that they'd seen his display of emotions.

"Could we talk at Jake's?" he asked. "I'll get a ride there. I've got to tie up a few things here."

She nodded and started to walk, but he stopped her briefly.

"Vic, I promise to never tell you to back off another investigation again."

On the drive back to Jake's, Victoria stared out the window until Jonathan broke the silence.

"Are you going to be all right?" Jonathan asked.

"I don't really know. I don't want to see any more dead bodies," she said. "Maybe it is time for me to move on. It's only been three months since the Blakes were killed. So much death, like Miss Myra said. Bennettsville was such a peaceful place in the spring."

"You wouldn't be making a fortune with me, but at least you could afford a nicer place to live," Jonathan said and smiled. "I know what you make now."

"I'm seriously considering your offer now," she said. "And I really don't know what happened here today. Liz said she probably didn't need stories on the funerals. She let me off the hook after this morning. I'll file something once Jeff comes to give me the official line."

"Jeff could be a little while," he said.

She had forgotten about what Miss Myra told her until that moment.

"Jonathan, Miss Myra told me to get you to remember what she taught you about Bennettsville's history."

He looked perplexed as he stared out the window. He glanced briefly at her before a broad smile came across his face.

"Let's visit the library," he said. "The thing about a cipher and the coded item are like your debit card and password. You never write your PIN on the back of the debit card. The cipher and the book wouldn't be hidden in the same place. I think what Miss Myra was trying to tell you is the cipher we found doesn't decode the book Jennifer left you. It decodes a book Miss Myra left you."

"Well, that's not confusing at all," she said.

"Come on, and let's have a look. There's another book in there," he said.

They rushed to the library. She followed Jonathan in; he went straight to the reference desk.

"Lovely to see you, Jean," he said to the librarian behind the desk. "Could you let me into the rare books room?"

He smiled. It was obvious he was well-known at the library. The librarian went into an office to get a key, and with it in hand, she headed to the rare books' room. She left, making sure the door was locked behind them.

"I just came here with Jeff not long ago. How did we miss something?"

"You have to know where to look."

Against one wall was a heavy curtain. Victoria hadn't paid much attention to it before. Jonathan partly opened it, and it revealed a hidden bookshelf - containing one book - Miss Myra's History of Bennettsville.

"This book will go with your cipher, and this book holds the key behind our Bennettsville mystery. Victoria, I think we might want to hold onto this quietly."

She nodded.

"I think you're right."

They headed to Jake's to wait for Jeff.

They arrived only a few minutes before he did.

Jeff sat down next to her. He handed her a toy sheriff badge. She turned and looked at him with her brow wrinkled.

"You're officially an honorary member of my investigation team," he said and winked at her.

"I didn't do anything," she said.

"Yes, you did. You helped me connect dots."

"What happened to Jackson? Is he dead?"

"He turned his gun on himself," he said. "As it turns out, Jackson was Mick's son. His real name was Freddie Jackson Evans. He dropped the Evans. Dad said he looked more like his mother and never put the two together. Jackson had plotted their deaths for a long time. He was angry The night Mick died was they were supposed to meet an informant at the mill, but things went horribly wrong. Dad arrived too late. Mick was dead. He took Mick's weapon and gave it to Sheriff Granger because apparently Dad knew the sheriff's secret. I can only think that Sheriff Granger must have known about his grandson and gave him the weapon, but I don't know why Dad wouldn't have known. Dad told me he had a suspicion that Billy Ray Spears was Mick's actual killer. Bruce Cannon was his partner. The charges that Evans had arrested Spears on had been dropped. He was out of jail and back on the force. Cannon was on a drunken bender the night Mick was killed. He couldn't remember any of the night. Dad's theory was that Billy Ray had stolen Bruce's gun and used it when Mick tried to expose him once more. Dad had told Mick's widow this. Billy Ray ended up drinking one night and was killed when his car hit a tree going 80 mph around a curve on the old county road."

"It's amazing the secrets this town can keep and the ones it can't," Victoria said. "I'm really confused about something. How could Jennifer Campbell have known about those deputies? She wasn't a psychic."

"She didn't. I don't think she was behind your mysterious book. I think she knew about it. And I think that the booby trap at the mill was a warning that what happened to the deputies could happen to whoever found the papers. That's not all that was in the documents. There's stuff to implicate a lot of other people. I haven't had a chance to wade through it. It seems a lot of people want to clean house in the department and in Bennettsville itself. Right now, I'm anticipating the next murder to take place. I don't think it's over yet," said Jeff.

Victoria glanced at Jonathan. He slowly shook his head. She didn't say anything about the other book and key they'd found.

"Jeff, I need to write a story. What can you give me?"
"Official line?"
"Right now, I'll take it."
She wrote down several notes.
"Let me out," she said to Jeff, and she slid out of the booth.
She looked at the toy badge for a minute.

"I have a story to file. It could be my last. I can't do this anymore. I don't understand all the killing, and I don't want to become the jaded journalist with no compassion."

She placed the badge in front of Jeff. She nodded at Jeff and Jonathan and walked toward the door.

Follow C.Z. Brackett on Twitter - @CZBrackett
Follow on Facebook at www.facebook.com/thekeyofelyon, or email czbblog@gmail.com.

Made in the USA
Charleston, SC
08 November 2016